HARD BOSS

IONA ROSE

SOME BOOKS LTD

AUTHOR'S NOTE

Hey there!

Thank you for choosing my book. I sure hope that you love it. I'd hate to part ways once you're done though. So how about we stay in touch?

My newsletter is a great way to discover more about me and my books. Where you'll find frequent exclusive give-aways, sneak previews of new releases and be first to see new cover reveals.

And as a HUGE thank you for joining, you'll receive a FREE book on me!

With love,

Iona

Get Your FREE Book Here:
https://dl.bookfunnel.com/v9yit8b3f7

CHAPTER 1

JULIETTE

*C*hoosing a dress for my first day at work is proving to be unnecessarily difficult. It's a hard choice since it has to be something between simple and professional. I stare at myself in the mirror and take in the black suit I have on. I look okay in it, but it's a bit funereal and okay isn't what I'm going for this morning.

Today is a day of first impressions, and I really do want to make a good one. I want to get in, do my job, and return home. Repeat the same process for as long as it takes to gather all the money I need. Jenny says I might spend my first day meeting with other girls and that's okay. I'm not emotionally invested or looking for any opportunities here. I just need to make more money and save enough to start my bakery.

My job is simple. I'm what Jenny calls a replacement secretary. There are men who are too important to survive a day without an assistant, and should a case arise where their regular assistant or secretaries aren't available, they reach out to my agency to hire a secretary on rental. The job description is simple enough. I'm to perform all the tasks required of a secretary.

I should go for something chic and simple. A powder blue suit, very demure. My intention is to look like a ray of sunshine, approachable and friendly, but still interesting, given the slit that extends a couple of inches above my knees. I hope it's not too much. I certainly don't want to offend anybody. For makeup, I go light like I usually do. Anymore and I'll be too busy trying to keep from clawing my face off from the tingling.

There, I'm ready for my first day at work!

Filled with excitement and intense anxiety I start the commute over. I really need this to work. I need the money so badly. The drive takes about thirty minutes, and Jenny is there to welcome me.

"Juliette, I'm glad you could make it," she says and pulls me into a hug as she leads me down the hall to join the other girls. It really helps to settle my nerves and is just what I need.

There are about six of them in an open office area and Jenny tells me they are all waiting on a call to serve as a short-term secretary. If today is a busy day, Jenny says we will all be out of the building in an hour. But she is pretty sure it won't be. I hope it is because the contract I signed, while I get a base fee, is based on commission. The more jobs I get, the higher my commission.

Juliette introduces me to the other girls, and it quickly becomes obvious that I have much to learn. I sit quietly and listen attentively to the girls talk, looking to see if I can make friends with any of them. They talk about their recent encounters with some of the bosses and complain about some bosses that are a pain in the ass to work with.

"All I'm saying is basic decency requires you address me by my name and not whistle to call me," one of the girls says with a shake of her head. "I have a name. It's Tessa. Call it."

Jenny excuses herself to get to work and I move closer to the girls so I can join in on their conversation.

"Hi, I'm Kendra," one of the girls introduces herself and then the other girls introduce themselves. I try to remember all of their names because they'll be colleagues for as long as I remain with the agency, and I know I need to form a good rapport with them.

"Hey everybody. My name is Juliette," I reply and ask a question that has been bothering me. "It isn't always like that, is it? You get decent bosses sometimes?"

"You get decent ones most times. They come in different flavors, but most of them are too busy to notice you. Some can be so stressed they are stuck in rude mode. You'll learn to tolerate and handle each of them very quickly. None of us plan to be here forever. It is just temporary. I'm doing this to put myself through college," Kendra says. She can tell I'm already worried about working with the kind of bosses Tessa just described. However, if anyone can handle such bosses, it's me.

This is consoling feedback. I don't tell her I plan on saving enough to open my bakery. I have a tangible amount saved already and if the payment scheme Jenny shared with me is correct, I'll need to do about eighty to a hundred gigs to get enough money to open my bakery. That is roughly a year's worth of work.

Jenny returns after a while and helps me through the registration process. After the registration, I join the other girls at the open office. The number has increased in the short time I was with Jenny. Having no intention of excluding myself, I join them and introduce myself to the newcomers. Some are cordial, a couple are cold, and a few are nonchalant. I don't really care. No emotional attachments, I remind myself. I have a goal, and this is all I should put my focus on.

Most of the girls get called to places that have requested them. I have no choice but to wait. After about an hour of waiting, Jenny comes outside with a folder in hand.

"We have a last-minute gig that has just come in," she announces, and the handful of us look up at in her.

"Who is it?" one of the girls asks.

"Aliya has called in sick."

"Again?" Kendra groans.

"Oh, I'm sure she is sick. Sick of his ass, no doubt," another girl says, and the other murmur in agreement.

I'm lost here, but I guess this is one of the bosses Tessa was talking about.

"Am I assuming there are no takers?" Jenny asks.

The girls look blandly at Jenny. I get the message. This is my chance to get my first job. But why are the others reluctant and unwilling to work with this man?

"Who is Aliya?" I ask Kendra.

"The right question is who is her boss," Kendra says.

"Hudson Sinclair," Susan, a petite red-head provides the answer. I catch the resentment in her voice.

"You don't want to be working for him, dear. And definitely not as your first gig," Tessa adds.

"Why not?"

"He's an asshole, is why," Susan explains. "He is a perfectionist to the letter. Difficult to work with and his assistant Aliya is always calling in sick. We all think she calls in sick whenever she doesn't want to put up with his bullshit."

"If it were me, that'll be every day," one of the girls mutters.

"He can't be that bad," I say.

"Oh, he's worse," Susan says tartly. "I made the mistake of working for him three weeks ago because I needed the commission. The worst day of my life. I counted down the minutes until my time was over."

Hudson Sinclair sounds like someone I should avoid, but beggars can't be choosy. A plan is fomenting in my mind. If Hudson has an assistant who calls in sick consistently, he must be a regular here and if no one is willing to take up his gig, it'll always be available for me.

"How often does Aliya get sick?" I ask.

"Maybe once or twice a month," Tessa answers my question.

They are all looking at me now, wondering if I will be crazy enough to risk working for Hudson Sinclair on my first day at work.

An average of five times a month gives me sixty gigs assured in the year. Couple that with other gigs I'll pick up along the line, and I'll hit the hundred mark and get the big bonus, which will be more than enough money to start my bakery.

Susan shakes her head with disbelief. "You really aren't thinking of doing it? You'll be crazy to."

"What's life without a little craziness?" I ask and pick up my bag, heading towards Jenny.

"I knew you'd say yes," Jenny says with a cheeky grin. "You never could resist a challenge."

"The other girls think I'm being a fool."

"Do you want the truth from me?" she asks with arched eyebrows.

"Go for it."

"Will it change your mind?"

"I don't think so," I reply.

"Good. They're right. Sinclair is a repeat client. He is terrible to work with and will constantly keep you on your toes. Nothing you do is ever good enough for him, and you shouldn't expect even the slightest bit of appreciation from him. It's like you don't exist to him. But we keep him because he pays well."

"Even if he's an inconvenience to the girls?"

"We try not to force him on any of the girls. We let them decide to work with him. The last two calls he made for a secretary were left unanswered because we were unable to assist him as no one was willing to work with him. We've explained to him why that is so, but he is unwilling to change."

"He sounds like a terrible person."

Jenny cocks her head and then shakes it. "He isn't terrible per se. I've worked with him when I was still a temp. He is straightforward and curt. If you try to stick to his rules, you won't get into any trouble with him. Of course, you won't enjoy the work, but are you here to enjoy it?"

I get the message.

"Alright. What do I need to know about the job?"

"It involves traveling," Jenny says. "So, it is a high-paying commission, and we don't know how long it'll last. He has left the contract open-ended. Of course, you're free to break it off at any time. But I'll advise you not to. You'll forfeit the bonus that should come with such a lengthy gig."

"So, I'm going to work with a man no one is willing to work with for an unspecified length of time, and your best advice is for me to leave unless the time expires."

"Pretty much," Jenny shrugs.

"This should be fun," I say and relax. The others might

have bad reviews for Mr. Sinclair, but I intend to have a good time working for him. It might not be enjoyable, as Jenny pointed out, but it won't be miserable.

I complete the required paperwork, and Jenny orders me an Uber to drive me to the office. Back in the open office, the other girls tell me they think I'm crazy. Kendra calls me cuckoo. When we arrive at the building, I walk up to the receptionist at the front desk and explain who I am to her.

"Are you new?" she asks me.

"Yes."

She gives me the direction to Hudson Sinclair's office. As the elevator takes me up to the floor his office is on, I have half the mind to stop the elevator, ride it back down and return to Jenny and tell her I changed my mind.

Jenny wouldn't begrudge me of the choice, I'm certain.

But I have never been one to chicken out of a tough situation. When life gives you lemons, you throw them into a blender and make lemonade. I get to the office and knock on the door. A husky voice calls from behind the door.

"Come in," it says.

I open the door and find a man busy at work on his laptop. Without looking at me he groans.

"They found someone for me," he mutters grumpily to himself. "I wonder if this one will be any good."

CHAPTER 2

HUDSON

"Mom, listen to me," I say to my mother over the phone, trying to avoid sounding angry or offensive. "I'll be ready when I'm ready. Your constant nagging won't change anything."

She still tries to get a word in, but I interrupt her immediately.

"Mom?" I groan again, this time more adamant, and I can hear the sigh of exasperation from across the phone, but I don't care. I don't have the time to pamper her now. Aliya's called in sick again. It's the second time this month, and I've made a pointless call to the At Your Service Agency, but I know they won't have anyone for me. They've been unable to provide me with an assistant the last two times I called for one. I need to find a new agency. And maybe a new assistant.

But I can't dismiss Aliya. She's been a great help to me. More importantly, she's able to handle me while keeping somewhat of a cool head.

After finishing the call with my mother and promising to be home for dinner after returning from Manhattan, I returned to work. Aliya would have helped with this if she were here. I need to find out some information about Frank Dubois, the man I'm to broker a billion-dollar deal with. I need to connect with Frank on some personal level, and I have never been one to get that personal with people.

"You can just take the easy route out and marry his daughter," I think out loud and crease my brow in frustration.

Yes, that won't be hard at all. Phillipa, Frank's youngest and favorite daughter, has an enormous crush on me. I could use that as leverage to tie Frank down. He would be more inclined to do business with his daughter's husband. But I don't like Phillipa. She is a sweet girl, pretty, will make a good wife and definitely make my mother happy. But she doesn't stir anything in me. She awakes no passion and ignites no lust. Marrying her would be subjecting me to years of torture I wouldn't be able to endure, and I would have to break up with her eventually. That, in the long run, will disrupt the business I have with Frank, so Phillipa was a no-go area.

I sigh in frustration and almost pick up my phone to call the At Your Service Agency. I need to know if they'll be sending someone over or if I was on my own this entire trip. Before I reach for the phone, I get an email from them. Someone is coming over.

Good, I sigh and look over at the paperwork they'll do for me.

Before they arrive, I make a couple of phone calls to confirm flight details to Manhattan. My pilot, Reece, who has been with my family for more than two decades, confirms that the jet has been fueled and that he's ready to leave whenever I'm ready.

At least that's someone who remains reliable always.

I have made many deals and led my family's company, which was close to ruin, back to becoming a force to reckon with, yet nothing has made me as tense as this meeting with Frank Dubois. The failure or success of that meeting will determine the trajectory of my company for the next couple of years. I need this to go right!

Frank is a very private man; his deals never make headlines, but they rock the financial world. No one knows what he's up to at any point in time, but everyone is always weary about his decisions. Tracking him down is almost impossible. If that were possible, I would have put some people on him to follow him to see what he does and the people he interacts with. But I'm not the only one who wants to put some men on Frank. He was as protected as the President of the United States. I'm still looking for information on Frank on the internet when the knock comes on my door. I know it's the assistant from At Your Service Agency.

"Come in," I say,

The door opens, and in comes a lady. She's wearing a light blue dress that hugs her body and highlights her hourglass figure. Her petite body immediately catches my attention but it's nothing I haven't seen before.

"Hello, I'm Juliette," she introduces herself. "I'm to be your substitute assistant for as long as you need me." She stretches her hand for a handshake, but I ignore it. Yet, the smile doesn't leave her face. I can't tell if it's perfunctory or genuine, but I suspect someone like her has no reason to have a perfunctory smile. The smile looks so natural and sweet on her. She's a happy soul, and I can glimpse it already. And her eyes also. Her eyes are a striking shade of blue, reminiscent of the deep ocean and the vast sky. Standing there before my desk, the light from the window striking her face makes those eyes sparkle with a mischievous glint.

All of that doesn't help me, though. Will she be diligent, and will her input come in handy when I deal with Frank Dubois in Manhattan?

"Sit Juliette," I say to her. She sits with a nod and watches me, waiting for me to introduce myself, no doubt. That won't happen until I read the brochure that At Your Service Agency would have sent to me, highlighting her personality and what to expect of her. I had gotten carried away by Frank Dubois and forgot to read it, as I usually do when they send me a temporary assistant.

While she sits just a couple of inches away from me, her legs crossed so that her dress hikes up a couple of inches, revealing the soft and milky flesh of her thighs; I read through her file.

She's new. This is her first job. That's not good. But then, it explains why she must have been willing to come to work with me. For me. The file says she is hardworking and always committed to whatever task is assigned to her. We'll see about that.

I read through her profile, and at the end of it, there is a bit that I don't find in other profiles. She says her motto is "If life gives you a lemon, make lemonade." Is she here to make lemonade of me?

The brochure provides some information about her, including that she has an acting degree. What good is that?

She seems nice, not my kind of woman, that is for sure. I prefer my women to be quiet, submissive, adept at giving me pleasure and gone the next day, never for me to see them again. Looking up from my MacBook, I find her still watching me, studying.

She's been informed about me, I can tell. Well, she is about to discover everything she's been warned about.

"Come with me," I say and stand up, leading her to one of the cabinets in the office. There are files for her to peruse before we leave for Manhattan to bring her up to speed about my dealings with Frank Dubois. There are also some files in there looking into Frank Dubois's personal life, the little information I can gather. I'll ask her to go through that and see if she's smart enough to give a fresh perspective. That will determine her usefulness. Let's see that commitment her files talked about.

She walks with me to the cabinet, and I remove the file and place it on a table nearby.

A degree in acting? Why can't I get that out of my mind?

"What do you need me to do?" she asks, and I watch her lips move as she speaks. The way her lips shimmer makes me hard.

She's not my type, I remind myself. And she's here for work.

"You'll go through these files," I tell her. "There is information on the man I plan on doing business within Manhattan. He's a mogul and it is imperative I strike a deal with him. I want you to familiarize yourself with him as we'll be spending a lot of our time in Manhattan around him."

"Okay," she says, opening the files. "Frank Dubois."

"Do you know him?"

"Never heard of him," she tells me.

It's just as I expected.

"That's okay. You'll have to know enough about him before our plane takes off in three hours."

"Shouldn't we be on our way to the airport then?" Juliette asks, looking rather concerned.

"Why should we? We can make it to the airport in thirty minutes."

"What if we get delayed at check-in?"

"Delayed at check-in?" now I ask, confused. I immediately understand where the confusion stems from. She thinks we're taking a public aircraft. "We're flying on my jet," I tell her.

"Oh," she catches on quickly and nods. "I didn't know you were rich rich."

"Well, now you know."

She looks like she will get snarky with me, but then she changes her mind. I can tell she's going to be trouble. But trouble I can tolerate if she'll make herself useful. I'm about to explain to her the other assignment I have for her when an idea crosses my mind. I let it out before I can dwell too much on it and conclude it is a bad idea.

I pull the files away from her.

A degree in acting? There is a way to put her skills to use.

"What did you do that for?"

"How good are your acting skills?" I ask her.

"What?" she says, confused.

"Can you act? Put up a charade?"

"I guess...I can," she says, her confusion persists.

"I have a proposition for you," I tell her, walking back to the table to sit on the edge. She stands back and eyes me suspiciously. "It's not that," I dismiss her worry. "You're safe with me. Don't worry about that."

"Well, I don't think—" she starts. I can see that she is preparing to argue. I don't really care to engage in that.

"No need to buttress whatever point you want to. I just need you to listen."

It takes a few seconds for her to process my reply but eventually she does and snaps her mouth shut.

"So, what do you want me to do?" she asks. "What's this proposition?"

"This man I want to make a deal with, Frank Dubois. He has a daughter, Phillipa. She fancies me."

"Oh, okay," she says, "You need my help on how to handle that?"

I don't miss the snarkiness in her answer but again I have no intention or desire to engage. At my silence she obviously gets the message though and keeps her mouth shut. I continue.

"As I was saying, Phillipa fancies me, but there can never be anything between the two of us. You see, she's not my type. She looks just like you."

"So… I'm not your type?" she asks.

I nod, and she chuckles.

"So, tell her you don't like her."

"I can't do that. It'll hurt her or whatever, and Frank is rather protective of her."

"You don't want the girl. You also don't want to offend the father."

"Yes," I tell her. "And you, you're unknown within my circle."

"What are you suggesting?"

"I want you to pretend to be my fiancée for the period we'll be in Manhattan."

"So, you really do want sexual favors from me," she snorts.

"No. Nothing of the sort. It's all going to be pretend," I tell her.

"Pretend, huh," she says, moving closer to me until she is just an inch away and I can look right into her eyes. They stun me. What is she doing? "Do you know what it is like to be a fiancé?"

"Of course," I hiss.

"Really?" she scoffs. "You know what it's like to love?"

"This isn't about love. It's about acting out."

"You can't act something you are clueless about," she says. "Have you ever loved someone before?"

"What does this have to do with anything? We'll pretend to be lovers. It is as simple as that. I can pretend to be your lover."

"How will you do that?"

"Excuse me?"

"How will you pretend to be my lover? I can look at you with longing," she says, and right before me, her expression turns to lustful longing. I see her eyes go watery, and her lips quiver. They tempt me, and I want to bite down on them. "You can't look at me like that, can you? You said it yourself. I'm not your type."

She is so straightforward, bold, and unlike any woman I have ever dealt with.

"You don't have to be my type for me to pretend to want you," I tell her. I lift her chin up and look into those dreamy eyes; I let my thumb pull down her lower lips, so her mouth opens slightly, looking to welcome my lips. I move closer to her so there is barely any space between us, and I can smell her. Her hair smelled of daffodils and sunshine, her neck of passion fruits. And her lips. Maybe I'll have just a taste. I let my lips brush against hers and then pull back. "How's that for pretense?" I ask.

She smiles. "Not bad. But I won't be complicit in your deceit."

"I'll pay you," I tell her.

"And that solves the problem, doesn't it?"

"Ten thousand dollars every day until the contract with

AYSA expires, which, give or take, I think will last for seven days."

Seventy thousand dollars. That gives her a pause. She needs the money. I can see her running some calculations in her head. Her mind warps and warps, and she says nothing.

"If you'll do it, we'll have to get you a total wardrobe revamp. If you're with me, there's a way you must dress. You get to keep everything you buy."

Everything?" She asks, her resolve breaking.

I nod.

"It's not really deceit, you know. You're just helping me out here and helping Phillipa not get her heart broken. I want this contract, and I'll do anything to get it. You really aren't losing here, you know."

She's going to do it. I can tell because she isn't protesting against it. I just have to push her a little bit more and I know just how to do that. "Or are you scared?"

"Of what?"

"That you'll fall in love with me?" I ask her. "Do you think you'll fall in love with me in seven days?"

She chuckles. "Or maybe I'll be your type in seven days."

"We both know that won't happen," I tell her.

"Okay, I'll do it," she says after a while.

"You know, sometimes, we'll have to kiss to keep up the charade, though; I want to get that out there before we make any conclusions."

"Yes, it has to look real, doesn't it?"

"Good."

I return to my seat. "I'll get an NDA prepared for you to sign and I'll put all of what we've discussed here in a contract. You don't have a problem with that, do you?" I ask.

"No, I'm fine with it. It's good to set boundaries now. My responsibilities do not go beyond being a pretend fiancée and whatever else At Your Service Agency's contract binds me to help you with. Besides that, nothing else."

"Yes. And when all this is over, we'll go our separate ways, never to speak again."

"I like the sound of that."

This should work, I hope.

"There's something I have for you, something to make all this look more genuine," I tell her and ask her to wait in the office for me. I walk into the inner office and return with a diamond ring. She gasps at the sight of it.

"How do you have that handy?" she asks, running her fingers over the diamond ring.

"It was a backup plan if everything else fails. I have a feeling Frank will be more inclined to work with me if I can provide myself as a husband to his daughter. It will make him feel his investment is more secure."

"You really do consider everything, don't you?" she says.

Should I take that as a compliment?

"I didn't get this rich without being meticulous."

"Are you always this boastful?" she asks me, her face telling me she's pulled back the compliment she just gave me.

"You don't like it? Why? Does it make you feel self-conscious about your position?"

"No, it just comes off wrong," she says while rolling her eyes.

"You've known me for just thirty minutes, and I am sure you already made your judgement of me."

She shrugs. "Some people are open books."

"Quite presumptuous, don't you think?"

"You got presumptuous when you assumed your boastful-ness makes me self-conscious."

"You complained about it,"

"I mentioned it. You assume it affected me. Nothing you

do affects me. I'm just here to do my job to the best of my ability."

I frown, wondering if this is all a mistake. I've never had someone talk to me without fear as she does and truthful, while it irks a part of me, it makes her interesting. She's someone I can have a real conversation with. Someone that wouldn't suck up to me in hopes they don't offend me.

"I think this is going to be fun."

"What is?" she asks.

"Our ruse. I think I'll have a swell time messing around with you, But I must tell you, I am a man with voracious needs. While we are in Manhattan, I must have sex."

She looks at me, flabbergasted. And disgusted. Yes, there is disgust on her face. Does she think I'll go seven days without having sex? I can as well drop dead.

"Not with you, of course," I add, and she relaxes.

"Of course. You're free to do whatever you want."

"I'm not asking permission from you. I'm just informing you."

"It's all pretend isn't it? Nothing matters. Like you said, it isn't like we can fall in love in seven days."

CHAPTER 3

JULIETTE

J sit in a corner of the office, watching Hudson work. The girls didn't exaggerate when they said he was a nail in the side to work with, but there is a side of him I'm seeing now that I'm sure none of them saw. He looks a tad bit desperate and is giving all he can to close this deal. I roll the ring on my finger. Even though the circumstance leading to me having the ring is all a fabrication, it still feels great to have such beauty on my finger.

Hudson is a handsome man, no doubt. His rugged features, chiseled jaw filled with unshaven stubbles, and rough hair all combine to give him a roguish look. Even though I could see he was older, I was surprised when a quick Google search told me he was thirty-two years old. That's ten years older than I am. That is a significant age disparity between us.

Why am I thinking about his age anyway? It isn't like anything will happen between us. Hudson's deal is simple.

We keep up the pretenses whenever people are around, but alone, we keep to ourselves. For ten thousand dollars a day, that is more than a fair deal. It's almost too good to be true even.

Seven days. That is all I have to endure. Seven days of his rudeness, his brash disrespect, and his disregard for others. If I survive that, then I'll have more than enough money to start my bakery and will be able to implement new menus that I hadn't even thought I would be able to include in my plan. I won't have to return to At Your Service Agency to work anymore. It is a good deal. A perfect deal.

But however, I cannot help but feel empty. I truly wonder why because it's almost as though I feel guilty about something, and I just cannot put my finger on what it is. Suddenly, the sound of the printer draws me out of my thoughts, and I look up to find Hudson walking towards me. He's about six-two, with a broad chest and muscular arms pressing against the shirt he's wearing. He has rolled up the sleeves of his shirt for comfort, and I have to admit despite the fact that I absolutely do not want to, that it makes him look sexier. More sexy than I will ever admit even to myself and this is because of who he is.

I am a man with voracious needs.

Those were his words. I still can't believe it. What a jerk.

Yet… it does make my belly flutter so maybe I am in some sort of a denial? I can't even dare entertain the possibility of what this denial might imply but the fact that I truly can't help but feel queasy whenever my eyes meet his. And then they drop to his lips. Those beautiful lips grazed mine a couple of minutes ago, and it took all the restraint within me not to reach up and kiss him back.

It truly baffles me just how one can feel such aversion for a person and a huge rush of attraction?

"I have the documents here ready for you to sign," he says, handing them to me. He walks back to his desk. I straighten, almost as though scared he can read my thoughts even though now everything between us is more or less mechanical. There had been a spark between us when we stood so close earlier on. There is no denying this. I can't even help but admit to myself now that I was teasing him to see if he'd break under pressure, but a small part of me, hidden in the dark crevices of my heart that I am not so proud of, had hoped he would kiss me. I also am not proud of how I would have responded had he kissed me. I can imagine the two of us on the floor, and then afterwards trying to get back into our clothes. I can unfortunately imagine much more than that- sweaty backs and hands clawing down skin, harsh breathing, fucking with complete and raw abandon.

I have to pause for a very long moment to catch my breath.

Not him, Juliette, I tell myself. You need to stay away from him. He might seem harmless now, but the fact of the matter is that he is a distraction. However, I do have needs myself just as he does, and so I cannot stop myself from thinking that maybe, just maybe I need to find a way to satisfy those needs when we get to Manhattan.

I read through the documents and find everything that we discussed in detail. He is thorough and I cannot help but admire him for this. He has painstakingly mentioned that the diamond is to be returned to him after the expiration of the seven-day contract.

Nice addition.

"I wasn't going to go away with your diamond," I point out.

"It's just business," he says, a cold as a viper.

I sign the documents and return them to him so he can

sign them as well. Now, I am contractually and falsely engaged to him. It still hasn't hit yet, and I hope it doesn't. I hope it feels nothing as a result and means nothing to me until the seven days are over. This is the only way I can be assured that I will be able to keep my head screwed on right. I wonder though how the next couple of days will go for me.

"You should get ready to leave. When we get to Manhattan, I'll take you shopping," he tells me. "We'll meet my project manager, Alison, on the plane. I have a meeting to attend before we leave. You can walk around the area for a while. I'll come get you when it's time."

All of these I have to admit sound incredibly appealing to me. I watch him leave and wonder what his type of woman is. I really don't want to assume but I can't help but peg him for the kind to especially go after the blonde and dumb types.

For some reason all of this makes me pissed, and I really can't understand why. I'm not supposed to be emotionally invested in any of this. You're here for a simple goal, remember? I admonish myself. Stay focused!

And so, I decide to take his advice and go for a walk. Soon, I find myself back in the parking lot with my phone in my hand, calling Lisa.

"Hey! I have been waiting for your call. How's the first day at work?" Lisa says immediately the call connects.

Truthfully, I really don't know where to start from, but I'm soon able to. "You're not going to believe this," I say and tell her how my morning went.

"Hudson Sinclair? I know him. My firm represented a client that filed a suit against him a while ago."

"Did the client win?" I ask.

"Oh, no. Lost woefully. The word around here is that you don't go up against Sinclair hoping to win. You go up against him to get your name up on the scoreboard."

"What kind of scoreboard?" I ask.

"The one that says you went up against him," comes Lisa's reply.

Hmmm... he is that fearless, huh? But there is fear in him. I saw it when we were talking earlier—fear and desperation.

"But did he really say you aren't his type?" Lisa asked with a snort.

"Yeah, the snarky bastard. Can you believe him?"

"Wait until he sees you dolled up."

"I'm not even into him. I just want seven days to be over and to get my money. Easy money, don't you think?"

"Yeah, quite easy money. But you have to be careful around him."

"Why? Is he dangerous?"

"From what I've heard, he can be very venomous when he doesn't get his way. I think he was raised quite spoiled, and he's used to getting his way."

Now, I feel terrible for giving in to his demands so easily. I should have made him sweat a bit more. I can't help but note I'm becoming more unusually feisty as well. He seems to bring out this side of me.

Lisa and I talk some more before I return to his office in case he's finished with his meeting. I'm barely back in the office for ten minutes when he shows up and announces that it's time to leave with barely a glance at me.

"Up, now," he says, and I can't help but blink long and hard.

And so, despite how shaky it makes me feel inside because I do have a lot to lose if this goes south, I remain rooted in my seat. I am indeed his staff, but I also can't have him making me feel like shit for the foreseeable future. Eventually, he notices I'm not behind him and turns back at the door.

"You didn't hear me?" he asks.

"You were speaking to me?" I retort, giving him the stink eye he deserves. I don't miss the fact though that my voice has a light shake to it. Damn it.

He scoffs and turns around to address me. "What is this? Some childish game?"

"No game," I tell him. "I just … I don't care where we are, public or private; I just truly hope that you can be cordial to me and not order me around like some maid."

He looks confounded. "Are you serious?"

I nod and remain in the chair, outrightly staring at him. If he isn't ready to do the right thing, we'll be here all day. I know he won't rescind the offer, or at least I hope so. He needs me.

"Alright," he says after a moment, a breath of exasperation rushing out of him like a dragon's breath. I can see the regret in his eyes. If he could go back on the contract we'd signed, I'm sure he would. "Alright, let's go, shall we? The jet is waiting for us."

Now, I stand up and follow him out of the office. We get into a waiting SUV, which drives us to the airport and to his private plane. Getting onto the jet, I meet Alison, the project manager, and from the get-go, I can tell she doesn't like me.

"Who's she?" she asks when I walk in with Hudson, eyeing me like I'm worth less than the dirt underneath her shoes. They are Louboutins, so I'll kill for them. But, still, the bitch air around her is so great it stinks up the whole place.

"My new assistant," Hudson mentions and points at an empty seat for me to sit in. I think about rebelling because I deem that disrespectful, but I know he'll ignore me. So, I sit anyway. Alison walks with him to his seat.

"What about Aliya?" Alison asks.

"Called in sick this morning. She said she might not be

available for the next three days, and I can't go to Manhattan without an assistant, so I hired her."

"I told you, you need to get a replacement for Aliya," Alison says, eyeing me.

Not me. I'm not fit to be his assistant.

"Why is she wearing the ring?" she asks, her face more or less accusing me of theft.

"I gave it to her," Hudson says. "She's my fiancée now."

"What?" she says, flabbergasted. "That is supposed to be for Phillipa. If all things fail, we resort to that. You know that."

"Well, the plan has changed. I don't like the lady," Hudson hisses

"So, you like this one?" asks Alison. I wonder if she actually considers me a piece of chewed gum.

Unable to keep quiet while they both talk like I'm some non-playing character in a video game so I say something.

"I'm sitting right here," I say.

They both ignore me.

"Alison, I do not feel like arguing now. I want to try to get some sleep before we reach Manhattan."

"You don't have anything scheduled when we land," Alison points out.

"Well, I am taking Juliette shopping."

"She can do that on her own."

What is this bitch's problem?

"Sure. But I just met her today. To give this a chance to work, we need to know a couple of things about each other. It should make the pretense easier. Taking her to get some clothes is one way I see we can get to know each other better. And the faster we get out there so people see, the better for us. Now, let me rest."

The last bit comes off as a command and Alison takes it as such. She mellows out but continues to fume in silence.

Seeing she's been defeated and silenced, Alison sits opposite me just as the announcement comes for us to buckle up. She glares at me throughout the takeoff, shifting her focus between the ring and my face. She wants the ring. Maybe she wants more than the ring. Maybe she wants the man, too.

Girl, you can have him.

I want to get some sleep, too, but I have a sick feeling that Alison will stab me should I close my eyes, so I keep watch on her throughout the flight, which lasts two hours. At the hotel, I get a room beside Hudson because he thinks it makes sense logistically and will help continue the ruse, while Alison gets a room on the floor beneath ours. That gets her riled up some more, but I ignore it all. Even when Hudson sends her away to prepare for a meeting, and she offers to postpone it and come with us to shop together, I sit back in silence and watch him chastise her.

"Why aren't we with a driver?" I ask as we head to a clothing store.

"Sometimes I like to drive myself," Hudson replies from behind the wheel. "You know I was serious about what I said earlier on the plane. We should get to know each other. At least superficially, so if people ask us questions, we won't be caught in a bind."

"The most important question they'll ask is how we met."

"That's easy. We met at work," he says dismissively.

"I don't think that will work. It'll come with too many questions. People will want to know what I do for you and how long I've been with you for."

"You're right," he says, and I can barely believe it. "There are people who will wonder why it is they've not seen you around before."

"Yes," I say, just glad that he's acknowledged that I was right.

"Okay, so we didn't meet at work then," he scoffs, clearly frustrated with the whole arrangement already.

"Where did we meet then?"

"You tell me. Where do you think it is possible for us to meet?"

"At a ranch."

"A ranch. Do you ride?" he eyes me and takes his eyes off the road for a while.

"Yes," I answer.

"You do?" he says, clearly not trusting me.

"Yes."

"You DO?" now he is serious.

"Yes, and I know you do," I tell him and show him a picture on his Instagram page of him on a horse. "So, we met at a ranch."

"Okay. Which ranch"

"Melinrad."

"I don't know it."

"Exactly, and neither do your friends."

He nods.

"You know how it goes. Boy likes girl; girl thinks the boy is a little forward and ignores him. Girl thinks boy should really chill out as he's being a creep now."

"Really? That's the story?" he says.

"It's a believable story."

"Not when I'm the boy, it isn't."

"Oh, you get all the women you want just by winking, don't you?"

"Something like that," he says in all seriousness.

"Well, not this girl. She's sassy."

"Yeah, that she is," he throws back at me.

"So, back to the story. Boy makes the girl laugh a bit, and that breaks the tension. So, girl thinks, maybe boy isn't so bad after all, and maybe she should give him the benefit of the doubt and voila, the rest is history."

"I don't like it," he complains.

"What don't you like about it?"

"Everything."

"Well, you come up with your own story then?"

"Will you accept whatever I come up with?"

"I'll gracefully reject it."

He scoffs. "Let's go with yours then."

I won this time, and it makes me glad.

"What other questions are there?" I ask him, and he passes his phone to me.

"Google gave me a list of right questions to ask one's girlfriend."

"Come on, we are not going to be that boring couple that is so mechanic. Let's be organic. We can think up our own questions."

"Like, what's your favorite color?" he scoffs

"Purple. More of lilac, really," I tell him. "What's yours?"

"I don't have one," he says as he turns the corner. We're driving down a road with shops selling luxury items on both sides.

"That's a lie. Everyone does," I say as we drive past a Gucci shop.

"I'm serious; I've always thought it silly to pick a color and make it your favorite. Colors are non-essential. I have my favorite liquor, my favorite horse, my favorite chess opening, but colors... that's silly."

I frown at that. It is sad to hear him speak like that. "Must life really be so rigid for you?"

"It isn't rigid for me," he says.

"You know what, let's play a game. Close your eyes."

"I'm driving," he says.

"Nonsense. Imagine your eyes closed. Have you done that?"

"This is silly. How does one imagine their eyes closed?"

"Just do it alright," I say, already frustrated with him.

"Alright, done."

"You walk to your closet, open the door, and reach for a linen shirt. What's the color of the shirt?"

"White," he says.

"God, you can't be saved," I mutter.

"Why? White is a good color."

"It's not," I counter and roll my eyes. "You can't say white or black is your favorite color. It's silly. They aren't even real colors. You know what, enough about colors."

"Thank you," he says.

We sit in the car in silence for a long time. It's awkward for a while, but then I start to feel comfortable in it.

"Do you think we should go back to the question Google suggests? It isn't like we want to actually get to know each other. We need a peripheral knowledge about each other, enough so our ruse won't be exposed."

"This is turning out to be more work than I imagined."

"Seventy thousand dollars."

"You'll squeeze every penny out of me, won't you?"

"You know that's not true."

"How much is the deal you're looking to broker with Frank worth?"

"About a billion dollars," he answered.

"Are you worried about it?"

He turns and gives me a look that tells me he finds my question ludicrous.

"What's this? You're trying to make me think you care about me?"

"Never crossed my mind. I'm just making conversations." I say.

"Well, conversation over then," he says with such caustic intensity that I instinctively move away from him.

Something about the deal made him get so defensive suddenly. I am right to think he is worried about it; he is so worried he's willing to make silly decisions like marrying Phillipa. Good thing he talked himself out of it. He talked himself out of it only to talk himself into me.

I decide to carry out a little research of my own on Frank Dubois. I do what I think will be a quick Google search on him, but soon, I find myself running down the rabbit hole.

He's a French American middle-aged man who amassed his wealth from electronic sales before pivoting to finance. He made himself a mogul after heading the purchase of two big American banks, one of which was acquired by a hostile takeover. Frank managed a hostile takeover while he himself was nothing but a millionaire with a big dream and a covetous heart. He's a ruthless businessman, so Business Insider described him. Wall Street Journal 500 called him *The Burning Star, Which Turned Out to Be The Sun*. After he bought over the two banks, a journey of ruthless takeovers and buyouts began. Once Frank has his eyes set on your company, consider it gone. He was a terrifying man.

Digging deeper into the man, I soon find something that catches my eye. It's a headline about six months old.

A savior meddling in the affairs of devils. The Sinclair fortune at risk of liquidation.

I barely read beyond the first line of the article when the story became clear to me. Frank got wind of the success that Sinclair has made with his company, and now, he wants it for himself. They've entered into a battle that has lasted over four months now, longer than any other hostile takeover battle that Frank Dubois has been involved in. Hudson isn't going out without a fight, but unfortunately for him, the fight is hurting his company terribly.

I take a look at the man with the set jaw, his eyes firmly on the road, his hands gripping the wheel so hard that I fear he'll pull it off. There is more to him than meets the eye. Maybe I have judged him too harshly. He is a fighter, apparently, and he's fighting tooth and nail for something he loves.

CHAPTER 4

HUDSON

*T*he rest of the drive to the store is silent. I can't say it's an improvement on the banter, but I like the quiet. I get to think. That doesn't come easily, though. All that's left is to play the game of offers and see who comes out at the top. When we get to the store, I can see how eager Juliette is to get out of the car. I might have been comfortable with the silence, but she clearly wasn't.

"You need to get a gown for a dinner party," I tell her as we walk in.

"We're going to a party?"

"Yes, tomorrow night."

"What kind of party? Who's going to be there? Is there a particular way I am to dress?" she asks, panicky.

"There's no need to panic. It is just some dumb party that Frank is throwing. I need to be there, and Phillipa will be there, so it's the right time to introduce you as my lover."

"Oh…"

That is all I get back. We start to walk down the aisle, and she picks up some clothes, showing them to me.

"What do you think?"

I shrug. "You're the one who knows how they fit."

"Is it the right get up for a future Mrs. Sinclair?"

"Get up?" I ask with a shake. She really is taking all this as a game. Well, she better be ready to play it well. "I won't know how it fits unless I see it on you."

"So, you want me to play dress up?"

"You asked for my opinion and I gave you the honest truth."

Grinning, she picks up some more clothes. "Okay, I'll play dress up for you. I'll play whatever you want me to play for seventy thousand dollars."

She takes me by the hand, and we head to the dressing room. I tap at one of the attendants and ask if they serve champagne.

"We'll be here a while, won't we?" I ask Juliette.

"Yeah. Get yourself something to drink."

The dressing room is a big squarish room with a big room and a smaller cubicle for changing. There's a sofa in the corner and a loveseat beside it. I choose the loveseat as Juliette packs her handful of clothes into the room.

"How many clothes do you have there with you?"

"Five or thereabout," she says.

"Will that be enough for a seven-day itinerary?"

"I guess."

"No, get some more."

She eyes me for a while, shrugs, and then heads back out into the store. She returns with more clothes and heads immediately to the changing room, while I wait for her.

"We can continue the Google questions while you wait," she yells from the room.

I had thought I'd have some quiet time, but then we need to know more about each other before the dinner party tomorrow. I get my phone and scroll to the webpage with the questions.

"They say we should tell each other our names. Full names," I say.

"Okay… I'm Juliette Marianne Nightingale. My grand-mother was called Marianne. She died a couple of days before I was born, so naturally, I got her name. I'm not complaining. I like it. Now, you."

I roll up the page to check the number of questions we still have to go through. It's a list of a hundred questions. This is terrible, I groan.

"Full name's Hudson Jonathan Sinclair."

"Is that all? No anecdote as to why you got the name?"

Is this going to be me for the next seven days? Telling stories, filling up silent moments? On one hand, I feel it might be tiring, on the other, it's something I've never done before, and there is a tepid excitement about it all.

"I didn't get any of my names from a dead grandparent. My mom wanted to name me Jonathan and my dad Hudson. So, they settled for a middle ground."

"That's boring," Juliette crones from inside the room.

"Well, not everything in life as—"

The door opens, and I forget what I intend to say. Juliette is standing by the door. She had made some changes to her hair. She's wrapped it up in a bun, but some parts of it remain free, dangling in a curl down to her ears. It appears like something that was done in a rush, but it highlights her facial features and gives her a more distinct look. I can see her eyes better now, but that isn't the only thing that has left me speechless. She's wearing one of the dresses she picked out. It was a dark green dress made of satin, and while it was free, it still wrapped around her body as though part of the cloth was wet. The short dress settles well above her knees and has an open neck shape, so her ample bosom is partly exposed to me.

This woman is different from the one who came into the office hours ago. She looked beautiful back then, but she looks like a seductress here. Her appearance suddenly fills me with the imagination I had put a leash on before. I hunger for the feeling of my finger on her thighs, tracing the soft and milky skin up until I get to her warm wetness.

Fuck!

What is this? I'm hard, and my cock is pressing against my zipper.

"What do you think?" she asks me and throws herself around, giving me a full view of the dress.

I think I'll have you right here, right now.

"You look good," I say, only to discover that I'm standing. I don't return to my seat immediately. Instead, to play it off like I stood up intentionally, I walk over to her and turn her around so she's looking into the mirror. I stand behind her, my hands on her waist, watching her. "It's a good choice."

"It's expensive," she complains.

"You are taking it," I declare.

"But I can't wear this to the dinner. It's too… I don't know the word for it."

"Sexy," I give her the word she's looking for.

"Yeah," she says, chuckling. "I know just what I'll wear to the dinner party," she says and pulls away. When she returns to the changing room, I stand there, looking at myself in the mirror.

What are you doing, Hudson? You're here to make a deal

and secure the future of the company and the future of the family. Not let yourself be beguiled by some woman.

How did she go from looking sweet to looking dangerous suddenly? I told her she wasn't my type, maybe that is quickly changing.

Still, I know nothing must happen between the two of us, especially because of the contract we both signed. I had indicated there that she isn't under any obligation to perform sexual acts that do not further the ruse before people. So, I have to push all dirty thoughts that involve her out of my mind and focus on the reason I'm in Manhattan.

My phone chirps and I check it to find I have a message from Alison. She's finished with her meeting and wants to know if I have any plans for dinner. If I have none, she'd like to make one. She's sent a list of restaurants we can go to.

I don't feel like talking business with Alison tonight, so I text her that she is free for the night and that work begins tomorrow. She'll brief me on how the meeting went, and we'll prepare for the dinner party later in the day. We'll prepare a dossier of the benefits we're willing to offer Frank Dubois and why he stands to gain more by partnering with us instead of buying us out totally.

If all my attempts to reason with Frank fail, I might have to do something unreasonable. I really hope it doesn't get to that.

"Hey, Hudson. Could you come in here for a minute?"

Juliette's voice breaks through my thoughts. I walk towards the changing room, wondering why she needs me. Is she all dressed in there or naked? I hope for the latter but quickly chastise myself for thinking that. I'll have to see some of my connections here in Manhattan. Juliette has stirred and started something in me that she isn't fit to take care of. I open the door to find her facing me. She's changed out of the former dress and into something else. This doesn't scream seductress like the first dress, but it still looks damn good on her. It has a classic look, perfect for the dinner party. She turns around and shows me her bareback.

"Can you help me pull up the zipper?" she asks.

"Sure," I respond.

I pick up the slider of the zipper, slowly pulling it up. My finger grazes her bare back, and for a moment, it causes me to freeze. I'm too close to her and she has too much skin exposed here. I can't trust myself to go any further. I want to pull the zipper back down, turn her around, and kiss her.

"Are you alright back there?" she asks, and her voice is all I need to get back in my right senses and pull it up all the way.

"I'm only familiar with the downward pull," I say and, against better judgment, spin her around. The spin catches her by surprise, causing her to fall towards me. I have to steady her so she doesn't fall any further. In doing that, my left palm finds itself pushing against her right breast. I let it linger for a while. The dress she's wearing doesn't need a bra, so there is only one layer of fabric between my palm and her tender breast. I can feel her nipples poking into my palm. I want more of it, to peel away even that last layer.

"Your hand," she said, looking down at my palm. I step back and smile at her.

"Sorry. I thought it was calling to me," I say.

"Alright, you've exhausted your usefulness."

I walk out of the changing still sporting a painful boner. I must do something about it.

A while later, she comes out with the clothes to solicit my opinion. I tell her it's perfect for dinner. We try some of the other clothes she picked, but nothing compares to the first two she showed me.

As we drive back to the hotel, I begin to wonder if she'd knowingly picked up those two dresses and showed them to me first to make a point. Was she tormenting me? Looking for a lick back because I said she isn't my type? Is this all her feminine urge to show herself as a suitable mate?

We make no effort to strike up a conversation during the ride back, and it's late by the time I pull into the hotel parking lot.

"Are you hungry? I'm starving." I ask her as we make our way back to our rooms.

"Yes, I want to eat."

"Alright, Why don't you clean up? Change out of that dress and wear one of the new ones. We'll have dinner at their restaurant here in the hotel."

"I wouldn't know how to make my way there," she tells me.

"When I'm ready, I'll knock on your door."

"How long do I have to prepare?"

"An hour at most," I tell just as we get to the door to her room. She heads in, and I walk into mine.

I get out of my clothes and hurry to the bathroom. I have more in mind besides having my bath and preparing for dinner. I let the lukewarm water run over me and reach for the soap bar.

I'd have preferred a lube, but I didn't plan for this, so the soap will do just fine. This is all her fault; showing me that dress and letting me pull up the zipper.

I step away from the running water and lather the soap, so I get good lubrication. I wrap my fingers coated with enough soap around my rock-hard dick, feeling it pulsating with need. I close my eyes, hand on the wall to keep me steady as I stroke myself, looking for relief. With my eyes closed, all I can see is her face. She smiles at me, bites down seductively on her lips, and stands on her toes to whisper in my ear. She doesn't say anything. Instead, she bites the lobe of my ear gently. I can't hold it back anymore. I cum, rope after rope of my seed spilling out with only one name on my lips, my face, on my mind.

Juliette.

CHAPTER 5

JULIETTE

I stand with my back against the door, taking a deep breath. It still confounds me how one man can strike two starkly opposing emotions in me. Hudson is the opposite of everything I have ever hoped for in a man. He is brashly proud, open sexually, uncouth, and disrespectful. Yet, there is a softness about him, the way he touched me when I asked him to help with the zipper.

Why did he spin me around, and why didn't he get his hands off my breasts immediately? Why did he linger? Does he want me?

He doesn't. He made that clear earlier on in the office. But then why did I make a show-off showcasing the clothes to him? I had restyled my hair and ensured the dress splayed on my body in the most enticing and revealing manner. And the zipper? I could have gotten to that myself. What game am I playing here? Why am I instinctively longing for his attention?

He's in the next room now. I wonder what he's up to. I don't want to delay him, so I hurry into the bathroom. He asked me to choose a new outfit from the set of clothes, and that's what I did. I choose a short black Chanel gown, with a matching purse, and I'm ready. Now, all I have to do is wait for him.

I wait a long time for his knock which doesn't come for an hour. When I open the door, he steps in like he owns the place. Well, he is paying for it, but he walks through like he's the king of the place, even though I didn't invite him in.

"Come right in," I say, letting my displeasure be obvious in my voice. He ignores it and looks around the room.

"Mine has a darker shade of brown for the wallpaper," he points out.

Making small conversations, are we?

"Are we going to eat?" I ask him. "There is no one around. You don't have to keep up the charade."

"I thought we were supposed to know each other better," he says, and for a moment, I think I see pain in his eyes. Did something I said get to him?

"Well. The shade of your room's wallpaper tells me nothing about you."

"I like it," he mentions and then immediately turns around, heading for the door. I follow him.

Oh, so that's it? This is about the favorite color conversation.

"Are you always this moody?"

"Moody? What gives you the idea that I'm moody?"

"I don't know. Look how quickly you turned the conversation on its head when I didn't seem interested in what you had to say."

"I don't care if you're not interested in what I have to say. I'm just making conversation, playing polite."

"Oh, you're far from polite."

"You are the queen of courtesy, aren't you?"

Why does everything always end up in a fight between us? We've known each other for about half a day, and we've spent the larger part of that time fighting and arguing.

He stops walking suddenly, and I almost bump into him. The look on his face tells me he's still in a foul mood. His anger now is just irrational.

"Did I say something or do something to piss you off?" I ask him, squaring up to him. But since he is significantly bigger than me, I cannot help but step back. It is embarrassing because I'm sure that he doesn't need this but because I really can't help it.

"Have you ever considered that not everything is about you?" he hisses at me. "You said, let's get to know each and ask what my favorite color is. I think to tell you a color, you dismiss me."

"You're just being petty now. How was I supposed to know you were talking about your favorite color when you mentioned the thing about the wallpaper? You waltzed into my room, said the most random thing ever, and got angry at me for not picking up on your cues."

He has a very cold look about him that for a while, I fear I had struck a nerve that he can't look past, but then he chuckles, turns away from me, and continues walking.

"Why are you laughing?" I demand.

"Look at us, bickering," he says. "No one will believe we aren't a couple."

I've seen couples bicker, and it's nothing like what we just did. There is hate laced in every word we speak. They sound like the words of people who can barely tolerate each other. I'm here for the seventy-thousand-dollar paycheck at the end of the seven days, and he's here, hoping to use me to divert an impending disaster. We are using each other, and that, I predict, is the root of all the troubles. There is nothing genuine about what the two of us have created here.

At the table, we have nothing to say to each other. The waiter comes around, takes our order, and then returns with the food; still nothing to say to each other. We dig in immediately as we are both hungry. Halfway through our dinner, Hudson passes his phone to me. It's opened to the webpage with the one hundred questions to ask a new potential girlfriend. I'm not going to do that with him. If we have a discussion, it'll have to be about genuine issues. I could ask him about his ongoing clash with Frank Dubois and how he intends to solve it. But he won't be willing to talk to me about that because it's too heavy. I should start small.

I push the phone back to him.

"We're not doing that," I tell him.

"Oh, but we need to. The contract says that you must partake in all activities that'll help further the ruse."

"But this doesn't do that. It's just a list of some stupid questions put together by someone who doesn't know you. Who doesn't know us."

"And you think you know me enough to ask me more personal questions?" he asks defensively.

"Why are you always so defensive?"

"Why don't you ever take anything seriously?" he countered.

"What do you mean?" I ask.

"You came. You came to me even though I'm sure all the other girls told you it was a bad idea. It was your first day at work, and you chose to fill the shoes others weren't willing to."

"Naivety," I say to him.

"That's not true. You're not the naïve kind."

"Oh, now, so you know me," I say mockingly.

"Enough to know that you're not an idiot, and neither are you naïve. But you're something else. Careless, I think, is the word I'm looking for. You didn't care for the pain and the difficulty that you might be presented with. You only think of forging on. That's all your life is about, forging on."

Which is similar to you, isn't it? I think, but I don't say. Total honesty isn't necessary yet.

"You say that like it's a bad thing."

"It's a bad thing if you have no sense of preservation at all. If you think you can forge through just about anything."

"You're taking pride in being the thing I can't forge through, right?"

"No… you're getting it wrong. I'm not saying this as it pertains to me. Just your person."

"But we're discussing, and everything we say is as it pertains to us," I say. "You say I'm careless, but you're diffi-cult. Even when you don't need to be. You don't seem to have any other mode but the difficult one. And you seem to take pride in it?"

"I am not difficult. I am meticulous."

"See, you won't even agree to a simple observation," I point out.

"Even if it is false?"

"It's not. Tell me the truth about Aliya, is she really sick? Why does she take many breaks?"

"I don't know; She has a family issue, I guess."

"You know why she does it," I say, maintaining eye contact until he admits the truth.

"Alright, she takes the breaks to cool off from me."

"And you think you're just being meticulous and not difficult?"

"Well, I can't help what I am."

"I can't help what I am either. So, you're an ostensibly difficult man who is almost incapable of forming any meaningful social relationship because people find you unbearable, too controlling, and annoying. And I am a woman whose motto is: when God gives you a lemon, you make lemonade out of it. A woman who never knows when to back down. It should be a fun seven days."

Hudson guffaws and takes a sip of his wine. He leans forward into me, still grinning.

"What do you need the seventy thousand dollars for?" he asks me, changing the direction of the conversation. I don't object to it because it is at least an avenue for us to know each other better.

"I want to start a bakery. I've saved some money, but not enough. But with the seventy thousand dollars, I'll have more than enough to get started."

"A bakery?" he says with a trace of disgust in his voice.

"What? It's too lowly for you, huh."

"Forgive me if it sounded like that. It was strange to me, was all."

Too tired to fight him, I let that go.

"How long have you had the bakery idea?"

"Since college," I tell him.

"You really want it?" he asks me, leaning even further and sipping his wine. There's a mischievous glint in his eyes. "Will you do anything for it?"

What is this? What is that look in his eyes? He's had more than three glasses of wine now, and I can see it's affecting him, causing him to set aside all his inhibitions.

"Anything like what?" I ask, not quite sure I know how I'll

respond to the answer he gives. I know what he'll say. His body is speaking louder than words he's yet to utter.

"Break the contract? Those wallpapers, do you want to see them?"

I stand up and pick up my glass of wine. "I think I'll just go to bed."

CHAPTER 6

HUDSON

I sit at the table for a while, basking in my foolishness. How could I let myself slip up like that? I can't understand the effect she is having on me. Whenever I see her, I lose all sense of composure and can't get my mind to function right. The whole night, there's been just one thought on my mind, and with the thought finally out, I can see how foolish it is and how much of a mistake it was to let it out.

After paying for the meal, I retire to my bedroom, exhausted. Tomorrow is going to be a long day, so I go to bed immediately. The next morning, Alison's call wakes me up. I get out of bed as I answer the call.

"When do we meet with the Fejitos?" she asks. I can sense hostility in her voice, but I can't deal with Alison's anger now.

"In an hour. Call them and text me the location they choose."

With that, I get ready for the day's work. I have good mind to leave the hotel and leave a message for Juliette at reception, but I figure that might come off as disrespectful to her. She's beginning to have tiny impacts on me. I shouldn't allow this. Anyway, I knock on her door—less because I want to tell her I'm leaving and more because I want to see her.

When she opens it, I remain by the door, having no intention of stepping in and cause myself to give in to temptation. She's wearing a nightgown, a sheer black one, and I can tell she has no bra underneath because I can see her perky breasts through the sheer material.

"Hi," she says, still sleepy. "Good morning."

"Good morning. Did you have a sleep well?"

She replies: "Pretty much."

"Good," I say, and then get down to business. I'll be in meetings all day today, so you have most of the day to yourself. Be ready for dinner by 7 pm. If I'm not here to pick you up, I'll send someone to."

"Not Alison, please," she says.

"Do you have a problem with Alison?"

"You mean other than the fact that she looks like she wants to kill me?" she says.

"Alison can be a little too protective of me sometimes, but she means well. No, she doesn't want to kill you."

"Protective is an interesting choice of word."

"I won't be sending Alison," I say, looking to end this conversation as soon as possible.

"What will you have me doing till seven in the evening," she complains.

"It's a big city," I tell her. "Go have fun. If you need some money," I say and start to reach for my wallet.

"I am not a charity case," she complains. "I don't need you to cater to me like a child."

"Well, I guess what you spend your day doing isn't any of my business then. I just need you to be ready by 7 pm. The contract binds you."

"All right, all right, 7 pm," she says and closes the door.

All the way to my car, I can't get the image of her breast out of my mind. I imagine what it will feel like to hold them in my hand, to run my finger around her hard nipple, to hear her moan my name.

God, what am I doing?

I get my phone out to make a call.

"Hudson," a soft voice says at the other end. I can hear soft and tender jazz music in the underground. Don't tell me you're in Manhattan."

"Hi, Jasmine. Yes, I am. How have you been?"

"You mean since you left me on my own?" Jasmine says.

"Don't play coy with me."

"Always so brusque," she tsks. "What is the call for?"

"I'll be over before the end of the day."

"You know I'm always available for you. What time should I prepare for you."

"Five pm, okay?"

"I'll be here then. You know how to find me."

"Yes," I end the call and sigh, feeling angry but not really understanding what the anger was for.

I can't dwell on that for too long anyway. I have more important business to handle. I get into the car and get a text from Alison. The Fejitos have decided to meet me at their home. That is a good sign, welcoming me into their home. She sends me the address, and I put it into the GPS and it leads me to their home.

The drive takes about fifteen minutes, and when I arrive at the mansion, Alison is waiting for me in the driveway. She's dressed smartly in a short skirt and silk shirt.

"What's the lay of the land like?" I ask her as one of the butlers leads us from the garage to the living room.

"It's hard to tell. The whole family is here, but we'll be meeting with just the father. I think they came to the US for the party."

"Dubois makes his demands."

"He runs his ship like it's the military. Disobedience is tantamount to insubordination."

Too much control, I hiss to myself. How was Frank able to amass so much control and so much impact in such a short period? He's been in the financial world for less than three decades, yet everyone treats him like he's some god, someone that mustn't be messed with. Crossing him sure means total annihilation.

I've been at war with him for the past three months, and here I am, standing strong. Maybe not as strong as I'd have loved. Maybe he isn't as powerful as he'd like people to believe.

The butler opens the door, and a big hall welcomes us. The grand hall exudes elegance, with its high vaulted ceilings designed with specially crafted chandeliers. Its polished marble floor glistens in the bright light of the afternoon that is let in by expansive windows with velvet drapes, and I can almost see my reflection through it while columns worthy of being in the coliseum line the walls. This extravagance, all delicately balanced, is a testament to the Fejito's wealth. Down the hallway, the butler leads us to a door, where he knocks twice and waits for a response.

"Come in," the raspy voice of Rakeem Fejito calls from behind the door. The butler nods at us and then walks away. I open the door and step through the study. It is a medium-sized room with a table and chair facing the window. The design is simpler than that of the hall we passed. While

Rakeem has an appearance a man of his position must maintain, in personal taste, he is simple. Rakeem is standing by the window, looking into the garden. He doesn't turn to acknowledge us but speaks.

"My wife loves coming to the States. It means two things to her. The garden in our mansion here and parties. I hate coming to the States. It means trouble. Too many people looking to show their prowess and gargantuan influence. It isn't good for my health. I prefer it back in France on my farm. The smell of cow dung and peace in the air. Nothing beats that."

"Mr. Fejito, thanks for having us," I say in response, not sure what else is appropriate to the harangue we just received.

"You know to call me Rakeem, Hudson," he says and finally turns around to face us. He has a handy smile for Alison and me. He walks over, hugs Alison with a kiss on the cheek, and shakes my hand firmly. He points at an empty couch by the wall and takes the loveseat opposite it.

"I hate the US, but I wouldn't dare miss a party thrown by Dubois. He calls, and everyone comes running with their tail tucked behind their ass."

"I don't think you're one to run with your tail tucked, Sir," I tell him and get a chuckle from him.

"Don't patronize me," he says with a wave of his hand. I must say, you look better than I expected. I was expecting to see a thin, wiry old man already."

"It's been just three months," I say.

"True but going up against a deep pocket like Dubois can age one fast. Trust me; I tried it once and learned the error of my ways."

"Do you think this is a mistake? You think I'm making a mistake?"

"Hmmm," he murmurs and stands up. He walks to his mahogany liquor cabinet. The shiny lacquer on the wood tells me it was recently polished. "Bourbon?"

"Just a finger for me," I say, knowing the foolishness liquor made me commit last night.

Rakeem turns to Alison, who shakes her head. Alison doesn't drink much. With a nod, Rakeem gets two glasses from the cabinet and returns to the loveseat. He hands me one of the glasses and running my finger around it, I can tell it's a fine glass. Only the best for a man like Rakeem. He pours me some and then pours himself some more. He finishes his drink in a single swig before he speaks.

"Mistakes are things perceived in hindsight. They don't exist in the present. I can't tell you if you're making a mistake now, but I can tell you a story. My story," he says and pours himself another drink.

It seems it's a heavy story.

"Ten years ago, one of my financial advisors came to me with a graph showing the steady growth of the American economy. Oh, God, how I have come to hate graphs. We should have a business here, he told me, and I agreed. We came down to America, met with some people, and started one. Unbeknownst to me, that was the beginning of my troubles. We had good returns in the first five years, and then we started to make headlines. One night, back home, I got a call. It's the middle of the night, so I ignore it. Whoever it is, must have the sense to call in the morning. But the caller was incessant and disturbed my sleep, so I was left with no choice but to answer. It was my financial advisor telling me I have a call from someone in the US. A man called Frank Dubois wanted to discuss my new business in America. I thought it was a good thing, people are noticing me and want to partner with me. Partnering is a good way to get myself strong footed over there."

Rakeem laughs maniacally before he continues.

"How wrong I was. Frank doesn't partner. He hates it. It disgusts him. He wanted the world to be about him and him only. He wanted the spotlight all for himself, yet this strange man hated the spotlight. I answered the call, and those five minutes I spent on the call with him were the worst moments of my life. His demands were simple. I sell to him with no struggles, and he'll buy me out fairly. He gave a delicious offer, but I'd never had someone threaten to buy me out before, so I refused. Who does he think he is? America is the land of the free, and I must exhibit that right. By morning, I got a different kind of call. My license to import in the US has been revoked. I understood the message. This man has a reach and power in the United States that I can only wish for. I wasn't fighting against snakes and vipers, not even giants. He was the leviathan beast. Well, I was one stubborn mule, though."

Rakeem smiles and drops his glass.

"But you, you're young. You're different. He can't wave his wands and get your license revoked. You're a citizen here. It is harder for him. You can give him the scare that no one has been able to. What, three months now, isn't it? You've got him worried, that I am sure of. But is he worried enough?"

"There's a hole in my company's finances. He's blocked my access to loans and funding. The longer I'm in this battle with him, the bigger the hole gets, and it's only a matter of time before the whole thing starts to sink," I confess my fears to Rakeem.

"That is his game here, isn't it? Time and money. He has an excess of it, and you, unfortunately, do not. He can wait you out for a year, but you don't have that luxury."

"We would if we had a golden chest," Alison says.

"And that is why you are here, isn't it? You see a golden chest in me."

"We know you still want to do business here in America. Frank might have snuffed out the dream once, but you know your financial advisor was right to draw your attention to it. This country is a viable organism that is assured to procreate in large quantities, and you want to be there to enjoy those fruits."

"How much are you talking?" Rakeem asks.

"Endless," Alison chips in.

Rakeem laughs. "My great-grandfather was a pirate. He made most of his wealth stealing what others wouldn't dare to go close to. He was a madman. I come from a place with so much sand. The desert is large, wide, and unending. He left it to seek a different kind of desert. His favorite words to me while he was still alive were: *What is so familiar is easy. What is strange is what is worth fighting for.*"

"America is your treasure trove," I say.

"True. But my great-grandfather died from a shark attack. He was seventy and just wouldn't give up the hunt. It filled him with life, yet it took that life from him."

I look at Alison and wonder where this harangue is leading to. To keep up this war with Frank, I need some leverage and backing with a lot of cash.

"I am sixty-five. My wife tells me it is time to retire. Let's come to America and live the rest of our lives here. She wants a lot of servants, big gardens, and parties. America is the ocean to me. It calls to me every time I step foot here, and whenever I do, I see myself going out just like my great-grandfather, bitten by a shark. Life is all about learning from the mistakes of others. I told you; mistakes are brought to light by the passage of time."

"You said it yourself. Frank's greatest leverage is time. His other leverage is money, and that provides him with time; if I can match him in money, I can match him in time."

"I've read your financials. You're doing good," Rakeem continues.

"And we are projected for a two hundred percent increase in ten years."

"That drew the sharks in, didn't it? Sharks like me," Rakeem continues. "Last night, Frank came to me."

My heart skips a beat. Frank is unbelievable. How is he able to move so fast, so easy, so wise? I know immediately the destination of this new information. Frank will match and outbid whatever my offer is. It's over.

But Rakeem is telling me something. There must be a reason he is. There might still be hope.

"His offer was simple. I do not provide you any support and I get my company back. My financial advisor, the one you've tagged as intelligent, tells me it is the best and safest bet for me. I get my treasure trove and stay protected. I don't have one of the biggest sharks in the water as an enemy."

I watch him intently and can sense the anger coming from him.

"How stupid. A man comes into my home and returns that which he stole from me and then makes demands of me. My great-grandfather will say: *Cut his legs off so he crawls out of your house and knows there is no mercy for those that pilfer.* Very wise words from a pirate, don't you think?" he chuckles.

Alison shifts to chip in, but I hold on to her thigh, This isn't the time to offer any advice. Rakeem has made a decision. We just have to sit here and watch him meander his way to it.

"Here is what I think I'll do," he says. "My financial advisor is right. I need peace to function here. But I am also a prideful man. He who hurt me must hurt back. You want cash? You'll get it. I want my company back; I'll get it."

"What do you suggest?" I ask.

He stands up and walks to his table. From one of the drawers, he pulls a folder out for me. "That's your treasure trove," he says.

"You want to play the game on two fronts."

"I want to play it safe," he says and returns to watching the garden through the window. "There are two ways this goes. No, three. And I intend to benefit should it go either way. Now, I'm sure I can count on your discretion."

"Frank will know I have met with you."

"Of course, I'll call him to tell him about this meeting. He must think we have a deal, he and I."

"But you do have a deal."

"And I have a deal with you also."

I smile, quite impressed. He's acted like the great-grandson of a real pirate. He has nothing to lose in all of this. The game is up to the players now. But this is good for me. Very good.

"Thank you, Rakeem," I tell him.

"It's just business."

CHAPTER 7

HUDSON

"*I* don't like it," Alison complains as we walk back to the garage.

"We got the money we came here for," I point out to her.

"Yes, but not his heart? He has a deal with Frank, the enemy."

"Frank isn't the enemy."

"He wants your company. I consider him the enemy. That aside, how do we trust him not to inform Frank of all that we did here today? All of this might be a ruse."

It seems everyone is keeping up a ruse these days, I think and sigh.

I open the file and scan through it. "He is staying as far away as he can from the mess but still has skin in the game. He is funding us through this company."

"Some fictitious Dominican company?"

"No, it's an actual company. It's been in existence for ten

years now. The CEO is a man named Jamin Rakan. They make fair money, but it's the value of the company that'll keep us afloat, and it's in India, where Frank's reach is little."

"What skin does Rakeem have in it then?"

"It's his company. It's all in here," I tell her. It's well hidden behind numerous other shields, but it is his company, and should we go down, this company does also."

"He gets a replacement company in America."

"Yes, but he loses ten years of work. I'm sure he doesn't want that. What I think is this: He wants me to win this however I can. My win gives him the leverage to do what he's always wanted. Start a company here in America without the influence of Frank. With the deal he made with Frank, he'll always be under Frank's thumb should Frank win. But he's not an idiot. He plans for all possibilities but knows which he wants the most, so he commits more to the one he wants."

Alison knows I am right, so she doesn't argue anymore.

"We should have gone for the easy route," she says after a while.

"I am not going to marry her," I insist.

"Of course not. You're engaged now." there is spite in her voice.

"Hate doesn't look good on you."

"It's not hate. It's confusion. You don't even know who this girl is, and you gave her the diamond ring. That thing is worth over two hundred thousand dollars. What if you get to the hotel and she's gone."

"The company will track her down."

"Like hell, they will. They'll call you a fool for giving a practical stranger your diamond ring and you can't take her to court because she didn't steal it from you. She's not liable for that."

"She won't run away with it," I tell her.

"You don't even know where she is right now. How can you be so sure?"

I don't know, but I feel like I can see right into Juliette's heart. Maybe that is why I chose to entrust this whole deal to her. She's different, unlike the others. She has her own dreams, and nothing will deter her from them—not even some diamond.

"I trust her," I say.

Alison is ready to argue again, but I stop her. "I trust her, and that will be the end of it. I won't have you second-guessing my decisions."

She groans and pouts. I know she has a point, but I can't help what I feel. Juliette seems like the right choice for this. If Rakeem's support proves useful, all of this won't matter anyway.

All these talks about Juliette cause my mind to stray again, and once again; I'm standing in front of the room, watching her in that nightgown, her breast calling to me. This time, I don't stand by the door. I wander in and have my seat on the couch. I watch her strip, dancing, gyrating to some music only she can hear. She lets the strap of her gown fall from her shoulder and then to her arm. The gown moves further down until her breasts are bare to me. I find myself moving, floating to them, my palms fondling them, pushing them against her chest and gently guiding her to the wall; she moans into my ears. I can't get enough of her breasts; I wanted them all over my face. I want my hands all over them. I want her all over me. I roll one of the nipples in my fingers, getting more urging moans from her.

"Hudson! Hudson!" Alison's voice drags me back to the present.

"What is it?" I ask, clearly irritated that she disturbed my imagination.

"Are you returning to the office?"

"No," I say. "I have somewhere else to be."

I have to see Jasmine now. I know I said evening, but I can't wait till then. I need some relief, now.

CHAPTER 8

JULIETTE

*A*fter Hudson left, I struggled to get back to sleep, but it just wasn't forthcoming. In the end, I had a shower, went down to the restaurant to get breakfast, and then returned to my room. Now, I'm here in the room, clueless about what to do next. I'm a total stranger here in Manhattan with nowhere to go. My options are limited, so to kill time, I decided to try on the gown I'll be wearing later tonight to the dinner. Knowing how important the dinner party is for Hudson; I want to be properly prepared for it. We tried to get to know each other better last night, but that didn't go well.

Last night, he invited me to his bedroom, and I was close to accepting the invitation. Having to go next door to sleep alone felt sad but not so sad that I was inclined to end up in Hudson's arms on my first night here. I have no intention of ending up in his arms at all, though. I will not lie and say I haven't thought of it. What would it feel like to have his lips brush against mine again, this time, making it last longer? Why else did I open the door for him in the sheer night-gown? Am I still trying to show him I am his type, or is there a hunger in me, a deep itching that I long to scratch?

I am playing a dangerous game here. But there are six days to go, and this will be over.

I smile at myself in the mirror, feeling sexy and powerful. The gown, while stopping just a couple of inches above my knees, has a long slit that I know will expose much of my thigh, making it even more inviting.

My phone rings and I answer it. It's my mother.

"Hey, Ma," I answer and set the phone to loudspeaker so I can obsess some more over my body.

"Juliette, how are you, love? I thought you were to call me yesterday, but you never did."

"I'm so sorry Mom. I got busy at work, and it skipped my mind. How are you?" I ask and move closer to the window, taking a look at the top part of the gown, trying to see if I really need a bra. My breasts are perky, and without a bra, they'd sit well in the gown. But then I'll have my nipples poking the dress. While I have a beguiled intent to torture Hudson, I don't want to go out there looking like a slut. A bra it is, then.

"I'm fine. How was your first day at work? Jenny says you got a big client, and you aren't in town."

"Yes, I'm in Manhattan."

"And you didn't think to tell me that?"

"I'm sorry, Ma," I say.

What about wearing it with no panties?

God, Juliette, get it together.

I move away from the mirror and jump on the bed to focus on the conversation with my mother. I need to get out of this room, see the town and keep Hudson out of my mind.

"How's the new work then?" my mom asks me.

"Going well, Ma. My boss is a pain in the ass, but I'm not new to dealing with pains in the ass."

"Stop calling your father that!" she chastises me.

"I'm just saying. He is why I am adept at handling difficult people like Hudson."

"You know I don't like your new job. It sounds too much like you're an escort."

My mother will lose her mind if she finds out that I'm a pretend fiancée to my boss.

"You don't like anything I do," I point out to her.

"I'm your mother. I'm not supposed to. Now, the bakery, it is a much better idea than this."

"I am doing this to get money for the bakery, Ma."

"Yes, I know that! That doesn't mean I have to be okay with it. All I'm saying is that there must be a better way to get the money you need, like a loan."

I sigh and turn on the bed. My mother and I have this conversation every time and I tell her the same thing every time. "I can't get a loan, Mom. I don't have any collateral or credit points to do that. They won't just give me a loan."

"I can talk to Benny. He'll help you know."

"You know what Benny wants, Ma."

"And what's wrong with that? Benny is a good guy. He makes good money and is a good man. He'll make a good father."

I sigh and rub my brow with my thumb in disbelief that we are having this conversation again.

"I tried it with Ben once, Ma. It didn't work out."

"Because you wouldn't put in an effort to make it work."

Benny was a good man, just as my mother said, but he isn't the man for me. He adores and dotes over me, but the whole time we were together, I felt amiss. He doesn't spark any passion in me.

Not like Hudson does.

God, no, not Hudson.

Whatever passion Hudson sparks, I must tame and kill it.

"You should call him and talk to him. He'll support your dreams. You two can get a house at the end of a cul-de-sac and start a family."

I close my eyes and try to imagine it. Benny and me, with a small house at the end of a cul-de-sac, with two kids, a dog and a happy life. It feels so empty, so strained and forced. It must be what Hudson feels whenever he thinks of a life with Phillipa. That's why I'm sympathetic to his situation. I know what it's like to be forced to start a relationship with someone you feel close to nothing for. With Benny, I'm sure there'll be stability and a sense of comfort in knowing I have someone who will be home, who will support and guide me, but I want more than that out of life. I want zeal and passion. I want to boil with lust and longing. I want to feel pleasure building up from the tip of my finger and filling me up entirely. I want to feel whole.

"Alright," I tell my mom. "I'll call Benny when I get back home."

"Thank you," she says. I can imagine the smile on her face, feeling confident that things will go better this time between Benny and me. I hear some whispers underneath. "Ma! Is Benny there with you?"

"Yes, I invited him to have breakfast with me."

"Jesus Christ, Ma. You'll break the poor boy's heart with hope."

"You promised to call him," my mother reminds me.

"Yes. Not marry him. I'll call him, we'll get coffee together and see if anything has changed."

"What is supposed to change?"

"How I feel about him, Ma. We've talked about this before. I don't like him like that."

"Give it time. Spend more time with him. See he is a sweet man, and you'll start to like him like that."

I know my mother means well when she insists that I go out with Benny. To her, Benny is the ideal man with stability and peace. Maybe stability and peace aren't what I'm out for. Maybe I need some rousing, a little storm in my teacup.

"I told you I'll call him. But now, don't you go giving him any reassurance. We are just getting coffee to see things, nothing more."

"Okay, okay. I won't tell him to pick his suit out just yet."

I shake my head and end the call with my mother, enjoying the feel of the cloth against my skin. I get out of the gown and stand naked before the mirror. I have no idea what Hudson is up to, but I imagine him with the arrangement he's made in town.

What are they up to now? Does Hudson have his hands all over her? Is he playing with her nipples, running them through his finger? Squeezing her breasts?

I close my eyes and try to imagine them, but I see myself with Hudson instead. He's naked from the waist up, and my fingers trace his toned muscles. Back in the room, my hand finds my breast and I fondle them. An unexpected flood of pleasure rushes through me and I can't help the moan that escapes my lips. Biting down on my lips to keep the moans at bay, I push my imagination further. Hudson kisses down my stomach and towards my sex. As I imagine that, my hand makes the same journey in real life so that as the Hudson in my head slides his tongue over my slit, I slide my index finger in, welcomed by sleek wetness and a immense desire for the actual Hudson's touch.

I open my eyes and know I cannot remain here with nothing to do. I'll lose my fucking mind. I'm already well on the way. I need some distractions. I need to get Hudson out of my head. I know that fantasy of mine will never be experienced, so I better shelf it as fast as possible.

I'll do some sightseeing and see what Manhattan has to offer. It's a big city, big enough for me to lose myself in and every thought of Hudson I have.

CHAPTER 9

HUDSON

*a*s Alison drives out of the garage, she leaves me with a warning.

"She's distracting you," she says. "This Juliette girl. I see the way you look at her. She's bold and daring and stands up to you. She's going to mess with your head, and I don't want that. I need you totally focused here, Hudson. This is the eve of the time of our lives. Don't mess it up."

She has a point. Juliette has definitely found a way to creep under my skin. I didn't intend for that to happen, but she's done it so swiftly and so precisely that it terrifies me. Yet, I like it. This is why I must see Jasmine before the party tonight. I walk into the apartment building, into the elevator, and up into the hallway. I stop at the familiar door and knock twice.

When the door opens, Jasmine is dressed in a short blue gown, which bares to me all the glory of her long legs. I can't get past how exquisite Jasmine always looks.

"I knew I'd see you before the time, you said," she says and steps aside so I can walk in. I'm welcomed by the sweet smell of her potpourri and potted flowers and the hiss of Slinker, who waltzes over to me, takes a look at me with his tired cat eyes, and then walks over to a corner of the room, returning to eating his toy.

"Looks like he missed me," I say.

"He doesn't remember you. He came to check if you have treats."

"Oh. I guess we have something in common, then. We both want treats."

Jasmine chuckles as she walks to her kitchen. "Do you want something to drink?" she asks me.

"Yeah. Water."

She hands me a bottle of water and throws Slinkers a cookie.

"You're here for the dinner party, right?"

"Yes," I tell her as I take my seat, and she joins me on the couch. She stretches her long legs over my thighs. "I think I might finally be able to convince Frank to let me go."

"Frank never lets anything go," she says with a chuckle. You're here for the distraction. To put your mind at peace."

"You know me too well, Jasmine," I tell her as I pull her closer. I bite down gently on her lips before kissing her.

Jasmine surrenders herself to me. The sweet taste of her lips, the soft flesh, and her tongue set me ablaze. Wanting more, I pull her even closer and get her to sit on my lap, my fingers finding her bare thighs. She pulls her thighs apart to give me access. I reach for her, for her warmth calling to me, but I just can't bring myself to go on. I stop and look up at her, feeling less than myself. She isn't the reason I'm in this bind. Only one person can free me of this sexual torment, and she isn't in this room right now. I don't know how long I can keep myself from touching Juliette. I lied to her when I said she isn't my type. The mere sight of her, her smell, sets my skin ablaze. She makes me feel wanton desire unlike any I have ever had before. It was unexplainable.

Jasmine takes the hint and pulls herself away from me. She settles on the chair, smiling.

"This is strange," Jasmine comments and stands up. She walks to her kitchen and returns with another treat for Slinkers.

"I don't want to talk about it," I say, feeling pouty. It has never happened to me before. I am so shocked by it I don't know how to react. No woman has ever had such control over me that I am physically unable to get pleasure from another. My skin burns for her. My need for her is so out of control that all I can think about is ramming my dick into her. Endlessly. Brutally. I want to fuck her so hard she knows I am mad at her for taking this sort of an asinine hold on me.

Fuck!

"That serious huh? So, we won't talk about her now. Let's talk about Frank."

"What about him?" I ask, the mention of the name rousing anger in me.

"What will you do?" she asks me.

"I have a plan," I tell her.

"What is it?"

"I can't tell you."

"You think I'll tell the enemy?"

"Why do you girls keep insisting he's the enemy?" I ask. "Even Alison calls him the enemy."

"He wants to take what you own. He is your enemy, and you're fighting him with all you've got."

"He doesn't seem perturbed."

"Oh, he is," she tells me, smiling. Then she takes a drink from the bottle.

"He is?" I ask, interested. "Tell me, what does he say?"

"Oh, so you want me to spill secrets, but you won't tell me anything."

I shrug.

"How about this?" Jasmine asks. "I'll tell you what he says if you tell who she is."

"She? What are you talking about?"

"The woman who has you all wound up?" Jasmine says. "I see it in your eyes. You came here looking for relief because you can't find it in her. Strange. I have never seen you pine for someone so hard before, not even me."

"I am not pining for her," I say rather defensively.

The evidence contrary to that is tucked into my trousers, deep dissatisfaction and a throbbing hard cock.

"Keep telling yourself that, but I know what I see. What's her name?"

"Juliette," I confess.

"Grand name. I used to know a Juliette. An old lady who makes music. She's in New Orleans now, happy as a bird. Will Juliette make you happy, Hudson?"

"Happy?" I ask with a cynical chuckle. "She's a pain my ass."

"Maybe she's a pain because you're hindering what could really be. She's supposed to bring you happiness, but I know you, Hudson, you believe and act like you don't deserve happiness but maybe you do."

"This isn't about happiness," I tell her. "It's about a girl who I'll be rid of in seven days, and all things will be back to what they used to be."

"Maybe that makes you sad. The return to the normalcy when she leaves."

I scoff. "You don't know what you're talking about."

"It isn't my embrace you longed for when you came here. It isn't my touch you hungered for; I know you, Hudson; I've been with you enough times to know when you're distracted."

"Of course, I'm distracted. Your lover wants to take my company."

"Not that kind of distraction," she says. "This kind." She reaches for my chest, and I pull her closer to kiss her. She pulls herself away. "I let that happen first because I had a yearning for you myself. That yearning isn't satisfied because someone else has you distracted, and I won't let myself be the distraction to that distraction."

"You're not the distraction," I lie.

"You say that like you really want to believe it. I don't know who this Juliette is. I don't know how you met her and what she's done to you. But maybe, in all of this storm, what you really deserve is the sense of calm she'll bring you—the peace, the pleasure, the joy."

Peace, calm, joy...those aren't words I'd associate with Juliette. She makes me angry so much, always ready to tackle me, never backing down, always fighting. I don't need that in my life. She is here because she is a necessity, no more.

"Tell me what Frank says about me."

Jasmine shrugs.

"He thinks you're more trouble than he bargained for. Going into this, he was convinced it'd be over quickly, but you've held on for longer than he had estimated. So now, he has to devise a new strategy to fight you."

"What's the strategy?" I ask.

"If I knew, I wouldn't tell you. I'd be betraying Frank's trust."

"You're fucking me. You're betraying his trust already."

"Frank and I, what we have is simple enough. He wants to own me, and I am not to be owned. He knows that, and being with me means he has accepted that. I made that clear to him."

"But you won't tell me what the strategy is?"

"Sincerely, I don't know it. If I did, though, I wouldn't tell you. I, however, do not want you to lose your company. I know it's the one thing you've ever truly come to love. If you lose it, you lose yourself. So, I'll let you in on one little secret. Frank is worried. He has money issues himself. I don't know the source, but it is significant, and he doesn't want to play a waiting game with you. He wants it done and done fast. He can't lose. Because if he does, he loses all the status that comes with being Frank Dubois. Playing a waiting game with you, however, means he'll win, but it'll be a victory that comes at a great cost. He's caught in a bind, Hudson."

Money problems. A Frank with a money problem isn't one that I would have ever envisaged. While it is good for me, it still doesn't make this battle any easier. I can already tell how the dinner party will go. Frank wants me to marry his daughter. That is this new strategy. He met with Rakeem to make him pull whatever support he intended to give me so I would have no choice but to marry his daughter, and with that, he'll pull a consolidation. If I marry her and break her heart in the future, he'd have solved his money issues, and then he'd be able to fight me till I'm dust.

No matter what, I can't agree to marry Phillipa, and this ruse between Juliette and me, we need to make it work, make it absolutely believable. This is the only way now.

"Thank you," I tell Jasmine.

"You men make wars over stupid things," she says, leaning over to kiss me. I let her kiss me. "You should leave now. Frank is coming here."

What if I remain here and let him find me. Maybe that will solve all of our problems. We'll fight it out and be done with it.

"Don't entertain silly thoughts," says Jasmine, like she can read my mind. "You can't be here when he arrives."

"It'd be nice to actually kick his butt you know."

"That'll achieve nothing," Jasmine points out and I know she's right. I leave her apartment, still feeling aroused. Once again, as I did yesterday, I'd have to seek relief by my own hand.

CHAPTER 10

JULIETTE

Spending the day walking through lower Manhattan was great. I had a little trouble finding the hotel on my return, but I asked around and found someone nice enough to lead me back to it. I got into my room at 6 pm, and by 7 pm, I was ready for the party, dressed up, dolled up, and perfect. I was barely able to take my eyes off my reflection in the mirror. When Hudson shows up at my door to inform me that it's time to leave, I get the reaction I want from him.

"You look amazing," he compliments me, stealing looks at me as he walks me into the elevator and heads to the waiting car.

"You look good too," I tell him, and he really does look good. For the night, he wore a charcoal-toned tuxedo and a brown bow tie. His shapely upper body frame provided a perfect carriage for the suit, and he walks with such regale that I feel great to be by his side.

The drive to the venue takes about thirty minutes, but it goes so fast because of the comfort the limousine provides, and Hudson seems to be in a chatty mood.

"You did your makeup yourself?" he asks me, still unable to take his eyes off me.

"Of course," I say. "It's all part of my superhuman skills."

"It's very good."

"Thank you," I tell him.

"You'll meet my mom today," he tells me.

"Wow, I don't think I'm ready for that," I complain.

"Don't worry, I'll tell her not to stress you so much. She'll know it's all a lie and will play along."

"Do you think that's wise. Won't she look at me like I'm some gold digger, just here for her son's money."

"Every girl I bring home, who she didn't suggest to me, is a gold digger."

"In this case, I am actually one," I point out.

"Well, while that is true, you are gold-digging but I approve. Don't you worry about my mother. She'll comport herself well."

"Alright. How did your day go?" I ask him.

He looks hesitant to answer the question but then shrugs. "Good, I guess. I was in a couple of meetings the whole day."

I see his eyes twitch as he says that. I have a friend who, whenever they tell a lie they're not so confident telling, has such twitches.

"Your eyes twitch when you lie, right?" I ask him.

"What?"

"Don't worry about it."

Why did he lie to me about being in meetings? Was he somewhere he didn't want me to know he was? Why should he care what I think about where he was or how his day went? I don't have the time to contemplate on this as the limousine pulls to a stop, and we get out. Immediately, we're welcomed by flashes of cameras and surrounded by what looks like a hundred paparazzi.

"Oh my god," I panic and want to turn around and head back into the limousine, but it's gone.

"What is it?" Hudson asks me as he holds my hand, and we walk on the red carpet.

"You didn't tell me there would be a red carpet, and you didn't tell me it would be something serious."

"Don't worry, You're doing great."

Doing great? I feel like I'm a step away from tripping and falling. I'm not scared of crowds, and I barely panic, but throughout the day, I imagine the dinner party to be small. A little gathering of, say, about twenty to fifty people. I didn't know it was such a big deal. This seems like too much of a big deal to me. A couple of people wave at Hudson, and some come over to say hi to him. Most look concerned as they hug him, asking him questions of the same variety.

"How's it going? Are you hanging in? You've got this. The villain can't back you in the corner"

They all encourage him about his legal battles against Frank Dubois. They all seem concerned for him and hold a prejudice against Frank. Still, I wonder, why are they all here? Why support a man they so much despise? Hudson answers as though he read my mind.

"They all don't want to be me. They hope cowering to him will give them at least a chance."

I understand that, but it still looks foolish.

"What if everyone comes together and fights against him? He definitely can't win against everyone."

"Fighting against him is like fighting against your money. He owns most of the banks these people do business with.

They don't want to be in his bad books. Where will they get the loans and financing they need to run their businesses?"

"Control the money, control the business."

"Pretty much," Hudson says. "Everyone's wondering who you are. You're practically unknown." He has a smile on his face, feeling proud.

I look around to see them all watching him, asking questions.

Poor Ma, I think. Good thing she doesn't read the papers or watch the news. Hudson hurries up, and we are out of the public eye soon enough. We follow a hallway that is lined with people meeting and greeting. I want to be out of here and into the hall as soon as possible. But that isn't possible as more people gather around to show Hudson their support. This is the only place they can do that, while Frank Dubois can't see them. I remain by his side, knowing he needs me to do nothing but be beautiful. Be beautiful then, I will be.

"Juliette?" a voice says behind me. For a moment, I think they're referring to me, but then I think I can't be the only Juliette here. Hudson himself turns around to see who here recognizes me.

"Juliette," the voice comes again, and this time, I'm sure they are calling me. "Juliette Nightingale."

Yup, that's me. I turn around to see who it is. It's a familiar face that I struggle to piece together for a while, but then it comes to me. Radder Bentley.

"I thought that was you I saw on the red carpet with.... Mr. Hudson."

"Hi, Bent," I say, looking at the woman I hadn't seen since she was a teenager. What are you doing here?"

"I'm one of the journalists covering the events," she offers. "What are you doing here?"

"I... huh," I struggle with an answer.

"She's with me," Hudson says, saving me the trouble of having to find an answer.

"Oh," Bent says, clearly in disbelief. She looks from me to Hudson, and unfortunately, her eyes pick up the ring on my finger. "Oh my god!" she gasps and points at it. "Can I see it?"

"We're in a hurry," Hudson says, wrapping his hand around my waist and pulling me away from Bent.

We are a couple of feet away from Bent before I finally can speak.

"Thank you," I whisper to Hudson.

"You're welcome. You looked like you needed rescuing," he says. "I take it you don't like her?"

"Oh, Bent? No, she's just… God, she terrifies me. I had no idea I was still so terrified of her. The last time I saw her was in high school. She was a cheerleader, one of those types who has the whole school worshipping them, and for some reason, she just seemed to hate me."

"I know her mother. They're the same thing."

"Thank you for rescuing me."

"Come on, I'm only just repaying the favor. You'll be doing a lot of rescuing for me later today," Hudson says as he pushes open the door. We are welcomed by soft music and lights. The hall is half full. Hudson immediately leads me down the hall, searching for his designated seat. He finds it in a corner, just beside a table that reads Dubois. It'll be a fun night, I conclude. The two tables are still empty for now. He pulls out one of the chairs for me.

"Gentlemanly, huh?" I ask.

A server brings us both glasses of champagne. I take mine, knowing I'll have to be careful about drinking. I don't want to drink so much that I spill what I shouldn't.

"I'll be back, I'm just going to say hi to a couple of people and be right back," he tells and to my surprise leans over and kisses me on the forehead. I watch him, feeling like a balloon floating.

It's all just part of the game I tell myself as I relax and sip my champagne. I watch people filling up the hall. There is an older couple on the dance floor, which is empty, just swaying to the music and all these people in their regalia and exuberance of wealth. I know now why he was so particular about getting a new gown. Just any kind of dress wouldn't have cut it here. I'm so engrossed by the caliber of people walking into the hall, a couple of them I recognize as celebrities, that I do not see the lady walking towards me until she coughs and draws my attention to her.

She's tall and moves with the grace and elegance of a god. She looks earthy in her green dress, dark skin, and perfect smile. Phillipa? I thought for a while and wondered if Hudson was dropped on his head as a child. This woman is the dream of every man. She looks exotic.

"You're Juliette, aren't you?" she asks, pronouncing my name correctly. Her voice sounds like the soft chitter of a bird.

"Yes, I am," I say, wondering if I'm in trouble.

"Can I sit?" she asks.

"Of course," I say, wondering why she'd ask for my permission to sit if her table is right beside ours. She doesn't sit at the Dubois's table. She joins me at mine, still smiling.

"I'm Jasmine," she says. "I know Hudson."

"Oh," I start. "You're not Phillipa?"

She chuckles. "No, I am not."

Then why does she look at me like that? With such wonder and satisfaction.

"Forgive me if I'm staring," she says.

"I think I'm staring also," I tell her.

We both laugh, and that eases the tension.

"It's just that I understand it," she says. I see why he's in a bind. You look like an angel."

"Who?" I ask, confused and barely able to feel good about the compliment.

"Hudson. He told me about you. He failed to mention that you're engaged, though," she points at the ring. "It's beautiful."

She knows about me? How's that possible? Well, the only way that is possible is if Hudson met her today. What does this gorgeous lady know? Everything? It doesn't seem like it. Is she the one Hudson was with that caused him to lie to me?

Well, he must have been having a good time during those meetings.

"I'm sorry if I don't know what to say," I tell her. "I don't know many of Hudson's friends."

"That's no fault of yours. Hudson, he's a hermit. It's a wonder how he rose in this world that tends to punish those who don't socialize."

"I think he socializes well enough. Just not with the intention to make friends."

"You're right about that," she tells me. "You see through his soul, don't you?"

"I don't know what you mean."

"The whole façade, the tough guy play. He really is just a big puppy, if you will. All you need to know is how to handle him."

And I'm sure you're quite adept at that, right?

Why do I feel jealous suddenly? I shouldn't care what Hudson does in his free time or that he fucks this woman who looks like a goddess, but yet, I do. I care, and that irks me. Where the hell is he, anyway? I wonder.

"Well, I know he's a soft man," I say, not quite sure I believe that. I've seen evidence of it, like how he jumped in to help me out with Bent a couple of minutes ago. But then, I haven't known him long enough to know all about him. But this woman does.

"Yeah, that he is. Anyway, I don't want to bore you with my presence. I have others to say hi to," she says, reaching over, kissing me on the cheeks, and walking away.

Is she mocking me? If she fucks Hudson and thinks I'm engaged to him, why is she so chirpy and happy about it. Why was she so free to talk to me? Is this all a game? If so, what game is she playing? It seems all quite confusing. I turn around to watch her and see her meet Hudson on the way. I watch them talking. Hudson looks suddenly tense and looks my way just after Jasmine looks at me, so I can tell they are talking about me. I hear her chuckle a little and then go her way. Hudson heads over.

"Who's she?" I ask.

"No one you should worry about," he says dismissively, looking to move past the discussion. She's not no one, that is for sure. But maybe he's right. I'm not to worry about her unless, of course, I am jealous that he's fucking her.

"You were with her today, weren't you?" I ask him. "She says she knows me, knows my name."

Hudson suddenly looks angry, and good sense tells me to abandon the conversation, but I don't see how I can.

"Yes, I was with her, and so what?" he whispers harshly to me. "I've told you, I have arrangements here in Manhattan for some needs. Or do you want to include that in your contract so I pay you more!"

"You want to talk to me like that!" I strike back at him. "And you'll apologize."

"For?"

"I'm going to leave," I tell him. "I was just asking you some questions, looking to find out who knows about our ruse. You won't be rude to me. We discussed that already."

"No one knows about our ruse. No one. And, we'll keep it that way," he says, and I eye him with dissatisfaction. The discussion isn't over. "I am sorry," he succumbs finally. "She got me angry, is all."

"Why?" I ask, relaxing.

"I don't want to talk about that. The Dubois will be here soon," he says. "Are you ready?"

"I think so," I say and breathe out. The Dubois—two Dubois in particular — are the reasons this relationship between us exists.

"Don't worry. It'll all be over pretty soon. Frank and I will excuse ourselves to go talk. You just need to survive—one hour or two with the others."

"They'll grill me to death."

"Phillipa will give you the glare of death," he tells me. But you don't have to worry; she won't attack you. She isn't that kind of girl. And also, my mother won't be here."

"Oh, why?"

"She couldn't make it," he says, but I can tell there is more to it.

"You told her to stay away, didn't you?"

"It's too much stress for her. Besides, she and her friends are now on their way for some night shopping. She hates most of the people here anyway, and I fear she'll say something to piss Frank off so badly he'll throw us out. It's a win-win."

It does feel like a win to me. I'm partially relieved because I was worried about what seeing his mother and keeping up the ruse would entail.

"They're here," he says, nodding his head at the door. I turn around to watch them walk over. Immediately, I know who Frank is. He's dressed simply in a white linen shirt and black pants, but there is such an aura around him, so palpable and maybe evil. Yes, it looks evil because people look up at him with envy, love, worship, and hate all mixed together. This is what power feels like. He walks like he isn't aware of the effect he has on them. Maybe he is aware, but he is so soaked in it all and has resigned these people to the back of his mind, so they look like ants to him. People that don't matter in the grand scheme of things. He and his family join us.

I don't know what to do. Sit or stand. It makes no difference. This man isn't royalty, so I remain seated. Hudson stands, though, to shake his hand. He does the introduction, but not before Frank interrupts.

"Where's your mother?" he asks.

"She couldn't make it; the flu got her."

"Oh, that's too bad, I wanted her to meet Phillipa," he says, and I look at the lady he points at.

She's a damsel, young like me, looks a little naïve but is beautiful. She looks like a well-treasured jewel. There is a delicateness about her, which must be what Hudson doesn't like about her. I'll also describe myself as delicate, but I have rough edges that make me a more interesting thing to handle. But with Phillipa, her delicateness makes her all-rounded. Like an egg that should be kept safe in a treasure chest.

"Who's your guest then?" Frank asks.

He likes control. He wants to be in charge of even something as little as a conversation.

"She's Juliette," Hudson says, and finally, I stand up and have to shake everyone's hand. They all eye my engagement ring, and their eyes say all that needs to be said. Phillipa, in particular, is shocked, and for a moment, I think she wouldn't shake my hand, but after a tiny nudge from her father, she reaches out rather shyly with her hand. I shake it, feeling sorry for her, but Hudson is right. It is better this way. The girl should be heartbroken now and heal quickly to forge ahead with her life. Now, her rough edges will start to form.

The elephant in the room is unspoken as Hudson introduces me to the family.

There's Frank Dubois, who I know a lot about already. Annie Dubois, Frank's wife. Whose troubled eyes trouble me. James Dubois, the first son, who, evidently, Frank doesn't think is capable of becoming his heir and who isn't interested because he has a fashion school to tend to. There's Elizabeth Dubois, cold eyes, calculative, and most likely to be a problem. Elizabeth's husband, Brendan. And then, the baby of the house, Phillipa, sticks close to her father and sits beside him.

Frank insists that Hudson and I join them at the table, but he doesn't stay around and pulls Hudson away immediately, no doubt to discuss business, leaving me with the people here. Just as I suspected, Elizabeth is the first to question me. She eyes the ring with jealousy. Her eyes have such fire in them, while those of Phillipa are sad.

"That's a beautiful engagement ring," she says. "Very expensive. How long has Hudson known you?"

Her actual question is: Why would Hudson give a woman he barely knows such an expensive ring?

I raise it and roll it around my finger, looking at it with joy. "I know, right? I told him it was too much, but he really wanted to splurge."

I don't answer her question. I turn to Phillipa and smile at her, but she looks away. I feel a responsibility to talk to her, to ease her of the pain she's going through now.

CHAPTER 11

HUDSON

I hope Juliette is doing ok. I've thrown her to the wolves, hoping she would be able to fend them off. The only people who can give her too much trouble are Frank and Elizabeth, and thankfully, I've pulled one away from her. Frank leads me down a hallway where the sounds of the party slowly recede from us until I can't hear it anymore. Then he opens a door, and we step into what I assume is a smaller hall like the one hosting the dinner. We go through that hall and into the dark night into the open, where I can hear the gentle lapping of the beach only a few feet away. We head to a park bench and sit. He gets a Cuban cigar out and offers me one. I'm not one to smoke much, but I take it anyway. I didn't know he smoked.

He takes a lighter out of his pocket, lights it, and then lights mine. Frank and I have never had the chance to sit down and discuss this for long. The first time I had a conversation with him was when he showed up at my company to talk to me about buying me out. After that, we discussed it through our lawyers.

So, this is the first time I'm sitting alone with Frank and so close. I can see the lines on his face, the bags underneath his eyes, and the wildness in his look. He looks like a tiger—a very old but very tired tiger, but a tiger, nonetheless.

"Hudson," he says after letting out a long smoke. "I knew your father," he finishes.

"My mother mentions it sometimes."

"He was like you, stubborn as a mule. He told me there was so much money in the sea, we just were looking in all the wrong places. He would find the right place. He was confident of it, and all his life, he chased it. Fishing with large ships. I never believed in him, and I felt justified when the company he started tanked. I like it when I'm proven right."

That much I had gleaned from his stories that are public.

"But what I hate more is when I am proven wrong," he continues.

My success has proven him wrong.

"The world has come far, though. This isn't the day of your father. You have better equipment, better fishing methods, and better marketing. But that doesn't explain why a fish company is making so much money like you are doing. I was curious. My people said you are probably skimming. The Mexicans need people to move their drugs here; you have a license to have ships in their waters. How much of the waters can the Coast Guard cover? Your ships pack tons of fish every day; it isn't hard to hide some items with them. I made some calls, had you searched some more, just hoping to find something."

I was aware of it and back then, I thought the Coast Guard was being more careful and tactical in their war against drugs, but I had long known it was all just Frank Dubois, sniffing around, asking questions about it.

"I wasn't shocked when they found nothing. You're your father's son, and I expect you to be clean. There must be something else. So, I dug deeper and found the truth. It was you all along—always you. Your vision, your ability to lead, and your desire to help others see that vision and make it come alive. I recognized something I hadn't seen in a long while. I recognized myself in you. It was absolute."

"But you didn't like it," I say, watching him, waiting for my time to chip in on why I'm here. He had the ground now and I must let him speak.

"Of course not. Having someone like you around is dangerous. You'll get hungrier. It is guaranteed, and then you'll come for me. The more you hunt, the more you'll see that money is exactly where money is—in finance. I couldn't let that happen. I must prevent it. You're making that hard."

"I'm just fighting for survival here."

"Rakeem called me," he says. "I knew you'd see him. I know all that you'll do because I am exactly like you. This game you're playing, you can't win. I have the money and the time. You might have the time also, but you will run out of money soon. You can't keep it up."

"My father taught me never to give up and to always find new ways to fight."

"Sometimes, giving up is the best thing to do. The wisest."

"I don't see why I should. We're both on even ground for now. You're losing money, and so am I."

"How much can you afford to bleed off?"

"As much as it takes."

"Don't be a fool. You have people working for you that you must care for. If you keep this up, how do you intend them to feed their family?"

"I'm not in this battle alone," I tell him. "Everyone who works for me knows we are in it together. They want me to remain at the helm."

"And I will ensure that happens. You'll have total control of everything: Hiring, processing, every day running, everything."

"But it won't be mine."

"What difference does it make? You've made your mark, you've made your name, and you've achieved more than your father could have hoped for."

"But it's not enough," I tell him.

"What is enough then?"

"I have a proposal," I tell him. This is my chance. "My office will send you the details of it tomorrow, but I can give you the gist of it now."

He watches me and smiles. "Go ahead," he says, taking a long drag from his cigar while mine burns away.

"You've offered to buy me out entirely and to transfer full ownership to you for three billion dollars. I think we can do one better."

"Way above the company's current valuation," he says.

"Potential is what you're looking to buy," I tell him. "Potential is why I'm unwilling to sell. So, we make a deal. We both become owners of the company. You buy out a portion. A billion dollars. I buy out a billion dollars also and we put the rest out for public sale. We are both major owners, and whatever I stand to gain in the future, you stand to gain also. And then, you go on with your life, and I continue running the company. You're making money without having to worry about anything. It's a good deal."

"No doubt about it. You've thought it out. Have your people send out the details. But you must know I have no intention of agreeing to it.

Goddamnit, I feel like strangling him. Why must he make everything so hard?

"I have never stepped into a battle and called a truce. That isn't the Frank Dubois way, but no one has ever offered me a deal as sweet as the one you just gave to me. That is why I will take it into consideration, but I won't agree to it."

"We're both losing money, Frank. You should agree to this and be done with it. Like you said, it is a sweet deal. You lose nothing at all."

"Except a billion dollars," he says in mockery.

"If you buy me out, you'll lose three. Think about it this way, Frank. If you succeed and buy me out, I won't work for you. I'll retire, leave the business, and go settle down. If you don't have me at the helm, you won't have the returns you're so hungry for.

"Are you threatening sabotage?"

"Of course not. But you'll never find someone like me who can run it as efficiently as I do. In the end, it bleeds money, and you lose. Maybe then, I'll return and offer to buy it back from you, for far less. Maybe a billion dollars or less. Then, you'll have no choice but to pay and count your losses. I do have time, Frank. I have time to step back and make that happen. I am younger than you are. Three billion is enough to retire and never work again in my life. But you're old. Death lurks in the corner."

"Now, you threaten me,"

"With a win," I tell him. "I threaten you with the win you want. You want to have my company, don't you? I'll fight you tooth and nail, but if I lose, you lose. Or rather if you win, I win."

If what Jasmine says is true, then I know Frank can't afford to have two sinking ships losing money. "Think about it Frank, you really do not want to play this game anymore."

"The girl," he says suddenly. "The one you brought with you. That was a nice play. You made it impossible for me to make a counter play and ask you to marry my daughter. You know I love her. You know I'll give up all of this for her, but I can't ask you to marry her when you have one already, you can't make her happy."

Good thing he figured that out on his own.

"I'll win this, Hudson. I'll win and harness the company's potential. You forget what I said at the start. You and me, we are the same."

"Maybe. But you don't know fish."

"I don't have to. I just have to know people."

CHAPTER 12

JULIETTE

*H*udson has one arm around my waist, holding me so close that I can breathe him in, and while his other arm rests on my shoulder as we dance. Strangely, I feel secure in his arms, all troubles matter little here, in the moment. I think we are doing more of a performance than actual dance because the Dubois have their eyes on us, watching our every move, tracking all motion, and looking for God knows what.

"How did the meeting with Frank go?" I ask Hudson, who looks a little distracted, knowing what reply to expect.

"Not so well. But we're not done. He's invited me to their ranch house here in Manhattan. We'll be spending a couple of days with them."

"What?" I ask, almost screaming. He pulls me closer to cover up for the scream. "We'll be staying with them? I don't want to do that."

"We have no choice. It's not like I like it myself, but I

believe if I spend some more time with him, he might change his mind."

"What about Phillipa? The whole family? I don't want to be under constant scrutiny. Look at them, they hate me already."

Hudson smiles, places his hands on my cheeks and pulls me closer. For a while, I want to pull away, but then I realize we are outside. This is part of the contract. I let him kiss me.

"For seventy thousand dollars, you'll do it," he says, his voice cold and detached. He doesn't care how I feel about spending a couple of days with the Dubois. And why should he? I signed my freedom away to him when I signed that contract.

"You'll be fine," he adds after a while.

I don't know about that; I think to myself. "Who else will be there with us?" I ask him.

"Alison will be around, but she'll be so busy you won't even notice her. The ranch should be fun for you. There are a lot of things to do there."

"Fun? If you call an anal probing the Dubois will subject me to like I'm an alien fun, then sure, I'll have fun."

"Come on! Where's that go-girl attitude of yours? We really need that now!"

I want to kick him in the nuts, but that, I know, isn't a fiancée-like attitude; instead, I throw him a terrible look that tells him to shut up.

Out of the corner of my eyes, I see the girl who came up to me earlier walk past us. The angelic Jasmine has a young boy's hand in hers and they start to dance. The boy, who looks no older than ten, has a big smile on his face, so happy to have such a beautiful woman dancing with him. I wonder who she really is. She doesn't have the boisterousness I've noticed in most of the woman here, who are so quick to show off their wealth or their husband's wealth. Her grace-fulness is her most alluring and enticing quality, and it seems like something she picked up naturally, not something money instilled in her. Her clothes aren't the most expensive at the party, but she's found a way to make them the most attractive. Simple touches with pieces of jewelry in her hair, ears and fingers make her appear like some earthy goddess. I can close my eyes and picture her sitting before a cauldron preparing a witch's potion.

"Who is she?" I find myself asking Hudson. I am very curious.

He turns around to see who I'm referring to, and I can see in his eyes that he doesn't like it that I'm asking about Jasmine.

"Don't tell me to forget about her," I say before he speaks. He sighs resignedly.

"That's Jasmine."

"I know her name. Who is she? Why is she at this party? Does she have a rich father, husband, or her own company?"

"None of those things. She's Frank's mistress," he tells me.

Mistress. I feel a little disappointed at that, but it passes. If this lady feels like the best position she can achieve is that of a mistress, who am I to be disappointed by that? She looks satisfied with life, and I can tell it's because she isn't the type burdened with earthly endeavors.

"Does Frank know you're fucking his mistress? I ask him, getting a gasp from him. He places his palm on my mouth, looking around to ensure no one heard me.

"Watch what you say," he hisses.

"So, it's not a lie."

"It's nothing. It's none of your business."

"It's dangerous, isn't it?"

"Frank isn't an idiot. He knows to separate business from pleasure."

"Have you seen her? She's the type of girl you destroy worlds for."

He chuckles, spins me around and pulls me closer. "Jasmine won't stand anyone destroying anything for her. People see her as Frank's mistress, but she sees herself as something else."

"I see," I say, watching her. Jasmine catches me staring at her, and she smiles. I smile back, not sure why. I have a seething feeling that I'm supposed to despise her. This is the woman my fiancé is having an affair with. I'm supposed to despise her, yet I can't find it in me to do that. It's not because Hudson isn't really my fiancé, but because Jasmine isn't the kind of person to hate.

"She knows the engagement is a ruse," Hudson confesses after a while.

"What? How? Did you tell her?"

"No, she figured it out. She's quite intuitive," he says, but I can tell he's lying. He must have said something she picked up on.

"What did you say, Hudson?"

"Nothing big. I told her I can't wait to be rid of you in seven days."

"Ouch," I mock.

So, that was what she was referring to when she said she understood how I had him in a bind. Do I really have him in a bind, or does he just want to have sex with me? I am something he can't have, so he wants me even more. Maybe there's not much difference between Frank Dubois and Hudson Sinclair.

"It's something we're both thinking," Hudson hisses back at me. "This relationship is artificial and is having a strong impact on us that we'd rather not have happening. So, in six days, it'll all be over."

"You're not the one who is about to spend those six days with a family that absolutely despises you."

"You'll be fine," he tells me.

"Hudson."

I hear a voice call to him from behind, and I turn around to see who it is. Phillipa stands with her hand out, asking for a dance.

"You don't mind, do you?" she says to me, smiling. I see no sincerity in that smile, and the sweet girl I saw earlier who looks hurt is gone, replaced by one with the cunning look of a serpent. I look beyond Hudson and to the table, not surprised to find Elizabeth watching us keenly.

"Of course not," I say.

Before I pull away from Hudson, I kiss him brashly on the lips,

I don't look back at them as I go outside the hall, intending to get some fresh air. I won't have them thinking they've gotten under my skin or that I fear that they'll steal Hudson from me. I don't walk past the family to get to the balcony overlooking the beach. Just as I step out, I get another glass of champagne.

It's nice to be away from the crowd and noise. Phillipa can have Hudson for the rest of the night. I like this peace and quiet. It doesn't last long, though. The door to the balcony opens, and I turn around to see Elizabeth walking towards me.

Oh, come on, give me a break.

I don't acknowledge her but continue to watch the lapping ocean.

She joins me and rests her back against the railing while watching me, studying my face.

"When I was younger and my dad bought this beach house, I'd bring boys here on the weekends when I knew he was out of the country," she starts, but I keep my eyes focused on the water, hoping she'll take the hint that I want to be alone and leave. She continues. "We'd have sex everywhere in the house, and sometimes, I'd leave evidence of my transgression lying around for him to find so that when he does, he'd get so mad at me. It happened so many times, I wonder how long it took him to know I was doing it intentionally. But that didn't matter; he was still always mad at me, and then he banned me from the house."

Why is she telling me this? I'm not interested in your teenage shenanigans.

But I cannot keep mum. I'm supposed to show them they do not terrify me.

"We all do stupid things as teenagers."

She chuckles. "No, I wasn't being stupid. I was sending a message to my father. You think I liked those boys I brought here? A good number of them irritated me, but I wanted to get my father to see me."

"I'm sure he does now."

"You think so?" she scoffs and turns around. She takes a pack of cigarettes out of her dress and a lighter. She offers me one, but I decline. She lights it and smokes before she continues. "I run a major part of his company, keeping him afloat, but all he talks about is his Phillipa. Phillipa this, Phillipa that."

What is this? Is this her way of befriending her way into me to find a way to pull me away from Hudson? Does she want me to become her friend?

"Every father wants a solid marriage for their daughters. You found a husband. Phillipa is still a spinster."

"My father hated Andrew so much. Almost didn't come to our wedding."

I don't know what to say to that. Why is this girl trauma-dumping on me? It makes me uncomfortable.

"I feel a little joy that Phillipa won't get what she wants, and if I didn't have a stake in this drama, I would have congratulated you."

Now we're getting to the reason she's here.

"But we need the deal with Hudson, and you're getting in the way."

"Hudson tells me he has a good offer for your father. Convince him to take that."

"Don't be an idiot," she says dismissively. "Do you know my father? He doesn't do deals. He takes. We need Hudson to lay his head down and let himself be defeated."

"Well, that isn't going to happen."

"Yes, because of you. There is only one person who could have made my father agree to a deal, and you've come and taken her place. You're causing more pain and loss than you realize."

"I think the pain and loss are all your father's doing. He's not unbeatable, and he isn't God. The faster he realizes that the better for the whole family and company."

Elizabeth takes another drag and shakes her head. "You don't know my father."

"I think I do. I think for all your protests as a teenager, you never really outgrew him. You still can't stand up to him to tell him the truth. If you could, you wouldn't be in this mess now."

"What are you saying? That I'm a failure?" she sounds angry now, ready to pick a fight.

"You've achieved more than I'll ever dream to achieve in

my life. You're no failure. But at heart, you're still a little girl terrified of her daddy."

She's silent for a while.

"Is your father alive?" she asks finally.

"No. He died when I was a child."

"So, you have no idea what it's like to have an overbearing father with such control and power. So, don't talk like you know me. You have no idea what my struggles have been about. You have no idea what it's like to be me!"

She's screaming now, so I know I've hit a nerve. I also know living with these people for the next five to six days is sure to test me. How I wish there was a way out of this.

"Now, let's talk about you," she says, moving closer. How did you get a man like Hudson, and how has he kept you a secret for so long? My father has kept tabs on him for a long time, and I'm sure if he had a girl, he'd have found out a long time ago."

"Your father isn't God," I tell her. "And how Hudson and I met is none of your business. We love each other, and we'll start a family together, and you and your family can do nothing about that. Hudson isn't a weak man who'll cower to your father."

Elizabeth sighs and drops her cigarette to the floor. She picks another and lights it.

"It should be fun having you around," she says and turns away. She smokes for a while longer before she turns around and heads back in, leaving me infuriated.

What is the problem with this family?! It is so dysfunctional.

I remain on the balcony for a while to cool my head off. When I get back inside, I can't find Hudson, but immediately, Jasmine finds me and pulls me to a corner. There is a look in her eyes that I can't place.

"I need to talk to you," she says.

I point at the balcony as a place where we can get some privacy.

"You need to be careful," she tells me. "Hudson says you'll be staying with the Dubois for a while."

"Yes," I tell her.

"You need to be careful with them. They are a crazy family. You should be wary of them."

"I know. Elizabeth, she—"

"No, not Elizabeth. She's the most sensible and balanced of them all. Phillipa is the one you should be worried about. She's crazy."

I find that hard to believe. Elizabeth has been aggressive and invasive since I got to the party.

"Don't let the sweet face and sweet voice fool you. Frank wants her married off and away for a reason."

"And how would you know that?" I ask, even though I know the answer already.

Jasmine stares at me. "You know why," she answers. "Anyway, someone will miss me at the party soon. I just wanted to warn you. You're messing with vipers. Hudson made a mistake bringing you here, dragging you into this mess of a family."

"But you've dragged yourself into this mess of a family yourself."

She smiles. "I'm like a moth to a fire. I can tell fire isn't good for me, but I can't help my nature. I'm attracted to what I'm attracted to."

"Men with power. It's the same reason you're sleeping with Hudson. You like that he has power."

"Are you jealous?" she asks with a sleek smile.

"Why would I be? I don't care about Hudson."

"You two really are playing this game well," she says,

shaking her head. I hope no one comes out of it utterly destroyed, and I hope for your sake it isn't you. Hudson, he's strong, he's hardheaded. He'll throw himself into some other venture and heal through it. What about you? What do you have to throw yourself at?"

I have my bakery; I think to myself.

"You're playing a dangerous game yourself."

"The thing with Hudson and me, it's carnal, nothing more. Hudson knows that."

"This thing with you and Hudson, is it just carnal?"

"To me, it is," she says.

"But Frank doesn't think so."

"He won't let himself think so. He likes control so much that he's convinced himself there is nothing he can't control. Do you see why I say this is very dangerous for you? There are so many avenues for things to go wrong, so much mess waiting to explode, and here you are smack in the center of it all."

"I'll be fine."

"Hudson will protect you," she tells me. "He doesn't acknowledge it yet, but he won't let anything bad happen to you."

"What about you? Will you be fine?"

Jasmine smiles. "I have always been able to take care of myself."

She leaves me, and I have no urge to leave the balcony this time.

What have I gotten myself into? I should be scared. I should find Hudson and tell him that I can't keep up this charade and that I want to go home. I should forget all about the seventy thousand dollars. There are other, safer ways to make money.

But I don't do anything. I watch the beach, and my fears

dissipate. For some reason, I want to be here. I want to see how all this plays out.

So much time passes before I finally walk back into the hall. The party is waning out already, and Hudson walks towards me.

"Where the hell have you been?" he asks me, watching my face.

"Out there, on the balcony, getting some air."

"We have to leave."

"Did something happen?"

"No. The Dubois are heading home. We ride with them. Are you okay?"

"Yes, I'm fine," I tell him. "I'm fine," I repeat to reassure myself.

CHAPTER 13

HUDSON

Throughout the drive, Juliette is silent and contemplative. She looks out of the SUV window that Frank provided us. I had argued that we should come in our luxurious limousine, but Frank wouldn't have any of that. He's made provisions for our transportation, and we must use it. Arguing with him is a pointless endeavor. He's in a sour mood already because the meeting didn't go as hoped, and Juliette's introduction seems to have made everything even more complicated. This isn't a win or loss for me.

"Are you alright?" I asked Juliette again, wondering what happened in the short time I stepped out to talk to Alison.

"Yes, yes. I'm fine," she repeats. "Why are so many cars driving to the ranch house?" she asks.

"It's a Frank Dubois party. It lasts all night," I tell her. "The one at the beach house is less exclusive. This one is for the top brass."

"I thought Frank was supposed to be someone who keeps out of the limelight."

"Yes, he is, but once a year, he does this. A reminder of his power and affluence. Frank is nothing if not tactical."

The drive to the house takes about half an hour. As we drive into the gate, we're welcomed by a view that seems to transport us to the nineteenth century. A mansion is seated on an expansive piece of land that seems to stretch on unendingly. The house has a grand exterior of buttress arches, columns, and stained-glass windows. Its architecture speaks of the opulence of the Dubois. Our SUV parks behind a lot of other cars, and we're led into the house itself, where we are met with a new wonder.

Large windows, high ceilings, velvet drapes, polished marble floors, and chandeliers that glistered like they are sprayed with stars.

"Wow," Juliette gasps. The purpose of this party is to show off. Out of the corner of my eye, I see Phillipa heading towards us. She's changed out of the clothes she wore at the first party and is now in a shorter dress, similar to what Juliette is wearing. Phillipa skips over to me, but before she gets to me, Juliette holds my hand.

Good call, I think. The smile on Phillipa's face fades, but she isn't deterred.

"Hey," Phillipa says when close to me. "I want to show you something. You have to come with me."

"We just arrived, Phillipa. I'd like to say hello to a couple of people first."

Now, Phillipa is frowning, and from the corner of my eye, I see Frank watching us. Juliette must have seen it, too, because she speaks up next.

"I think you should go with her, Hudson. She looks excited to show you whatever it is."

"But I don't want to leave you here on your own. You've been on your own most of the night," I complain. I really don't want to go off with Phillipa because I can tell by the look in her eyes she is up to no good.

"Don't worry about me. I'm a big girl. I'll take care of myself."

Before I follow Phillipa out, Juliette kisses me again. This time, it isn't just a normal kiss. She pulls me in, her tongue seeking mine. I let the kiss linger a while, savoring the sweet taste of her lips before we pull apart; I can swear I see hunger in her eyes. I dismiss it and go with Phillipa. All the way, Frank's eyes track me.

Phillipa leads me out of the house. We follow a cobblestone path by the side of the house, which leads us down a dirt road, and soon, I can hear the gentle neighing of horses. We are well separated from the party now, and the light from the house looks distant. Phillipa opens the stable and pulls a light switch that turns on a small bulb to light our way. The horses notice our presence and start to neigh louder. As we move in, we hear the door open, and I turn around to see a man at the door with a flashlight in hand. He must be the horse groomer I figure.

"Go back to bed, Benjamin," Phillipa says. "It's just me. I want to show Hudson Misk."

"Alright, ma'am," Benjamin says, bending an imaginary hat to me before he walks away.

"Benjamin is very protective of the horses," she tells me as we go even further, moving past more horses, some of which have moved closer to watch us.

"Where are we going, Phillipa?" I ask.

"You'll see," she says and stops in front of a compartment soon enough. She hits the wooden door, and a sleeping horse stirs. It raises its head to see the cause of the noise. When it sees Phillipa, the horse pulls itself up and walks to the door, setting its nose down so Phillipa can pet it.

"This is Misk. She's mine," Phillipa announces.

"Oh, hello, Misk," I say, not quite interested in her horse. Also, I get the feeling we aren't here to see horses.

"You can pet her," she tells me.

What I really want to do is to be out of here, out of this whole compound and this whole mess. I don't want to play a stupid game with their father, who doesn't know what a compromise is. I am compromising hard here, and her father acts as if he has a right to my company.

I pat the horse gently on the nose and rub her neck. The horse snorts and moves closer to me, her dark, soulful eyes looking into mine. It is a beautiful horse with luscious, brown and thick, black hair.

"She likes you," Phillipa says. "Tomorrow, you and I will go for a ride on her."

"I don't think that'll be possible, Phillipa; I have a lot of work to do."

"Come on," Phillipa insists, shifting closer to me. "You can have Alison do all your work for you. I want to spend time with you. Alone."

She is insistent, almost like she's giving me a command. That is Frank speaking through her.

"I can't be spending time with you alone, Phillipa. That isn't gentlemanly."

"Why? Is it because of her?" the spite in her voice can't be missed.

"My fiancée?" I ask. "Her name is Juliette."

"I don't care what her name is. She isn't supposed to be here. This week was supposed to be about you and me—just you and me, not her."

"I'm sorry if your plans have been disturbed, Phillipa.

Neither you nor your father made me aware of such plans. I didn't know I'd be spending the week here at the ranch."

I've surmised that is how they wanted it. That she's hurt and disappointed is no fault of mine; it's just her and her father's doing.

"Why do you hate me?" she asks, pulling my hand away from the horse. She touches my palm so delicately, her finger running across the lines of my palm.

"I don't hate you, Phillipa," I tell her.

"Then why won't you have me? You know I want you. Why then won't you have me?"

This is embarrassing, I think. Here is the daughter of one of the most powerful men on earth, throwing herself at me.

She places my palm on her breast, and I can tell through the clothes that she isn't wearing her bra. Her breast feels tender and soft against my touch. I could have her here in the stable, satisfy an urge, but I have no urge. I watch her, looking at me with stark hunger in her eyes. She looks so desperate, and it irritates me.

I pull my hand away from her breast and watch as her face takes on a crestfallen look. For a while, I think she'll break down, but then something emboldens her. Maybe it's just desperation.

She tugs at the strings on the shoulder of her dress, pulling both together so they come free simultaneously, and her dress falls to her feet. She is fully naked before me, no bras, no panties. Her nipples are rock hard in the chilly night, and I can see she is moist.

Her nubile body stirs nothing in me.

I move closer to her, and her breath catches in her throat. Her eyes track mine with hope and hunger. I hold her by the neck, letting my hand fall from there downward to her breast, where I catch her left breast in my hand and roll the nipples in my finger. Phillipa bites her lips and moans.

I stop and move away from her.

"You should get dressed," I tell her. "You're making a fool of yourself."

Suddenly, she gets upset. She screams and jumps at me, hitting me.

"Why do you hate me! You hate me! You hate me!"

She repeats, hitting my arm, my face, and just about any part of my body her arms connect to. I let her hit me until she tires out and then falls to the ground, crying. I squat before her and hand her dress to her.

"Put your dress back on. We need to get back in. You'll catch a cold standing out here naked."

"What do you care, you bastard," she curses me.

I stand up and watch her. I have half a mind to leave her on her own here in the stable, but I don't. Instead, I remain until she gathers herself and picks up her dress. She covers herself with it.

"Turn around," she says.

I do, thinking about how foolish it is to ask me to turn around when, just moments ago, she had willingly undressed herself before me.

"Let's go," she says after dressing and walking past me.

I look at her. She wiped her eyes and pulled a stolid look about her. It feels almost like she didn't break down a moment ago. Maybe there is something sinister about this girl I've missed all along. She is one to watch out for, I conclude and make a note to warn Juliette about her.

We walk out of the stable and back into the hall. Juliette isn't there.

CHAPTER 14

JULIETTE

A party after a party feels like too much stress to me. All I really want to do now is sleep. I look around me at all these people who are still agile and up. The number, which was small initially, has progressively dwindled again; maybe soon, everyone will leave, and they'll finally show me to my room. Or they'll show me to a slaughter room where a guillotine waits for me. They'll chop my head off, present it to Hudson in a box, and force him to marry Phillipa.

God, my exhaustion is starting to get to me. I groan and look at the door through which Hudson and Phillipa walked out a while ago. They are yet to be back. I wonder what she has to show him. All her goods, that's for sure. The disappointment the poor girl will be met with at Hudson's hands makes me feel sorry for her.

Why do I feel so confident that Hudson won't be an idiot? What evidence do I have to back that up? He, after all, slept with Jasmine while our ruse was on. Why can't he find some relief in this Phillipa girl and be done with it? Having sex with Phillipa will no doubt further complicate things and make Phillipa more attached. Hudson is smart enough to see that and refuse whatever advances Phillipa brings.

"They'll be back," I hear Frank's voice beside me and look up to find that I have been so lost in thought I didn't notice him walk up to me.

"Yes, of course. I just miss him is all," I say, pushing a smile to my lips. Is this all still an act, or do I really miss Hudson? I've spent much of my time looking at the door, waiting for him to come walking through it.

What does this man want with me?

"He's a good man, isn't he, Hudson?"

"Yes, he is," I reply.

"Come, walk with me. I'd like to talk to you. You don't mind, do you?"

Of course, I do mind. You're an egotistical maniac who can't take a loss and is out to destroy someone else's life just because you can.

"No," I say, letting him lead me out of the house.

Where are we going? I wonder. To the room with the guillotine?

It's been a very long night, and my tiredness is really showing. I follow Frank through a dark path that leads us to a separate house.

"You know, good men have demons also," he says as he opens the door. We step into the dark and musty room. When he hit the switch, I could see that we were in an old house that hadn't been used in a while. It gets cleaned regularly, but the dust and the cobwebs that have gathered tells me no cleaning has been done here in a while.

What are we doing here?

"What's this place?" I ask him and he must have read the fear on my face.

"I'm not going to kill you," he says, but his tone isn't reassuring. "I know what people say about me. Trust me, I am not that unhinged. As I was saying, good men have demons. Do you know what Hudson's demons are?"

I know for sure that that wasn't among the hundred questions we tried to answer. I try to imagine Hudson's reaction to the question would be dismissive, of course.

"I should have known. Your fiancé and I have too much in common. It's one of the reasons I won't accept a deal that doesn't transfer total control of his company to me. I fear that if I let him have this win, no matter how irrelevant it might be, he'll use it as leverage to grow himself so much, and one day, he'll come for me."

"You're scared of someone doing to you what you've done to others," I hiss.

"Fear, no. Worry, yes. What's a businessman's life without a couple of worries."

"Why am I here?" I ask again, not really comfortable with the environment. Why couldn't he talk to me somewhere less spooky?

"I want to talk to you about Hudson's demons. See if you can help him see reason. Has he ever told you about his father?"

I shake my head. "No."

"His father started this company. I used to know the man. He was a headstrong one with big dreams. But those dreams never got realized. He wanted a company that would get so big that the whole world would have some sense of reliance on it. His dreams were wild. I remember when I met him for the first time. It was in this house."

Ha, so that's why we're here.

"Hudson's father, James, had heard about me and wanted me to lend him money. I was the new banker who was bankrolling everyone. He thought he'd have a chance convincing me to give him money. I met him in this house. The house there was under construction at the time."

"How long ago was this?" I ask him.

"Twenty-five years ago. I remember the day like it was yesterday. How can I forget him when he is the reason I won't collapse this structure even though it is no longer safe for accommodation."

I look at the building, a new fear emerging. We really should be having this discussion someplace else.

"We shared coffee by this table, and for a while, we had random discussions about world history. He was a well-read man and always had an opinion about everything. I was so blown away by him that finally, when he got down to the reason he was here, I was so sure I would give him what he came for."

"But you didn't?" I ask.

"No. A leopard can't change its spots. I watched him describe this business and the hopes he had for it, and I thought to myself—"

"You must have it," I finish for him, the disgust obvious in my voice.

"Yes. I must have it. But I am no fool. I knew his dream couldn't be achieved. Fishing? It sounded too abstract to me. He was chasing dust and I set him on his way. I'll fund him under one condition: he shows me actual data backing up the claims he's made. He went away and never came back to me. He couldn't achieve it, not until he died. When I read about his death, I felt like I was dealt a deadly blow, yet somewhere in my heart, I was satisfied. I had been proven right. His dreams were unattainable."

"How did James die?"

"Drugs," Frank says. "He got so depressed by his constant failure he took solace in drugs and alcohol. He was always an emotionally weak man, and it didn't take long for those vices to take over. I heard he tried to fight it but didn't have the strength to do it. Poor Hudson. He watched his father dig a hole for himself, fall into it, and struggle back up, only for him to dig it again and fall into it. You ever wonder what such a thing does to a child?"

He isn't asking for my opinion, so I keep quiet and watch, knowing he'll answer the question himself soon enough.

"It can do two things: create a weaker man who follows in his father's footsteps and loses himself in places that provide little to no solace. Or it can create a man like Hudson, intent on never becoming his father, struggling against all odds to build that which his father failed to build."

"And he did. He succeeded, yet you want to steal it from him. Why?"

Frank shakes his head. "I hate to be proven wrong."

"That's it? That is what all of this is about. Your ego?"

Frank laughs at the distaste in my voice. "Everything is about my ego, young lady. Do you think I would be the man I am today without that ego?"

"You know what losing that company will do to him. You know what it did to his father, yet you won't back down? Why? That's cruel."

"The world is cruel, and I'm a part of it. I told you this: if I don't now cut the legs underneath Hudson, he'll grow to be the monster that devours me. I can't let that happen."

"Why did you call me here then?" I ask him.

"Because I want you to talk to him," he says. "I want you to convince him. I've made him a proposition. I buy the company from him, but he remains in charge. That way, he doesn't lose what he has created."

I know that isn't the reason this man is offering to keep Hudson at the helm. He is too selfish to consider that. There must be some other reason. Maybe Hudson is the only one who can run the company as well and continue to bring in profits.

"You know I won't do that."

"Then I fear for you. You'll start a family with the man soon. You need him stable and clear-headed. If he drags this game out much longer, I see him quickly becoming his father. He'll lose his head, lose his mind, lose his being. If this goes on much longer, what you'll be left with won't be Hudson. It will be a shadow of him."

"I don't think so," I tell him.

"Then you're a fool. A bigger fool."

"Do you know what I think?" I ask, feeling suddenly confident. "You're worried. You're scared he'll beat you at this. And you should be. You can't win this. You'll never beat Hudson. He's unbeatable."

CHAPTER 15

HUDSON

*W*here the hell is she? I wonder, searching for Juliette. Phillipa is with her sister, who is in a corner, watching all that is happening. I walk over to the pair of them.

"Hey, Elizabeth. Do you know where Juliette is?"

"What's this? I'm supposed to dog-sit your little bitch now?"

I think about walking away but then I change my mind. I move closer to Elizabeth, my body language threatening. She gets the hint and moves away, but I follow her until she runs into the wall. She looks around her for a way to escape, but I move my body in the way, so she doesn't move. I don't care that people are watching us now.

"You'll show Juliette respect," I tell her.

She nods.

"What is that?" I ask, even further closing the space between us.

"I'll respect your girlfriend," she repeats

"Good," I say and walk away.

I can't believe I just did that, threatening Elizabeth Dubois for Juliette. It was dangerous and spontaneous, but it felt right. I won't have anyone disrespecting Juliette.

I get out my phone, planning to place a call to her, only just to realize I don't have her cell number. How careless of me. I have nothing else to do but wait. I sit in the corner, not interested in any of the shenanigans going on around me. Not the party, music, or even ladies who seem particular in making eye contact with me. I just want to see Juliette and make sure she's alright. I made a decision to wait just ten more minutes, and then I'll go out there to look for her. I don't think they could have done anything to her, not with so many people around, but I also can't put it beyond the Dubois to get so desperate for what they want.

I check the time consistently, and with just about a minute left for the designated waiting period to run out, the door opens, and she comes in. She has Frank alongside her. Without thinking much about it, I'm at her side immediately.

"Where did you take her?" I demand from Frank, who looks at me, shocked at my outburst.

I need to get myself back in order. Why do I feel so protective of Juliette?

"We were just talking," he says with a smile. "What? Are you worried I'll hurt your little toy? Come on, Hudson. I'm not a savage."

I do not know. I've folded my hands into fists until I relax them, and Frank chuckles as he walks away from me.

"Come here," I say, pulling at Juliette, who comes willing. When we are far from the family, I let her go.

"Jeez, don't you think that was too much acting?" she says

flexing her wrist. "You would have bruised me if we stayed any longer."

Acting? I scoff out loud. She thinks I'm acting. Of course, she thinks I'm acting. And was I really not? Was I worried something had happened to her? Do I care so much about her welfare that I'm filled with trepidation just at the thought of something terrible happening to her? No, that wasn't it. I was just acting.

"Well, you were gone a long time," I say. "I've been known to be a little possessive of my women."

"Please," she says with a roll of her eyes. I get my phone out and hand it to her. "I need your cell number."

She eyes me. "What for?"

"So you don't disappear on me like that again," I blurt out, saying what seems ridiculously obvious.

"You were really worried about me," she says, sounding chirpy.

"Just put your number in there."

"Macho Hudson can't admit that he was worried about anyone, so he doesn't appear weak, huh."

"I was just fulfilling my part of the contract," I hiss. "Now tell me, what was he saying to you."

Before she can answer, one of the butlers walks up to us.

"Mr. Dubois has asked me to show you to your quarters, Miss, Sir. Unless, of course, you still want to hang around for more partying?"

"Nope, that's enough partying for me for the day," Juliette says and turns around, eager to leave. But then she internalizes what the butler said and blurts out: "Are we staying in the same room?"

"Yes, Mr. Dubois assumed so, seeing as how you are engaged," the butler informs us. "If you want separate quarters, I'll have to consult with Mr. Dubois."

"Don't worry about that. We'd love to sleep in the same room," I say, smiling, but Juliette frowns. "Contract," I whisper to her, and she scoffs.

The butler leads up the stairs to a suite at the far end of the hallway. Stepping into the suite, we are welcomed by a luxurious display. The suite is a haven of luxury, a testament to Frank's proclivity to show off. The living area is about half the size of the hall we just left, and every inch of the floor is laid with a plush dark green rug, which softness I can attest to even through my shoes. The large velvet drapes that line the windows tell me that during the day, the room will be flooded with bright light, but now, at night, there is a cascade of soft night lights with a yellowish-to-orange ambiance that weaves themselves into the night. It feels like we've walked into a palace.

"Thank you," I say to the butler who steps out and leaves us alone.

"What about our clothes?" Juliette says suddenly.

"I'll have Alison retrieve them from the hotel room."

"But I don't have any clothes to wear tonight."

"We'll have to make do tonight," I say with a shrug.

"Make do. How do you suggest we do that?"

"Huh," I look around. "Okay, you take the bed, I'll take the couch. You can sleep naked in the bedroom, can't you?"

"And risk you snooping around to take a peek in the middle of the night," she says maintaining a straight face, but I can tell she's joking.

"Lock the door."

"Look at that, you're not even saying you won't take a peek."

"Will that change anything?"

"No."

"So, lock your door. I promise not to pick the lock. If you don't feel safe enough, put a chair behind the door, alright?"

"I don't like this arrangement. None of it at all."

"Sorry about that," I say not really feeling sorry. I am secretly having a good time with all of this.

"You're loving this, aren't you?"

"Caught in the same room as you? God, no."

I walk past her to check the bedroom. I check all the utilities to ensure they are working well and check to see if the door can be locked.

"It's all safe for you to use now," I tell her. "But before you retire for the night, you must tell me what you and Frank talked about."

She looks reluctant. "I think I'd rather just have a shower. It's been a long night. I really need to sleep.

"No, you're telling me about it now. I need to know if it's something I can use against him."

"No, it's not something you can use against him."

"Alright, But I still want to know what it is."

"He was telling me about your father," she says softly.

"Oh..." I say, not sure how to proceed. "I, huh, what did he say?"

"He told me how he died."

"Did he tell you he was the reason he died? I mean, my father went down the path of drug abuse and alcoholism, and that's on him. He made terrible decisions with his life. But Frank refusing to give him the money he needed and making him chase his own tail was the push that led him down that terrible path."

"Yes, he mentioned it. He didn't look contrite about it, though."

"Frank is never contrite about anything," I hiss. I don't

want to get angry, but I'm working up towards it already and I feel no inclination to put a leash on it. "My mother hates him because of it. She blames him for all the misfortune in our lives, and here he is again and at the forefront of it."

"I don't want to tell you what to do or how to react, but..."

"Then don't," I cut her off. "I know exactly what you'll say. Is this healthy for me? Am I not worried about going down the same path as my father."

She nods.

"I have done something my father couldn't. I made it work," I tell her. "I have that to rely on. I can't make the same mistake that he did."

"But it's Frank Dubois. I don't know that much about him, but what I've learned in the last two days tells me he isn't someone to be messed with."

"Yes, but I'll show him I'm not one to be messed with either."

She still doesn't look satisfied.

"What?" I joke. "You suddenly care about me now?"

"You just had to say that didn't you?" she says and hisses. "I'm going to take my shower."

I watch her walk away from me. For a moment, I feel like reaching out to her, pulling her back by the fingertips, and kissing her. I want to be the one to get her out of that gown. I had imagined what it'd look like all night. I let her go, though, and the door slams in my face soon enough.

I turn away from there and find the liquor cabinet. Frank was sure to provide one. He wants to impress. He might hate my ass now, but he would hate it even more if the word got out that he didn't treat his guests to the best.

The liquor cabinet is beside the fireplace, which I keep

myself busy with. After a swig of rum, I finally start the fire. I stand by it for a while and watch it; the gentle warmth wafting out from it is lovely. I take another swig of the rum, and I feel it sweep all my worries away. For now, I'm just a boy wondering at the wonders of the flame. It feels good to let it all go, to surrender in entirety to nothingness.

CHAPTER 16

HUDSON

"*Y*ou started a fire," Juliette's voice breaks into my trance. I turn around to see her with a towel wrapped around her chest.

"Yes. And I found a liquor chest."

"I see," she says. "I wanted to see if you want to take your shower. There are two more towels unused."

"Yeah, sure, why not," I say and hand her the rum bottle. "Watch over my fire, alright."

"Alright, Sir," she says. I don't walk away immediately. I watch her for a while. The light from the flames casts her in a glorious glow. The towel is short and doesn't cover much of her body. It extends from the lower region of her breast and to her upper thigh. Her eyes drink mine in. She doesn't shy away. She doesn't cough. She just stares at me. I can see the longing in her eyes, the urge, the hunger. Can she see them in my mine also?

"I better get into the bathroom," I say, breaking the connection.

"Yeah, you better do that."

I walk away from her and immediately head into the bathroom. It takes me about fifteen minutes to take my shower, and I come out, wrapping one of the towels around myself. I see that she's moved some cushions to the floor so she can sit comfortably. There is also another glass for me.

"Hey!" she says, calling at me. "I thought we'd get comfortable before the fire. It's a really nice fire."

I join her. There is a silent communication between us. We pass it without using words. We are both in towels, drinking alcohol, sitting in front of a fire. It's a precedent to dangerous things. The thing, judging by the look on her face, what we both hunger for. I had tried to distract myself, to find relief someplace else, but yet, here I am again, hungry for her.

This is dangerous, we both know.

We should retire to the bedroom. We both know.

But we don't move.

I grab the glass from the floor.

"Pour me some, will you?"

"Gladly," Juliette says with a chuckle.

We quickly finish the first bottle, and I move to open the next one. I can feel the effect of the alcohol spreading through my nerves, calming me, relaxing me.

"You know about my dad. I don't know about yours," I say as I pour Juliette another round. "It's only fair if you tell me about yours."

"There's not much to tell you about my dad. He died a long time ago, when I was a child, so I never knew him; I have a single memory of him, and it was of him lifting me up and singing to me. We stood by the window, watching the rain together. That was it."

"I'm sorry," I find myself saying.

"For what?"

"You didn't get to know your father. I think everyone should get to know their father. That's a relationship that can't be replicated. I know my father wasn't the best man, but he was my father, and I loved him. I learned a lot from him. He taught me how to be a man, and there are lessons I got from him that I'll transfer to my kids."

"You want to have kids?" she asks, eyeing me skeptically.

"What? I don't look like I want to have kids?"

"I don't know. I never pegged you as someone who wants kids."

"You don't know me that well."

"We don't know each other that well," she amends.

We sit and watch each other in silence for a while. The tension between us gradually intensifies, moving from subtle want to roaring hunger. We've delayed and waited, but there is no denying what we both want now.

We've exhausted the small talk, and now, we find ourselves here.

"Come here," I tell her. For a moment, I think she'll be the wiser of the two of us and decline my invitation. But she doesn't decline. She sets her empty glass down and glides across the floor to me.

Now that she's closer, I can see her skin better, the amber light from the fire casting a soft, deep, and sensual glow on her. I know this is the right choice. I place my hands on her cheeks, and she rubs against them, her skin warm and inviting.

There's still time to stop this. One of us only has to move away. I pull her face towards mine, so her lips are just inches away. They're red and inviting, and I can feel her breath mingling with mine. I don't kiss her immediately. Instead, I let my palm fall to her chin and then use my thumb to part her lips. She opens them up for me, and when I finally kiss her, I slide my tongue in first. Juliette welcomes me with a moan, her body, which feels taut to my touch, relaxing instantly. She falls like a deck of cards, totally letting herself go. I pull her closer now, and the towel she has wrapped around her body slips open. She makes no effort to cover herself. She's too busy warring with my tongue inside her mouth, her hands clutching at my shoulders, pulling me closer.

This feels better than I could have ever imagined. I want more of her, need more of her. I wish she could melt and fuse with me so we could become one, our pleasure aligning in a perfect symphony. I want her to feel how much I've hungered for her, how much I need her. My cock is rock hard, straining painfully against my towel, begging for release. But beyond the hunger, I want her to feel how much I want to please her, to make her body vibrate with unending pleasure.

She pulls away from me and looks into my eyes. Her gaze is heated, desperate, telling me that she wants me just as much as I want her, if not more. But I want to savor this moment—not because I fear it might not happen again, but because I want more out of it.

I don't want her to be just another girl in the long line of girls I've fucked. I want to make love to her. I want to make love with her.

She tugs at my towel with her finger until it comes off, and then she moves to pull it away from me, but I stop her.

"Why?" she groans, her voice hoarse with hunger. "I need you," she confesses to me.

"I need you too," I tell her. "But wait."

She doesn't look satisfied, but I know that's about to change. I help her out of the towel, and she's finally naked before me, her skin glowing in the firelight. She shyly covers herself, crossing her arms over her breasts and closing her thighs.

"I want to see you," I tell her, but she doesn't pull her arms apart, not until I tug at her hands a little. Then, she lets them fall to her side, revealing herself to me completely. Her breasts, which I have longed to see without any covering, are open to my gaze. I hold her left breast in my hand. It's full and tender, the skin soft under my touch. I run my finger over her nipple, causing her to tremble with pleasure.

"Do you like that?" I ask her, a teasing tone in my voice.

"Stop it," she says with a chuckle, playfully pushing my hand away. But I catch her nipple in my mouth next, sucking on it and running my tongue over it repeatedly. She loses herself to me, her fingers combing through my hair, urging me on. Her skin, so supple and warm, motivates me even more. I want to touch every part of her, to kiss every inch of her, to make her mine completely.

Easy there, tiger, I tell myself.

I shift my focus back to Juliette, who is writhing with pleasure under my touch. I move to her other breast, rolling the wet nipple between my fingers while I lavish attention on the other. Now, she's moaning uncontrollably, her voice louder, more desperate, pleading for more. I don't chastise her to keep it quiet or worry that our host will hear her cries.

I want them to.

CHAPTER 17

HUDSON

Slowly, I guide her to lay on her back, and finally, I peel the rest of my towel away from my body. She sees my hard cock, standing proudly, and reaches for it, but I push her hand away.

"Not yet," I tell her.

"You're punishing me," she groans.

"It's what you deserve," I reply, biting down on her lips before returning my attention to her breasts. I don't stay there long before I start kissing down her midsection, leaving a trail of wet kisses in my wake.

Juliette's eyes are closed, her fingers clamped against the rug, pulling at the fibers in anticipation. I take my time with her, kissing down her thighs, dangerously close to her core that's already dripping with arousal. The heat and sweet scent of her sex call to me, but I resist the urge to dive in just yet. I lick around her thighs, moving as close as possible without ever making contact with her aching clit. I can tell by the way her body shivers and writhes whenever I get close that she's desperate for it, but I delay, toying with her, building the anticipation.

"Just do it already!" she cries. "Just fuck me already."

I ignore her pleas and move to her other thigh, torturing her the same way. After what feels like an eternity of teasing, I stop and look up at her, watching the frustration and need in her eyes.

I smile and lift both her legs, exposing her completely to me. She's glistening, wet and ready, and finally, I allow myself to indulge. I position myself between her legs and breathe her in first, memorizing her scent, knowing I'll want to remember this moment long after it's passed. A pang of regret hits me, knowing in a few days she'll be gone, but I push it aside as my fingers find her slit.

Juliette trembles as if a million volts of electricity just passed through her. I rub my fingers over her clit, catching the swollen nub between my fingers, making it more prominent. Then, finally, I lower my head and let my tongue run over her clit, slowly sliding a finger into her at the same time.

She goes stiff, her body freezing as the pleasure overwhelms her. For a moment, she's completely still, and then she explodes with a scream, her juices gushing out as I lap at them greedily, my tongue working her clit while my fingers pump in and out of her.

Juliette's moans grow louder, echoing off the walls, no doubt waking the entire mansion. She shows no sign of restraint, and I don't want her to. I continue pleasuring her, alternating between sucking on her clit and thrusting my fingers deep inside her, playing her body like an instrument, coaxing out more and more of those beautiful sounds.

This goes on for several minutes until Juliette can't take it anymore. She pushes me away, her body trembling, her breath coming in ragged gasps. She's drenched in sweat, her skin glowing, her eyes glazed over with pleasure.

"Your turn," she says, her voice barely above a whisper.

I don't argue. I lay back and let her take control, eager to feel her mouth on me. She doesn't punish me the way I punished her. Her hunger is too great for that. She starts slowly, though, rolling her tongue around the tip of my cock, collecting the precum that's already leaking from me, a sign of just how much I need her. She keeps her eyes locked on mine as she does it, the sight of her mouth on me, her lips wrapped around my cock, is the most erotic thing I've ever seen.

Her fingers wrap around the base of my cock, firm but gentle, as she slowly takes more of me into her mouth, her tongue swirling around the sensitive head. I let out a deep groan, unable to hold back, and that encourages her. She starts bobbing her head up and down, taking me deeper each time, her saliva coating my cock, making it easier for her to slide me in and out of her mouth.

The sensation is incredible, her mouth warm and wet, her tongue skilled and teasing as she works me over. I grip the rug beneath me, trying to hold on as she pleasures me with a combination of her mouth and hands, her movements deliberate and precise, driving me closer to the edge with every stroke until I explode in her mouth.

After what feels like an eternity, she pulls back, her eyes locking onto mine as she wipes her lips with the back of her hand.

"Now, how was that?" she asks me, her voice sultry, laced with the satisfaction of knowing just how good she's made me feel.

"I see I'm not the only one capable of great things," I say, my breath still heavy, heart still pounding from the way she worked me over.

"You flatter yourself too much," she replies with a playful smirk, but there's a fire in her eyes that tells me she's far from finished.

I pull her closer and kiss her, this time harder than before, my hunger for her intensifying with every second. We aren't done with each other. The hunger persists; it's a wanton beast that won't go away until it is fully satiated. And satiate it, I intend to do.

I set Juliette down beside me, positioning her so her face faces the fireplace, the flickering flames giving her blue eyes an almost otherworldly glow. The sight of her, bathed in the warm light, only fuels my desire further. I kiss her deeply as I set myself behind her, raising her legs up for easier access. She bites down on her lips as I slide myself in, her wetness immediately welcoming me, wrapping around me in a warmth that sends a shiver down my spine.

I don't move for a while, simply letting myself savor the sensation of being inside her, the tightness, the way her body grips me, contracting and relaxing as if getting used to my presence. I can feel every inch of her, every subtle movement, every heartbeat that pulses through her. It's intoxicating.

I hold onto her waist, my fingers digging into her soft skin as I finally thrust myself in, hard and urgent. Juliette screams, the sound raw and primal, and then she turns to look at me over her shoulder. There's wildness in her eyes, a plea for more, and she gives me a gentle nod, urging me to continue.

And so, I do.

It becomes a dance of hunger, a rhythm that we fall into naturally, our sweaty bodies slamming against each other with a desperate intensity. The world outside ceases to exist; there is only us, the heat of the fire, the slick slide of our bodies moving together, the sounds of our moans and gasps filling the room.

I thrust into her over and over, each movement more powerful than the last, driving us both closer to that inevitable edge. The muscles of her walls tighten around me, gripping me as I push deeper, hitting that sweet spot that makes her cry out, her fingers clawing at the rug beneath her.

Her back arches, pressing her ass harder against me, and I take the invitation, pounding into her with everything I have. The force of it drives her forward, but I pull her back each time, keeping her locked in place, her body at my mercy.

Juliette's moans become louder, more desperate, her breath coming in ragged gasps. She reaches back, trying to grasp at anything she can, her hands sliding over my thighs, my hips, urging me on, needing me to take her even harder. I oblige, my pace quickening, the need to push her over the edge driving me wild.

The sound of our bodies slapping together is loud, echoing off the walls, mixing with the crackle of the fire. I'm lost in the sensation, the feeling of her tight and wet around me, the way her body moves with mine, the way she moans my name as I push her closer and closer to release.

I reach around, my hand finding her clit, rubbing it in time with my thrusts. The effect is immediate—her body tenses, her breath hitches, and she lets out a scream that echoes through the room as she comes, her orgasm crashing over her in waves. I don't stop. I keep fucking her, driving her through it, her body shuddering beneath me, her walls clenching and releasing around my cock.

She's trembling, her body spent, but I'm not done. I want to feel her come again, to feel her fall apart in my arms. I keep thrusting, my pace relentless, pushing her beyond what she thought she could handle. Her moans turn into cries, her body quaking with the force of another orgasm building inside her.

I can feel myself getting close, the pressure building in my core, but I hold back, wanting to draw this out, to make it last as long as possible. I want to see her completely undone, to know that I'm the one who did this to her, the one who made her feel this way.

Juliette's fingers dig into the rug, her knuckles white as she tries to ground herself, but there's no escaping the pleasure that's overtaking her. Her body is a live wire, every nerve ending on fire, and I'm right there with her, my own body trembling with the effort of holding back.

Finally, I can't take it anymore. I grab her hips, holding her still as I drive into her one last time, hard and deep. She screams my name as she comes again, her body convulsing around me, and I let go, my own orgasm ripping through me with a force that leaves me breathless.

I spill into her, my cock throbbing as I release everything I have, my body shuddering with the intensity of it. We collapse together, our bodies still connected, still pulsing with the aftershocks of our pleasure.

The fire crackles beside us, the only sound in the room besides our ragged breathing. I'm still inside her, still hard, but neither of us moves. We're spent, completely sated, and for now, that's enough.

The world could end tonight, and I won't care. I'm here, deep inside of her, and blissful. This is the best feeling in the world.

CHAPTER 18

JULIETTE

I stir awake to find myself in bed. I remember how last night went and truthfully, I hoped it never ended. Hudson and I moved from the floor when it got too uncomfortable to the bedroom; we continued to learn more about each other's bodies. I just simply couldn't get enough of him, and now, I slowly force myself to wake; I turn to find him standing by the window, sipping from a mug. He looks beautiful in the morning light. The way the beams slightly strike his face renders him in the fashion of a Greek god. His rumpled her, his quiet smile and mournful contemplation. This is all beautiful, so beautiful that I don't want him to turn around and notice me awake. I want to watch him by that window forever.

Last night, I had given in to a hunger deep inside of me. I could lie and tell myself that alcohol is to be blamed, but it isn't to blame for the lust I've felt since I saw Hudson in the tuxedo he chose to wear last night. It isn't to be blamed for the risk I took coming into the living room in just the towel; it isn't to be blamed that I hoped, and I would have gone ahead to make it happen—that my towel fell. Yet, things had gone better than I could have ever imagined them.

"You going to just lay there and stare at me forever?" Hudson asks, turning around to look at me.

"I wasn't staring at you," I lie.

"Now, you know that's just a lie. Do you want coffee? I got them to make you one. I don't really know how you like it, so I just told the cook, black is fine."

"Are you having it black?" I ask him.

"Yes, I am."

"I'll have it black then."

He picks up a mug from the ottoman and walks over to me. I sit up on the bed, using the duvet to cover myself. He grins at that but says nothing. Last night, we had no clothes to wear to bed, but he's wearing some shorts this morning.

"Where did you get new clothes?"

"I had Alison bring our clothes from the hotel this morning," he says. "It's all in the closet."

"Alison came in here?" I ask, feeling self-conscious.

"No, she didn't," he says, then he adds in a serious tone. "We have to talk."

I know what the discussion will be about, and I agree with him before he says anything. He sits beside me on the bed, his eyes drinking me in.

"You're a beautiful woman, Juliette, a passionate lover. I won't lie and say I didn't fancy you since you stepped into my office."

"I thought you said I wasn't your type," I tease.

"That's not what this conversation is about," he replies.

"Okay, okay," I say with a silly grin. "Go on."

"Come on, you know I said all that just so something like this doesn't happen."

"I know," I say, still smiling. "So go on."

He sighs before he continues.

"I had wondered what it'll be like to have you in bed, but I also knew it was something I mustn't do. You tortured me even when you didn't know you were. And I know this probably isn't what you want to hear, but this can't happen again. Last night has to be a one-time thing. I have always had a rule never to go to bed with people who work with me and for me. It complicates things."

"I know," I say, and I'm not surprised he looks shocked by my response.

"You do?" he asks.

"Yes. I was sent here to work. The scope of my work has expanded beyond what it should normally be, but I can't include this. Like you said, it'll muddy everything up. We need straight heads to survive the next five days, don't we?"

"Yes, we do," he agrees.

"Staying away from each other is one way to do that."

"Yes. So, I checked the couch this morning, and luckily, it is a pull-out couch and very comfortable. Frank doesn't leave anything to chance."

"We agree that we keep our hands off each other, right?"

"Yes," I tell him. "But not yet."

I look down from his face to his toned muscles. It's the right thing not to let sex muddle up the ruse we are building, but then I'm not ready to let go of him just yet. I want more this morning. Before I can tell him what I intend, Hudson kisses me. The hunger and ferocity in the kiss tell me he has been thinking just what I've been thinking.

He helps me set the mug down on the side table, and soon

enough, the duvet is pulled away from me entirely, leaving me completely naked beneath his gaze. There's no need for foreplay, no need to explore our bodies further. The only thing that matters is quenching the fire that's burning through us both. Hudson strips off his shorts in one swift motion, his cock already hard, pulsing with need.

He grabs my waist, his fingers digging into my skin as he pulls me closer. Then, with a sudden, rough motion, he turns me over, pressing my chest against the mattress while lifting my ass high in the air. My heart races, anticipation building as I feel his breath on the back of my neck, the tension in the room so thick I can barely breathe.

With one hand, he grips my hair, pulling it back to expose my neck, while with the other, he guides his cock to my entrance. He pushes into me with a force that steals my breath, stretching me open until I'm filled completely, every inch of him buried deep inside me.

"Fuck!" I moan out in pleasure, my voice hoarse and desperate as he begins to move. It feels like the first time all over again, the sensation of him inside me so intense that my mind goes blank, and all I can do is feel. He starts slow, each thrust deliberate, giving me just enough to crave more. But soon, his restraint snaps, and he starts ramming into me, his hips slamming against mine with a ferocity that makes me cry out, the sound echoing in the room.

Hudson spanks my ass hard, the sting of his hand sending jolts of pleasure straight to my core. He pulls my hair tighter, using it as leverage to drive himself deeper, and I arch my back, meeting his thrusts with equal desperation. The room is filled with the sound of our bodies colliding, the wet, obscene noise of his cock sliding in and out of me as he fucks me relentlessly.

Every nerve in my body is on fire, the pleasure so intense

that I feel like I'm going to shatter. My legs begin to shake, the strength leaving them as he continues to pound into me, and I collapse onto the bed. But Hudson doesn't stop. He follows me down, his body pressing me into the mattress as he keeps fucking me, his pace brutal, unyielding.

I'm lost in the sensation, my mind a haze of lust and need as he takes me over and over, driving me higher and higher until I'm teetering on the edge of oblivion. My orgasm hits me like a tidal wave, crashing through me with such force that I scream, my body convulsing around him as the pleasure rips through me. But he doesn't stop. He keeps going, his thrusts never faltering as he pushes me through another climax, and then another, each one more powerful than the last.

My nails dig into the sheets, clawing for purchase as I'm overwhelmed by the sheer intensity of it all. My body trembles uncontrollably, every muscle tensing as Hudson fucks me into oblivion, his cock filling me completely, owning me in every way. His breath is ragged, his movements frantic as he nears his own release, and when he finally comes, he does so with a deep, guttural groan, spilling himself inside me, his cock throbbing as he fills me with his warmth.

We lay there, tangled together, our bodies slick with sweat, both of us spent and sated. Hudson kisses my forehead softly before he slowly pulls out of me, leaving me feeling empty and fulfilled all at the same time. I can barely move, my body completely exhausted from the intense, primal fucking we just shared.

When I wake up again, the sun is shining brightly outside, and the bedside clock tells me it's midday. Hudson isn't in the room, but he's left a note for me, telling me he had business to handle in town and will be back in time for dinner.

He confesses he had a good time last night and this morning, and as I read his words, I can't help but smile. I miss him already, my body still humming from the aftermath, yearning for his touch, craving the feel of him inside me again.

"Get it together, Juls," I tell myself and get out of bed. My mug of coffee is still on the table. I take a sip of it and find it cold. I'll have to find someone to heat it up for me. I get into the bathroom to take my shower. Having the water cascade down my body reminds me of Hudson's tongue loving every bit of me, reaching into crevices I didn't know existed in my body and giving me pleasure from it. How do I go from experiencing such bliss from him to never experiencing it again? It'll be a tough job, especially given that we'll be staying so close to each other, just a couple of feet away from each other. It'll be hard, but it's what I must do. Things would have been easier to navigate if I hadn't given in to my lust.

After taking my shower, my stomach grumbles, telling me I'm hungry, so I dress, pick up my mug and search for the kitchen. The house is mostly empty, or at least in this wing where Hudson and I are situated; it looks that way. A couple of times I almost lose my way, but in the end, I find the kitchen. The sound of clanging utensils leads me to it. There is someone standing by the stove cooking. He's dressed in chef's clothes, and coming from the oven is the smell of freshly baked bread. The chef notices me and smiles at me as he pulls his bread out of his oven.

"Hi," I say to him.

"Hello," he says, walking over to me. "You must be Miss Juliette."

"Yes."

"I'm Alejandro. Mr. Dubois told me you might find your

way to the kitchen at any time. I trust your night was splendid."

The glint in his eyes and the way he cocks his head to the side gives me the suggestion that he knows about the activities Hudson and I performed during the night, but then I realize he's just making polite conversations.

"Yes, it was thanks. I woke up to find this by my side. It's cold already," I show him the coffee mug.

"Give me that. I'll heat it up for you," Alejandro says, putting my coffee in the microwave. We both stand in silence for a while as the coffee heats up. He gets it out and hands it to me a couple of minutes later. I take a sip. Perfect.

"I met Mr. Sinclair this morning on his way to work," Alejandro continues. "He told me to feed you properly; that last night must have left you famished."

I almost choke on my coffee, and he stares at me in confusion. "Are you not hungry?"

"Yes, yes, I am hungry. It was just… you know what, never mind. Are you making something?" I ask, pointing at the bread he's letting cool off.

"Yes. Bruschetta. Have you ever had it before?"

"I don't think I have."

"You're in for a treat then. It's one of my favorite meals to prepare. It's simple, but delicious."

"How do you make it?" I ask him.

"I'll show you, come. All you need is bread, tomatoes, garlic, basil, and olive oil."

I join him at the counter, glad that I have a way to spend my morning.

"Do you cook?" Alejandro asks me as I help him slice his tomatoes.

"Yes, I bake. I plan to open a bakery soon," I tell him, and he looks impressed.

"That's great," he says.

"I don't know how to bake so well. Especially American confectioneries. I have always wanted to learn, but there's no one to teach me and no time."

"Luckily for you, what I have in excess now is time."

CHAPTER 19

HUDSON

*W*ith a frown on her face, Alison drives while I try to focus on developing a strategy to get over my Frank Dubois debacle quickly. I keep getting distracted by images of Juliette splayed naked on the bed. There is a reminiscent taste of her juices on my lips, and I can smell her. Even though she's miles away, I still yearn for her. I wonder how we will survive the next few nights in the house. We've both agreed to keep our hands off each other, and I agree it's the best decision for us. Shaking my head and forcing myself to focus on work, I turn to Alison.

"How are we doing this morning?" I ask. "It's the end of the month. Let me see the sales report."

"Sales are up ten percent this month," she says and turns the corner, beating the traffic light just in time. "What we should worry about is cash at hand. We are leaking more than we are keeping in."

"The reason for that is obvious. I wouldn't stress myself

over that if I were you. As long as we are making good sales, once this whole trouble with Frank is gone, we'll be back on our feet in just a couple of months."

She doesn't look like she believes that.

"What if it doesn't end soon?" she asks.

"What will you have me do? Give up and sell to him?" I demand. She's getting on my nerves, and I know her sour disposition isn't entirely about the company sales or Frank.

"No," Alison hisses. "I don't want you to sell to him. That would be stupid. You went into the stable with Phillipa last night. What happened in there?"

I raise an eyebrow at Alison. "How do you know I was in the stable with her?"

"Elizabeth told me."

"You're buddies with Elizabeth Dubois now?"

"No, not buddies. But we have similar worries. We are caught in a fight between two men who are more interested in measuring dicks than finding a lasting solution to the issue at hand. We both don't want to see our respective companies go up in flames."

"Measuring dicks. You think that's what I'm doing with Frank? Playing a game of egos, huh? You think I want to be caught in this game for too long with that narcissist? You think I love that? Oh, you fucking love the company so much! You love the company more than I do." I sound angrier than I intend and it causes her to tremble.

"You know I didn't mean it that way, Hudson," she says.

"So, tell me. What did you mean? I want to know."

She looks at me, worried about speaking her mind, but whatever she sees on my face tells her she best speak instead of being mute.

"I just don't understand why you don't want to marry Phillipa," she complains. "If you marry her, we have a way out

—an easy one. We've done so much to make that possible. You've sacrificed a lot, but then you just want to abandon all the work we've put in. You can marry her, you can decide to marry her today, and you'll be married before the end of the day, but you just won't."

"The girl stirs nothing in me. You want to know what happened in the stable? I'll tell you what happened. She stripped for me. She got naked and begged me to fuck her. All I could think about when I saw her was how unappealing she was to me. The girl is a fucking child!"

"And what about Juliette? They're the same age."

Now, we're getting somewhere, I think. This is why she's had a frown on her face the whole time.

"This is really about Juliette, isn't it?"

"No, it's about the company.

"Don't fucking lie to me!"

"Okay, okay, I'll concede. It is about her. I don't like her, and I told you, she's a distraction, so what do you do? You fuck her, like that will help at all. I don't care if Phillipa is appealing or not. What does that matter? You make the girl your wife, you get Frank Dubois as your father- in-law, and you get a free pass to so many funds, you grow your invest-ment. You know I'm right. You see what I'm saying, yet you wouldn't make the right choice. You know why? You agreed to go with the Phillipa plan if nothing else works. We both talked about it and came to an agreement, but then that bitch came in, and she destroyed everything, set it all on fire. So, yes, this is about her. She's ruining everything for everyone. Every goddamn thing!"

Alison rounds up, hitting her fist on the steering wheel. I let her cool off before I speak, and because I worry that I'll speak out of order and then we'll get into a fight, I don't let the anger her stupidity stirred in me force me to speak. So, she waits for me anxiously.

Alison has been my personal assistant for over eight years now. She was there when I got the first round of funding to revive the company. I remember the night like it was yesterday, the happiness in her eyes, the look of hope and assurance of the beauty the future holds. We both knew we would shake the world. I had hired her out of college, a bright-eyed lady, eager to work, eager to impress and impress me she has over the years. But I sense her heading down a dangerous path and must steer her away before it's too late. There is only one way I know to do that.

"Listen, Alison. You've been an immense help to me, and I appreciate that, but the next time you raise your voice to me will be the last time I consider you an employee. The next time you call Juliette a bitch will be the last time you ever talk about her in any context whatsoever. The next time you think yourself bold enough to tackle my opinions aggressively will be the last time you have the chance to speak to me. Do you understand that?"

She nods.

"Good. Now, I'll tell you again why marrying Phillipa would be disastrous," I tell her.

I go over the same conversation I've had with her so many times. If I marry Phillipa, I can't assure her happiness. I can't give her the attention she so hungers for from me. I can't love or cherish her. I don't see that ever happening, and that begins a slippery slope that I am sure will leave her heart getting broken and her father, who dotes on her, seeking to punish me. A Frank that I don't deal with today is a Frank I get to contend with in the future. I can't go through this dance twice.

"You could fake it," Alison suggests. "Fake it just as you are doing with the new girl."

The new girl. She still won't mention Juliette by name. She must despise her so much. Juliette called my attention to it, but I didn't think it was something to worry about. I still don't think it is. Alison wouldn't dare do something stupid.

"How long do I fake it for? Ten years? Twenty years? Phillipa isn't a fool, you know. She'll catch on."

"It won't matter," she says. "You said she threw herself at you in the stable. That's a move from someone very desperate. You can make her your wife, and that will keep her satisfied."

"I don't think it will. I know you think of her as some overpampered dove, but there is a cynical side to her. I've seen it in her eyes. She's trouble, and she's the worst kind of trouble—the kind no one pays attention to. Marrying her will be a distraction. She'll be a hound constantly nipping at my heels."

"You can't bring yourself to fuck her? There are ways, you know? She won't mind. She loves you and just a touch from you is all she needs to survive on."

"I know what you're suggesting. You want me to get her pregnant, so she has that to keep her busy."

"Yes."

"You seem not to understand me. I do not want to dally with Phillipa because to do that will yoke me with her father. I do not want to be yoked with Frank and I do not want Phillipa to be the mother of my kids. I'll be subjecting the poor child to dysfunction."

Alison sighs and turns her focus to driving.

"You don't think I can beat Frank?" I ask her.

"I think you can. But I don't think we have the luxury of time to wait and find out. Frank knows that."

"We have the Fejitos, remember?"

"Yes, we have the Fejitos. But I don't trust him."

"Work on the company alliance he's provided us. Keep it very secret. If we can support ourselves with that and use their revenue to improve our cash at hand, we'll be good for as long as it takes."

"All of a sudden, we have good revenue. Frank will get suspicious. He'll take a closer look."

"And he'll see nothing. We're making good sales, and from next month, we'll make even better sales. I'm meeting with Randall this morning. He has a fleet of restaurants here in Manhattan and Dallas and all over the country. If we can get him onboard as a new customer, we can push our sales up more points."

"We'll have to cook the books a little," she says.

I say nothing to that. Going to war with Frank is telling on me more than I wish it was, but then I'm just a fish company going against a finance giant. He has an almost endless supply of funds; I do not.

Then, I remember what Jasmine told me. Frank is having some money problems, and Elizabeth getting cozy with Alison suggests that might be true. Elizabeth has no emotional attachment to this tug-of-war between her father and me and wants her company to stop bleeding money. She wants it to end, and if things were up to her, she'd take the deal I have offered.

"I want you to meet with Elizabeth," I tell Alison.

"Why?"

"Talk to her about the deal I offered her father. The one he declined."

"She can't change his mind."

"Maybe... but there's no harm in trying. That's not why I want you to meet with her. I want you to siphon some information out of her. I heard Frank has money issues lately. I don't know the source. If it is investments gone bad, we might have some new leverage to work with. But I hope it's something more juicy. Something he doesn't want out there. He's done a good job of keeping it hidden."

"How did you find out then?" Alison asks.

"I have my ways. Just prod Elizabeth a little. See if she'll budge. If she wants her father to give up this game, she must be ready to let go of some information."

"She'll want something in return," Alison says.

"Tell her about the deal."

"She's no fool. The deal is information she can get from her father if she asks. The deal is just a reason for me to see her again. We need to give her something tangible."

I think over it for a while, and I know what Alison is suggesting.

"I don't trust Elizabeth," I tell her.

"She's a Dubois. She's not to be trusted. But you'll agree, she is the only one in the family with a level-head."

She has that correct. I know Elizabeth is the one who suggested to Frank that inviting me to the party is a good move and fraternizing with me might make me pliable. I can almost see her whispering to Frank: "Play the father figure." Frank had failed woefully at that. But that isn't Frank's fault. He doesn't know what it's like to be a good father.

"Tell her we have a source of funds that Frank can't touch. Be ambiguous about it, nothing concrete."

"I think you should meet with her instead," Alison says. "It will look more believable from you."

She's right. Besides, I haven't ever had a real conversation with Elizabeth Dubois. She is married but opted to keep her father's name. The wise choice. The Dubois name opens so many doors.

"Set it up," I tell Alison. "Set it up soon."

CHAPTER 20

HUDSON

*W*e arrive at Sinclair's corporation soon enough. I step out of the car and send Alison on her way while I walk into the building. She has some more work to handle. I have two meetings today, and the one with Randall must go well. I went to college with Randall, so there is some hope there.

Getting into the building, I notice the eyes on me. It is usual for my workers to get self-conscious and try to act busy whenever I walk through the corridor, but this time, they all are watching me out of the corners of their eyes. I don't have the time to wonder what that's all about, so I head into my office immediately. I make myself a cup of steaming coffee and return to my seat, but I realize I'm without a secretary. The secretary I got from At Your Service Agency is at The Dubois ranch house, playing fiancé.

It's just meetings. I'll survive without a secretary.

About an hour later, with my coffee ingested, I get a knock on my door. It's Randall. He's about fifteen minutes early. I have nothing else to do, so I welcome him into my office.

"Hey man," he says, giving me a firm handshake before taking his seat.

"Can I get you anything to drink? I have some good Arabian coffee."

"Yes, some coffee will be nice. I can smell it already."

I nod and walk to the machine to prepare the coffee myself. This is something I learned from my father. Always treat a prospective client like they matter, and they're not just some entity you're looking to leech money off. Make their coffee, provide them with whatever they require, listen to them, and provide appropriate feedback. Business is beyond throwing money around. It's also about throwing a reputation around.

"How do you take it? Black or with milk?"

"Black," he says.

"With sugar?"

"Two cubes?"

I prepare his coffee.

"How are the restaurants?" I ask Randall as I hand him his cup of coffee. It's too hot for him, so he blows on it.

"Man, who knew running a business can be so hard," he says with a shake of his head. "What am I saying? I have it easy. You're up in the same pants with Frank Dubois. That's a stress level I never would want to perceive. How are you handling that?"

Make the meeting about them and not you.

"Oh, Frank and I will find a level ground, I'm sure. What's the number of restaurants now, fifteen?"

"Eighteen. We're expanding to Kansas this summer. We

have the locations set and are just waiting for the summer rush to open them."

"Sounds like a lot of work," I tell him.

"I mean, I meet with so many people in a day that I lose count: contractors, constructors, food merchants, and hiring firms. It is crazy. But that's the price of running a business. The grind never stops."

Be relatable.

"It just never stops," I say.

"I like this coffee," Randall chips in when he finally takes a sip from the coffee.

"I can have it sent to your office. I have a connection who brings them to me right from the Saudi."

"That'll be great, thank you! I guess we better get down to business then," Randall says. He reaches into his bag and pulls some files out. He passes them to me. Since we have a standard menu in all the restaurants, the requirements are mostly the same I'm referring to the kind of seafood we make and the products we'll require from you. But quantity varies from city to city and restaurant to restaurant."

I nod, perusing through the file. "Fifteen products," I say.

"Yes, but my partners say we start with eight."

"Why?" I ask.

"Come on, Hudson. You know why. We can't transfer all of our contracts to you and break off contracts with previous suppliers."

"Judging by the numbers I see here, of the eight products we'll be supplying you, we'll be providing just twenty percent of the total number your restaurant consumes."

"Yes," Randall says. "Playing it safe."

"Come on, Randall. You're losing money that way. If you give me all fifteen products and kick the percentage up to eighty percent, you save over a million dollars monthly on sea products. You know how much that racks up to in a year. Fiscal improvement."

"Yes, we know that. And I pointed that out to my partners, but there are talks that you might not be here by the end of the year. Now, if we lose a major supplier, we lose production and more than we would have saved if we had got onboard with you. They're not comfortable with that risk. I'm here because it's you and I would love to do business with you"

"I'm not speaking to your partners," I say, knowing those said partners do not have any say. This is Randall expressing his fear. "They sent you here because they believe in your choice, and I'm telling you, shifting to us is the best choice for you."

"What about Frank?"

"He's nothing to worry about."

"Come on, man, he's not nothing to worry about. We see the numbers. You're bleeding."

"Yet, we have a record-high sale this month."

"The money from those sales can't plug the hole Frank has dug."

"Yet, here I am, standing stronger than ever. Why do you think that is, Randall? If Frank could annihilate me and not kick himself in the nuts in the process, he would have a long time ago. I'm at a stalemate with Frank, Frank Dubois. No one has ever done that before."

"But can you stay in stale mate forever? Someone will shift. The market says you're more likely to."

"The sea says otherwise. It's a bountiful season for catch."

"You have fish. Frank has cash."

"But does he? If he does, why am I still here? If Frank is the big bully everyone fears him to be, why can't he buy me out? My company is valued at six billion dollars. He can pull several levers to get that off, buy me out, and toss me to the dogs, but that hasn't happened. Old Frank would have done that months ago. But he's stuck."

"What are you saying?" Randall asks. I have his attention now. If I close this deal with him, it will send a message to others out there that doing business with me isn't as riddled with risk as they think it is. If I get new customers onboard and improve sales even more, I will get more customers, and we will get more leverage and can play the waiting game for longer with Frank.

"I'm saying you're not paying attention. How about I make this deal less risky for you?"

"What are you suggesting?"

"I deliver to eight restaurants at fifty percent. If my fiscal accumulation by the end of next month goes up, we improve the deal to ten restaurants at sixty-five percent. If it goes down, the deal becomes five restaurants at twenty percent. If, in three months, I keep a steady fiscal balance or improve, I get the whole deal. You're still saving and bearing little risk."

"There's something you know that I don't," Randall says.

"What I know is simple. I am not losing this war to Frank. That's why I said to pay attention, Randall.

"How will you do well in the market when Frank is on your ass? It's not possible."

"I'm Hudson Sinclair. I can make anything possible."

Randall smiles, clearly impressed. "I think my partners will like this deal very much. You send the paperwork to my company tomorrow, and I'll get my legal team to go through it."

"Good. I'm glad we could do business."

"Yea, that aside. Let's talk about your girl making the news," Randall says, shifting into a comfortable position as he gulps his cup.

"Girl? What girl?" I ask.

"What do you mean what girl? Your fiancée. She's the talk of the town. Everyone is steaming like trains trying to find out who she is."

I frown, lost. I pick up my phone to find out what Randall is talking about. And there it is, the news of the day.

What Do We Make of Her: She Seemed to Have Dropped From An Obscure End of The World.

The first news article I read has a picture of Juliette and me walking down the red carpet holding hands. Juliette looks a little dazzled by all the lights, but her exquisiteness is captured. She has the grace of an angel learning to walk on cobblestones. Everyone is asking the same questions: Who is she, and how did I keep her a secret for so long?

"She's a big catch," Randall says. "That picture of hers absolutely blew me away."

He continues his compliment while one thing runs through my mind.

I have to call Juliette.

CHAPTER 21

JULIETTE

J'm having a good time with Alejandro, who has so many recipes to teach me. Unfortunately, we can only make two today because I have to teach him how to make a cake also. Today, he'll teach me how to make the puttanesca and ribolita while I teach him how to make black forest cake. Alejandro goes first and in two hours, we have a meal ready.

"God, I'm so excited to try it," I say, setting my plate of puttanesca on the kitchen counter.

"Hold on," Alejandro says. "It is best paired with a wine. I know just the right wine for this."

I wait in the kitchen, and he excuses himself to go to the wine cellar to get wine. Now that I'm alone, I find that Hudson hasn't crossed my mind. Yet, immediately, I realize that the fact falls on its head, and I start to think about him. I wonder what he's up to. He told me he had a couple of meetings today and would be back at night. Would he be meeting with Jasmine again? The earthy goddess. Jealousy burns through me like green fire, and I hope Alejandro will come back fast.

I don't want to think about Hudson. I want to think of the meal before me. I haven't had as much fun as I had today with Alejandro. I did something new, something exciting. Once we're done with this meal, we'll start to bake. That will take the rest of the day and then we'll get to making dinner. It's been a while since I dipped my fingers into flour, and I can't wait to bake.

Maybe my time here at the Dubois ranch house won't be so bad after all. As long as I spend it with Alejandro. I know the possibility of that is slim, but my fear is satisfied when Alejandro walks back into the kitchen with Phillipa. She's dressed in a riding getup, which explains why I haven't seen her the whole day. There's a look in her eyes that I can't place, and for a moment, I want to feel sorry for her. Here I am, the girl who has stolen the man she adores, waltzing around the house, messing up the kitchen like I own the place.

"I see you're having a splendid time," Phillipa says, joining me across the counter.

"Miss Juliette and I have had a busy morning," Alejandro answers innocently, not aware of the sarcasm in the tone of the question. "She's made puttanesca. I taught her how to. She'll teach me how to bake black forest cake soon enough."

"Oh, you are domestic. That must be it, then, huh? Hudson wants to marry you and stick you in the house, filling your stomach up with babies."

Now, Alejandro hears the spite, and he wonders what that is about. He doesn't speak up against his mistress, though, which I appreciate. I don't want him to get in trouble because of me. He sets the bottle of wine on the table and steps back.

I watch Phillipa intently. She wants to hurt me with her words, and while her face is mucked with hate, I can't help but see the pain behind the mask. The thing she mocks me for is what she'll kill to have.

"I have no intention of becoming a baby machine. Hudson knows that."

"So, what's all this then? The baking, the cooking?"

"I plan on opening a bakery soon," I tell her, holding my head high. She must not have expected that reply because she looks lost for a moment and can't find a reply.

"I think she'll run a good business," Alejandro says, picking up a hint to rejoin the conversation. He picks up his bottle of wine to open it. "Do you want to join us for, well, I can't call it breakfast or lunch, Miss Phillipa?

Phillipa glares at me, hate wafting off her like smoke from a fire. After a while, she smiles and shakes her head.

"No, I think I'll just go bathe and have a good nap. And by the way, Juliette, you've become something of a star. Do you know that?"

"What are you talking about?" I ask her.

Now, she grins, enjoying the moment. She chuckles and walks away, not providing me any additional clue. I glance up at Alejandro, who looks just as confused, and I run up the stairs past Phillipa, who is still chuckling. I get into the suite and shut the door behind me. Immediately, I pick up my phone and find out I've had multiple calls from my mother, Sophie and Hudson.

God, what is going on? I wonder as panic sets in. I try to open my phone, but my hands are shaking, and I have to take a couple of deep breaths to calm myself. No one is in danger; I feel confident about that. Finally, I open my phone and go online to see what all the hullabaloo is about. I get a pop-up notification and immediately click on it. Someone has written an article about me and my engagement to Hudson.

Oh god, no, I whisper as I read through the news. They described me as unknown, ordinary, and a possible mismatch for the billionaire playboy Hudson Sinclair. They even go so far as predicting a breakup very soon as I won't be able to handle the level of fame that comes with dating and marrying a billionaire.

A paragraph in the article jumps out at me.

I don't know what either of them is thinking. This relationship is doomed before it even begins. Juliette, with the personality of a squeezed sponge, can in no way keep a man as sophisticated as Hudson Sinclair. Juliette. That is all there is to know about her. Juliette Unknown.

Ouch.

It sounds to me like whoever wrote this article has some personal beef with me. I scroll to the end immediately, and I'm not shocked to see the writer's credit.

Bentley.

That bitch, I curse under my breath and pick up the phone to call Hudson. I wonder what this means now. If we are out there and public, our relationship will be under more scrutiny. It won't be long before someone finds out that Hudson and I have no prior relationship before At Your Service Agency sent me to be his temporary secretary.

Hudson picks up my call on the first ring.

"Where have you been?" he seems angry.

"Without my phone," I say.

"Have you seen it?"

"And if by it, you mean the scalding description of me as, Juliette Unknown. Goddamnit, that isn't my last name."

"This isn't a time for jokes, Juliette."

"Joke? Oh, you think I'm joking? Of course, you think I

am. They did describe you as the perfect gentleman, so all is peachy on your end."

"All isn't peachy, and disregard whatever adjectives were used in that write-up. You're not a child. You know all of that is just for shock value."

"Doesn't make them less mean."

"I didn't know you had such a thin skin."

"It's that bitch Bent. God, how can one be so vile?"

"You two must have kicked it off nicely in high school."

"Yeah, we were best friends. We made friendship bracelets and all that," I say. "How are we going to deal with this Hudson?"

"I've thought about it, and there is nothing to deal with," he says.

"What do you mean?" I ask, surprised. What does he mean there is nothing to deal with?

"We'll go about our lives like the article was never published. You ignore these things, and they very much fizzle out on their own. And I think this helps us—it helps me."

"How? How in the world does this help you?"

"Frank can't have me marry his daughter now, not even if Phillipa insists on it. It'll be ridicule for him. Because this, in a sense, lends validity to our engagement. People will repeat it so much it'll become the truth."

"People will ask questions."

"Yes, but you know these people. They don't ask any tangible questions. All they're interested in is the juicy tidbits that'll sell headlines. They'll get that and nothing more."

"What happens when this ruse is over then?"

"We go back to our lives, and if someday in the future someone wonders why we didn't get married, I'll simply talk about how our wants for the future didn't align, and that's that. I'm not an A-list celebrity, just some billionaire, so they won't pursue any further story, and if they want to, I have ways of blocking them off."

"You really have thought of everything, haven't you?"

"Is that mockery I hear in your voice?"

"No, it's a genuine wonder. So, why don't you tell me what to tell my mother and my friend?"

Oh, God, my mother. She'll be devastated. I broke Benny's heart, and Sophie will wonder if I've lost my mind.

"That's your headache to manage," Hudson says. "I have to go."

CHAPTER 22

JULIETTE

*H*e ends the call, and I stare at the phone angrily, wanting to squeeze the life out of him. I call my mother next, hoping she won't answer. She disappoints me and answers on the third ring.

"Juliette!" she calls me like I'm a child whom she's caught hand-deep in a cake. "What is this about some billionaire? It is a lie, isn't it?"

"Ma, listen."

"Don't Ma me, alright. Tell me the truth."

"It's not a lie."

"It's not!" she exclaims. "Why didn't you tell me you had a man in your life?"

"I wanted it to be a surprise Ma. But these blogs don't know how to shut their trap. I was going to tell you, Ma."

I hope she buys that lie.

"When?" she asks.

"When I return from Manhattan. I wanted to come home to tell you."

"Don't tell me lies, Juliette!"

"Ma, why would I lie? It was supposed to be a surprise, I promise you."

"A billionaire. Who is this man anyway? Is he a good man?"

"Yes, Ma, he is a good man," I tell her and find myself believing it also. I really do think Hudson is a good man. He has his issues, and God knows, sometimes I want to strangle him, but no matter how hard he tries to hide them, I can tell he cherishes those he loves and adores those who are loyal to him.

"So, this billionaire, is he the one you're working for?"

"There was no work, Ma, it was all a lie," I find myself sliding comfortably into the lie.

"A lie!" now, the exclamation is back.

"Ma, I'll explain everything to you when I return, alright. I promise. I have to go."

I end the call before she can say anything else, and thankfully, that is before she says anything about Benny. Poor Benny. I don't have the mental fortitude to think about him now. My mother was the one who got his hopes high, so she should be the one to let him back down gently.

I call Sophie next and that goes more smoothly.

"Girl, what is happening? You have me losing my mind here. My Juls is engaged to a billionaire?"

I consider telling Sophie the truth. But then I remembered I signed an NDA, and I am legally bound to keep this ruse a secret. I know Sophie wouldn't tell, and Hudson won't be mad if I tell her, yet I decide to keep it to myself. I owe Hudson that much. I know what is riding on this lie and how much he needs it to stand.

"All it took was for me to get dolled up once!" I say, and then I fall on bed, as Sophie screams and chuckles.

"When are you coming back to town? You've got a lot to tell me!"

"Soon. In a couple of days. When I get back, we'll go out for coffee. We've got to avoid paparazzi, though. They seem to be everywhere these days," I say laughing.

I spend the next half hour on a call with Sophie and in the end, all the worries I have disappear. I feel reassured and certain that all will go well. Just like Hudson said, we don't need to talk to anyone. The basis of our relationship was privacy, maybe secrecy to some extent. We will keep that up. Feeling better, I prepare to join Alejandro in the kitchen and eat the meal I made. But my phone rings again, and there is no caller ID this time. I answer the call, thinking it might be Jenny. Whenever she calls me on her office line, there is no ID.

"Hello, is this Juliette Nightingale," a male voice asks at the other end of the line, and I almost say yes before it clicks that it's probably a journalist. I remain quiet and listen. The man must have heard my breathing from the other end because he goes on. "My name is Teddy Wan. I'm with the Times magazine and calling to see if you'll be available for an interview with me. We're looking to do a piece about you and your fiancé, Hudson Sinclair. You can text me on this line what time you'll be available and where you'd like to meet."

"We're not giving interviews," I say.

"Oh," the man says, sounding a little disappointed. "May I ask why?"

"No, you may not. You might not be aware of this, but not everyone likes every part of their lives printed on paper. So, please stop calling and respect our privacy."

"Miss Juliette, the people feel like they are owed a story. They are interested in knowing how you came to know a man like Hudson Sinclair, seeing that—"

"Seeing that what? I ask. "I'll advise you to keep whatever sentiment you have about my relationship with Hudson to yourself. I now have your name Mr. Teddy Wan. I'll advise you do not call me again," I say and just for the fun of it, I add: "For your own good. Respect our privacy."

"Of course, Miss Juliette. I am nothing if not understanding," he says, immediately ending the call. I watch the phone for a while, shaking my head. I know it will be a long day of receiving such calls. Absolutely lacking the stress to deal with any of them, I make the decision to turn my phone off.

Cut off from the outside world, I walk out of my room and back to the kitchen, surprised to find Phillipa sitting by the counter, eating the meal I prepared with Alejandro.

"Miss Juliette," Alejandro says when he sees me. "Are you alright?"

"I'm peachy," I say, joining Phillipa at the table. "Can you pour me that glass of wine now?"

"Of course," Alejandro says, glad to serve me. "Will you also have the puttanesca now?"

"Yes, please. I've worked up an appetite. Popularity can do that, apparently."

Phillipa throws me a dirty look but says nothing. She focuses on eating. After Alejandro serves me my food, he excuses himself, stating that he has something to do in his room, so that leaves Phillipa and me alone in the kitchen. This is the first time I've been alone with her, and she doesn't look like the petite girl I saw at the party last night.

"Hudson told me about what transpired between the two of you last night," I say, biting into my meal while keeping eye contact with her. She looks away, shame clouding her face, but it lasts only a moment. When she faces me again, her face is as stolid as ever, and she shrugs.

"Can't blame a girl for trying her luck," she says with a sly grin.

"I don't understand it," I say, taking a drink from my glass. "How is it that you're obsessed with Hudson when he made it clear he doesn't want you? It's embarrassing. How did you two meet anyway? You seem like an unlikely pair"

"He hasn't told you?"

I shake my head. "He doesn't like talking about you at all," I lie. But it isn't an entire lie. Hudson really doesn't like talking about her, but I never asked him. It never crossed my mind to.

"Why don't you ask him? Transparency is important in a marriage, isn't it?"

"I'm asking you now."

"If you insist, then," she says, smiling. I guess this is one story she will enjoy telling. "Hudson pursued me."

I find that hard to believe, and my face must have communicated that because she laughed.

"You think I'm lying?"

"I'm not thinking anything. I'm just listening."

"Whatever. If you choose to, believe me. But I am telling you the truth. It was around the time he and my father got into this silly clash. He was very doting on me. We went on a couple of dates, he called me the most beautiful woman he'd ever seen, and we shared a couple of kisses. Very passionate kisses. I know he acts now like I'm some vermin he mustn't get close to, but he won't deny that there wasn't a time when my touch set his skin on fire. He told me that himself."

"Did you ever think he could be lying?"

She smiled. "A woman knows. Don't you know? Didn't you feel the passion in his hands when he touched you the first time? I knew. For all the pretense and lies he parrots now, I knew."

"What happened then? How did he go from that man who adores you to one who can't stand you?"

"What? Are you worried it'll happen to you, too? You got the ring, didn't you? You've won the game," she laughs hysterically and shakes her head. "I'll answer your question, not because you deserve an answer. You stole my place. I'll answer you because I know he'll do the same thing to you, and I want you to anticipate it. I want you to wake up at night, your eyes opened, wondering if your fiancé, your husband, is slowly hating you, and the mere thought of your skin brushing against him will come to irritate him."

I watch her as she speaks, brimming with spite.

"What happened was Hudson's nature taking over. He can't help it. He finds a new thing and obsesses over it. His obsession feels like love. Maybe to him, it doesn't, but to the receiver, it could be nothing but true love. But soon, the obsession wanes. Something shifts in him. He can't understand how he ever thought the world of you, and then he discards you and goes hunting for a new obsession. It is just the way he is. I thought I could make myself his forever; I wanted to be the obsession that lasts forever. But I was a fool. I see it now, there is no changing him. The leopard doesn't change its spots. He's like my father. They're at loggerheads because they are just alike. Two men who get sucked into an obsession and become engrossed until it tires them out. With my father, it's the companies. With Hudson, it's women. And don't you think it is just poetic for me to end up loving a man like my father?"

Poetic? No, I won't use the word poetic. Expected sounds appropriate.

"What?" She asks when I say nothing. "Cat got your

tongue now?" she adds with a laugh. "Poor Juliette. Can't believe the man she's to marry."

It is hard to believe any of what this woman says. She might be lying through her teeth because of all the spite in her, or her spite might be a result of the pain Hudson has caused her. Whichever it is, I don't care. In five days, I'll be out of here and put Manhattan behind me forever.

"You don't believe me, huh?" she asks.

"It's hard to believe someone filled with so much vitriol," I tell her.

"Okay," she says. "Why don't you ask him about this then."

She stands up and pulls up her gown. She turns around and shows me the back of her thigh. There's a tattoo there. Half of a butterfly.

"You'll find the other half on your fiancé's thigh."

A tattoo. I tried to imagine if I saw one on Hudson's thigh last night when we were locked in coital bliss, but I had other things on my mind and wasn't focused on what ink art he either had or didn't have on his skin.

"There's always some other woman, Juliette," Phillipa says and stands up. She taps me on the shoulder as she walks away. "It's just your turn for now. The bliss will soon turn to ash in your mouth."

CHAPTER 23

HUDSON

*T*he rest of the day goes slow. I have another meeting that was delayed till evening, and by the time I drive out of the parking lot, it's late at night. The first meeting with Randall has set a precedent that I hoped it would. Now, people are getting more confident about getting into business with me. The fear of retaliation from Frank has more or less become nonexistent. I've targeted my new customer base to include corporations that Frank failed to provide funds to—people he has no leverage over and that he can't bully. If all turns out well, and I am confident they will, the money to have inexhaustive cash at hand won't be an issue.

I get back to the ranch feeling famished as I had just had a single meal throughout the day. As I open the door to the suite. I feel elated at heart as I would be seeing Juliette again. The day had been so busy that I had kept her out of her mind, but on the ride over, she found her way back to my mind. The living room is empty, and without thinking much about it, I walk towards the bedroom to see if she's there, expecting her to be asleep. As I open the door, she lets out a scream and turns around to face me to see who it is. She is naked, except for the panties she's wearing.

"Jeez, you ever heard of knocking?" she complains.

"Sorry. I thought you were sleeping."

"No, I'm preparing for dinner. Frank says we're having dinner outside in the field. They set up a table. They're expecting us."

I walk into the room, gravitating towards her, my hands itching to reach for her breast, but I stop.

"I guess I better head to the bathroom then," I say, dropping my suitcase on the bed.

"How did your day go?" Juliette asks, reaching for a bra. I expect her to send me out, but she turns around and asks me to help with her bra clasp. Is that a call to touch her? My finger brushes the bare skin of her back as I help clasp the bra together. I control myself and do nothing beyond what has been asked of me.

"Good. I closed some deals today," I tell her as I take my seat and take off my shoes. It feels so good to have someone to talk to at the end of the day, and truthfully, it feels even better to have her to talk to. "We're expanding our cash source."

"That's sounds like you had a good day. But do you think one or two new sources of cash are enough sustenance? If I know nothing about the business world and Frank, I know he has a lot of cash and has access to more funds than you do."

"Yes, you're right. More customers isn't the best way to fund ourselves and keep us stable at this moment, But it isn't the only avenue we're exploring. We're getting external investors."

"From around here?" she asks, opening the closet to choose a dress. I point at a red dress.

"You should wear that," I tell her.

"Alright," she doesn't argue.

I returned to her question. "It's not easy getting big investors here in the country. They're all terrified of Frank. So, we sought one out from outside the country. They'll provide us with the necessary funds to keep the battle on. We're accumulating more customers around here, though."

I watch her slip into the dress delicately, in such a sensuous way that I can't tell if she was doing it knowingly to turn me on or if it is inadvertent.

She walks over to me and turns around again so I can help her with the zipper. I stand up to do that, pushing her hair aside, my thumb brushing her neck, and this time, I don't stop myself. I kiss her, tasting her skin. I hear her moan and want to take that as a message to go on. The talk we had in the morning has all been forgotten. She turns around so her lips are just inches from mine.

"We have to get ready for the dinner. We don't want to keep them waiting."

"They can wait. I don't care," I tell her.

She stands on her toes and kisses me. "We said never again. I think we should stick to that."

I groan. She's right. What am I thinking? We can't keep relapsing. I step away from her.

"I'll go take my shower." I tell her as I continue to get out of my clothes. It's her turn to watch me, with hunger in her eyes.

"How did your day go?" I ask.

"Well, it was great. I had a good time with Alejandro."

"The chef?"

"Yes. We made lunch together and made the dinner we're eating tonight, too. I taught him how to bake."

"A chef who doesn't know how to bake? That sounds ridiculous to me."

"No, it doesn't," she says. "Baking is procedural while with cooking, there is more leeway to be inventive."

"They both use heat to turn something inedible, edible."

"That's a simplistic way to view it," she chastises me.

"I like things simple."

"That's just not true," she retorts as she sits before the mirror to apply her makeup. I stand behind her naked, my cock hardening. She eyes it through the mirror and shakes her head. "Go into the bathroom, Hudson," she hisses.

"You sure? You don't want to have a taste?"

"God, you're unbelievable," she says, but her eyes tell a different story.

"Oh, you definitely want to." I chuckle, turning away from her and finally walking into the bathroom. When I get back out, she is ready and waiting for me. I spend the next couple of minutes dressing. I choose a white linen shirt and black pants, and then we head outside, where we can see the whole family waiting for us.

I hold Juliette's hand as we approach them.

"We're sorry for keeping you waiting," I tell them as I pull out a chair for her to sit. She smiles sweetly at me and thanks me.

"That's fine," Frank says.

"We were about to start without you," Elizabeth announces.

A table has been set on the lawn, and light streamers hang above us, illuminating us. The setting is idyllic and beautiful, and I wonder what it'll look like to have them all gone and for it to be just Juliette and me here.

A romantic dinner? I shouldn't be having such thoughts about her, but I can't help it when I find talking to her so easy and always want to be around her.

I look around the table at the people present; Frank and his wife sit side by side, and the lady is quiet and collected as usual. She has a perfunctory smile on her face. Elizabeth sits beside her, looking bored with all of this. That I know, of course, is an act. Elizabeth isn't one to be bored of anything. She runs a large chunk of Frank's consolidation and has a knack for picking up on subtle signals. There are whispers that she'll make an even more brutal chairman than Frank because the company is an entity to which she has no emotional attachment besides wanting to see it grow. They consider her more dangerous than Frank because she owes no one allegiance and thinks only in numbers and percentages.

Maybe Alison is right. It is time we shift focus from Phillipa to this woman.

Frank claps, and the butlers start to serve the meal.

"I heard you had a great time today in the kitchen, Juliette," Franks starts a conversation. "Alejandro says you're a fine cook."

"He flatters me. He taught me all I know."

"We really don't know anything about you," Elizabeth shifts the conversation away from talks about cooking to something more serious. I can tell this is the scrutiny that Juliette had been worried about being subjected to coming up. During the party yesterday, no one had the time.

"That's because there's nothing to know," Juliette chuckles. "I'm not like you people. I don't have rich or influential parents. My mother is a florist in Dallas, and that's about it."

"The articles they released today must have been the highlight of your life then," Phillipa says and from her tone and look, I can tell something had happened between her and Juliette while I was away. She is even colder and detached today.

"You know what, I think that's right. When I was in high school, I was featured in the magazine because I won the school's spelling bee competition. That was the last time anyone ever took so much interest in me and thought me worthy of an article," she says with a chuckle and takes a drink from her glass. But the rest of the family doesn't share in her joke. They all looked disturbed and sad. But I can tell she is messing with them. Quickly, Elizabeth shifts the conversation to something more comfortable.

"You guys should tell us how you met. That's one I've been thinking about," she says.

"We met at the ranch," I offer to answer that and spill the lie Juliette, and I have cooked up for moments like this. Juliette is good enough to chip in one or two whenever the lies try to catch up with me.

"You rode with her?" Phillipa asks, infuriated. "You never rode with me."

"There were circumstances beyond my control then."

"Don't lie to me. There was nothing like that. You just hated me. Did you ever love me? Did you even ever consider me human? You told me you don't like riding with people because it doesn't make you comfortable. But that was a lie. You rode with her. I fucking hate you. I hate you and hope you die!"

She stands up and storms away.

"I'll go with her," the mother says and goes after Phillipa. There is silence at the table for a while, and no one seeks to break it. We all just focus on eating.

"Dad and I were talking about this sale predicament," Elizabeth said and looked at her father for the order to go on. He nods. "We've done our research. We know you'll have increased sales for the month but a massive drop in cash you can spend. That's a discrepancy that the SEC will be interested in, don't you think? How do you make much more money but don't have any available to pay your investors with?"

"They tend to look away," I say. "It's only the first time we've recorded such a discrepancy. It'll correct itself."

"Maybe it will. But then again, what if they get a call from a concerned citizen, someone who thinks that they owe the nation's citizens a responsibility to investigate that unbalanced book? To some people, it might be a move for tax evasion," Elizabeth continues. Frank watches on, impressed.

"But it isn't," I say, knowing the direction of the conversation.

"You say that it isn't. They won't come to that conclusion unless they conduct the interview," Elizabeth says.

Why is Frank letting her speak now? Is he trying to pull back from this deal and let her handle it? I hope so.

"You know what we're saying, Hudson," Frank says, shattering my hope.

"No, I don't."

"You want me to say it, don't you?" Frank says.

"If you intend to pull sabotage, I think you owe me that. Be straightforward."

"Fair enough. I'll get the SEC to investigate your work processes. They'll make the point that all operations must stop for the investigation they want to carry out to be correct. I'll pull all resources available to me to make that happen. Cash inflow must pause and then and only then can they begin. And these things take weeks, sometimes months."

And in the meantime, I'll be losing even more money. It is a heartless tactic, no doubt, but it also tells me something else. It's a move that Frank has never taken before. If word gets out, it'll sow a seed of distrust in people and cause them to move their money away from his bank. The people will analyze the level of risk that comes with enjoying the loans he provides or a halt in their production and choose that which they feel more comfortable with. The jig is up. Frank is desperate.

"You do what you have to do. I have nothing to hide and will be available to help the SEC," I tell him.

There's no going back now.

"Your childish foolishness will be your ruin," Frank says, his facial muscles tweaking with anger. "You think the world functions without one person bowing to the other. Nothing works that way. You have to let go of what you have presumed to love, or you never really will achieve anything. You pose yourself like you're unbeatable, like you're the newly crowned prince of the business world, and I better learn to accept you. It will cost me little to ruin you. But I don't want to do that. I recognize talent when I see it. It'll be a waste to destroy you and send you down the same path your father took. It'll be a shame.

"I think the shame is you are unable to accept that I might be better than you at this. Did it ever cross your mind that I wouldn't back down because I see beyond the façade of unperturbedness that you put on? I see your worries. I see your fear. You are not unbeatable."

Frank stands up suddenly, pushing his chair backward. He leans into me, his smile wiped off and replaced by anger and frustration.

"You should learn," he says and walks away.

I return to eating my meal.

"Hmmm," Elizabeth says. "You've succeeded in getting my father mad. You know that gives you some sense of power over him, right?"

"I'm not interested in having any power over him. I just want him to back down."

Elizabeth relaxes in her chair, picks up one of the wine glasses, and takes a drink.

"In war, in the kind of war my father fights, there is a winner and a loser, no in-between. When it's over, only one person will be left standing."

"Do you want to be left standing?" I ask her.

"I have no fight with you."

"But it is your company as much as it is his. You don't want me to ruin that work you've spent so much of your life maintaining, do you?"

"You think my father will lose?"

"No, I think you're smart enough to make the right bet. As you said, there can only be one winner. And your father isn't acting like one who wants to win. He doesn't want to see beyond his nose that the world isn't what he used to know."

"He has control," Elizabeth mentions.

"Maybe. But also, there are companies out there his claws can never reach. Companies looking to solidify their financial standing that can't afford loans from your father or that your father denied loans."

"No one will dare fund you."

"We are a high return on investment company. A steady source of cash. Everyone in their right mind wants to fund us."

"No one will dare go up against my father,"

I smile at her, passing my message. It isn't that no one will dare to up against their father. It is that people are already

175

willing to go up against their father. Frank made himself Machiavellian, someone who can't be bargained with. It was only a matter of time before someone decided they'd had enough of his bullshit and call him out on it

"Who is it?" she asks.

"I don't kiss and tell."

Elizabeth is quiet for a while, no doubt considering her options.

"What will you have me do?" she asks me.

"I'll have you do nothing. Alison will contact you, and we'll talk more then."

She nods and stands up finally.

"You're a force to reckoned with, Hudson, I like that."

She walks away, leaving Juliette and me at the table full of food.

"Good," I say smiling at her. "I wanted them all gone."

"Do you think antagonizing him is a smart move?" she asks.

"I have no idea what the smart move is or not. But I know I'd be a fool to fall to my knees to Frank. He's played his card. And I've found him wanting. He's in some kind of trouble. I'll have to find out what it is and use it."

She's smiling.

"Why are you smiling?" I ask.

"You worry him," Juliette says. "I can see it in his face. He is scared of something."

"Yes, and I'll find out what it is soon enough when I meet with Elizabeth. Her father isn't the strong man he once was. He's gotten shaky, and Elizabeth must worry about him destroying everything because of his pride, only to leave them with nothing. She wants to guard against that. It is her responsibility to."

"What if she's playing a double agent."

"She won't have any information that can hurt me."

"I think you'll win this. I believe in you."

I wished I shared in the faith she had, but how could I? While I feel fairly confident about some of the things I said, I am making conjectures here, and if it all turns out false, I'll be the one out on my ass. That wouldn't be nice.

"I didn't think I'd enjoy my stay here, but it's not half as bad," Juliette breaks into my thought.

"You're enjoying it so much you'll be willing to extend your stay?" I joke.

"Oh, no. I want to return home to the things that feel familiar to me."

"What feels familiar to you?" I ask her.

"My bed, for one. I miss it. I miss the smell of my room, the bodega down my street, and the feel of my satin nightgown on my skin."

"I think you have a nice nightgown now."

"Yes, it's nice, but it just isn't the nightgown I love. It's a different one with different feelings. I'm sure you understand."

I look at her without replying, wanting to get some reaction from her.

"Of course, you don't. You don't know how such simple things can be so wonderful and—" she stops, realizing that I'm teasing her. She picks up a piece of bread and throws it at me as I start to laugh.

"You are always ready to give me a piece of your mind."

"Someone has to do it," she says with a hiss.

CHAPTER 24

JULIETTE

*T*he night is a wonderful one. Sitting here, having dinner with Hudson, as the rest of the family left pissed off or to pacify the ones that have been pissed off. I have no idea how much time passed as we talked on and on in the open air and we wouldn't have bothered leaving if Alejandro hadn't come over and relayed to us that the butlers would like to retire for the night, and they couldn't do that unless they clear off the table and clean up the dishes..

So, unfortunately, we had to finish up.

"Should we go with this?" Hudson asks, lifting one of the opened bottles of wine up.

"No," I tell him. "No more alcohol."

"Yeah, you're right, no more alcohol," he says, and we walk towards the house.

The quiet night, the gentle chill, and the beautiful stars all make for a good memory. We take our time, counting our steps and enjoying each other's presence the whole while.

Having Hudson here made me realize how much I missed him during the day. We say almost nothing to each other, but the bliss of being around each other seems to be just enough. I dare to break the silence as we get closer to the house.

"I got a call from a journalist earlier today," I tell him as we walk on.

Hudson looks back at me. "What did they want? And did they leave a name?"

"Yes, Teddy, I think. He wanted to talk to me about our relationship. I told him I had nothing to say to him and would rather be left alone."

"Did he pursue?"

"No,"

"Was he the only one who called?"

"I don't know. I was worried more of them would call, so I turned off my phone. I didn't want to repeat the same thing to more of them."

"I understand. Don't worry, I'll take care of it. No one will call you. I made some calls and got through to Bentley's agency. They are pulling down the story she published. One of the chief editors owed me a favor, and I called in on it."

"Will that help?"

"Yes, without that major source, the other news outlets that carry it will have no solid source. If the initial outlet pulls the story, it is possible for the story to die a natural death. That way, when all of this is over, and you're back home, you won't have to deal with more calls about a relationship you've moved on from. Whatever story they want to spin, I'll control the narrative."

"That's ingenious, thank you!"

Hudson shrugs, telling me it's nothing. "I did it for myself also."

We continue to walk in silence.

"I want to ask you something," I say as he opens the door for me, as we enter the house through a backdoor.

"What is it?" Hudson asks as he leads the way up the stairs. The house is strangely quiet. The drama must have sent everyone to bed early.

"Did you ever pursue Phillipa?"

"What? Why would you ask that? No, I never did."

His ears are twitching, so I know he's lying.

"Did she say something to you? Did Phillipa say something to you?"

"Yes, in fact, she did. We talked this afternoon after the whole issue with the journalist. I asked her how she knew you and she told me you sought her out."

"You know she's a lying bitch, right?"

And what about you? What are you?

"I believe her," I say as we get to the door to our suite.

"What? he asks, his mouth hanging open in disbelief. "You'll believe her over me?"

"Yes," I say, and now I'm beginning to wonder if she told the truth about his obsession with women and how he uses and dumps them. I'm not worried about myself getting used. The brevity of our deal gives me great confidence that I will be out of Manhattan before Hudson can think up anything silly.

"You're unbelievable," he yells. "You know the kind of girl she is."

Why is he lying about this? He has nothing to gain or lose if he tells me the truth. Because the truth is, I don't matter in the grand scheme of things. Why is he so invested in keeping up this charade?

"I don't feel like arguing about it. I just want to go to bed."

It looks like he still wants to argue, but then he shrugs and walks away, heading towards the bedroom.

"You should have the couch tonight," I tell him.

"What's that about?" he complains.

"It's the deal we made. You'll keep the couch, and I'll keep the bedroom. Unless, of course, you want to make an exchange, which I'll gladly do."

"No, don't worry about it. I am nothing if not flexible."

He storms into the room and returns with a pillow and a blanket.

"I thought you and I were finally getting along, then you go ahead and pull this," he sounds angry.

I ignore him and head into the bedroom to sleep.

We had a good time, especially after the rest of the family retired after the failed attempt at dinner. Why did I bring up the conversation I had with Phillipa when everything was going well? Why didn't I let myself be happy, at least for tonight?

I turn around on the bed, trying to get myself to sleep but failing. I can't seem to understand why he would lie. He has no reason to. None at all.

I sit up on the bed, looking out through the open window. Last night, I shared this bed with Hudson. The memory of that night is forever ingrained in my memory. I remember every single moment of the night, the way he touched me and reached deep into the crevices of my soul and made me feel pleasure in places unknown. If he wasn't Hudson Sinclair and we didn't have the written deal, I'd go out there to the living room and throw myself into his arms. If he was some random man who I met at the club or at the store, I'd have easily given myself up to him totally. But this is an important man. Women like me don't get to fall in love with such men. They remain elements of our fantasy and never grow beyond that.

All of that doesn't matter anyway. I don't know what the

recent soft feelings I have in my heart for him really are, but whatever it is, I have to ignore it and kill it. I can't let myself be a pawn in his game. If Phillipa is telling the truth, I can't let myself love Hudson Sinclair any deeper than I already do.

What if all of this is part of the game? The contract, the schtick about me not being his type was just some elaborate play to get at me? What if he saw me walk into his office and decided that he must have me, and this is his way of going about that? In seven days, he'll have a tangible reason to do away with me, never get in contact with me as his obsession and pleasure will have been satisfied. Is this all a game to him?

Why do I worry so much when the one who can answer the question is a couple of feet away from me?

I pull myself up from the bed and head to the living room, where I find Hudson lying on the couch. He's covered by the blanket, but I can tell he isn't asleep.

"What do you want?" he demands. "To berate me with more questions."

I stand a couple of feet from him, watching. There's a full moon outside, and the moonlight shines into the room, providing partial luminance.

"Do you have a tattoo on your thigh?" I ask, and he jumps up immediately.

"What did that Phillipa tell you?"

Even in the semi-darkness of the house, I can see his countenance take on a dark tone. He isn't angry at me, but that doesn't make him any less scary. This is a new version of Hudson I haven't seen. It sends fear down my spine, but I stand my ground.

"Can I see your thigh?" I ask, trying to turn around to get to a position where I can get a better look at the back of his thighs. Hudson has a menacing look about him, turning around so I can't see it.

"There's nothing on my thighs," he insists.

"Then show me."

"No, I won't be showing you anything. You'll get back into that room and go to bed. Tomorrow, you'll act according to the contract, and that is all I will say about it."

"No," I say, shocked at the sound of the sternness in my voice.

"Excuse me?" he says.

"If you have nothing to hide, you'll show me your thighs. If there is something there, I deserve to know."

"No, you don't."

"Yes, I do. Because it will determine whether or not I'm safe with you."

"Safe with me? What the hell are you talking about? You know I won't do anything to harm you."

"I know that. I know I am safe from any physical harm from you. But I don't know otherwise, and I won't know otherwise unless I see the tattoo."

"There is no tattoo," he says again.

"Let me see. If there isn't, I'll apologize to you, return to my bed and be the obedient and perfect fiancé you want me to be. I'll never bother you for anything else, and in four days, I'll be gone. You'll never hear from me again. I'll never pick up a gig to work for you. That'll be the end of it."

Hudson is quiet for a while, and I wonder what is going on in his head.

"So? What if there is a tattoo there?" he asks me. "What will you do about it?"

"I want to see it."

"Why?"

"Because I need to. Please, Hudson, just show it to me, okay?"

He glared at me, no doubt trying to understand what all of this was about. After a while, he sighs and turns around so I can see his thighs. The right thigh is clear and filled with springy hair, but looking away from that and to the left, I see a scar. It is about the size of a thumb and the size of the tattoo I saw on Phillipa.

He once had the tattoo, but he had it removed, and all that is left now is an ugly scar. A reminder of it.

She was telling the truth. That crazy bitch as he called her, was telling the truth.

CHAPTER 25

JULIETTE

*H*udson and I stand in silence for a while as I watch the scar on his thigh. He waits for me to speak, but I'm at a loss for words. How do I go on from this? I can't say he has betrayed me because, in the larger scope, I really don't matter. But I can't help but feel that way. Rage and spite run through me. In a way, Phillipa has won this moment. She had mocked me, and with everything I had in me, I hoped she was wrong. I prayed that she was wrong and expected her to be, but it wasn't so.

"So, you lied to me," I tell him, and from the look on his face, I can tell he is tired of this. This isn't how he expected the night to go, That sentiment applies to me as well. I had a good day, an absolutely terrific day, and I was eager to have Hudson back home so I could tell him all about it. Yet, after Phillipa talked to me, I had to throw myself into helping Alejandro make dinner because letting myself be jobless for a moment threw me into wondering if there was any validity in what Phillipa told me. I knew she didn't tell me that to help me, and this right now, the anger I'm feeling, the urge I feel to attack him and hit him till I'm satisfied, is the reason she told me. She doesn't want to suffer alone. Well, she wins.

"I didn't think you needed the truth," he says. "Why did you pursue this? You should have let it go."

Maybe he shouldn't have shown me. Maybe he should have insisted on not showing me.

Yet, I want to know more. I don't want any lies between us. I want to know what he did to her and how they really came to meet. I walk towards him and stand before him. I can see the lethargy in his eyes and can tell he really wanted nothing more than to just go to sleep.

"Let's forget about this night, Juliette; we'll go to sleep. I'll take the couch. We'll talk with focused heads tomorrow when we both feel better."

"No," I refuse. "I want to talk about it tonight."

"Come on! What the hell is wrong with you!" Hudson's outburst doesn't shock or deter me; in fact, I expect it. He would protest having any conversation regarding the matter again tonight, but I don't see myself sleeping or resting unless we iron things out. We need to have this talk, no matter how uncomfortable it might be. It doesn't matter if it opens old wounds and cuts new wounds into my skin. I know if we don't, Hudson will make a run for it tomorrow morning, and then we'll continue this dance tomorrow night, and he'll give the excuse that he is too tired to talk about it again, and then we go on and never speak of it.

Maybe I can do that. Maybe I can act like all of this never happened. Do my part of the contract for the rest of the days as required by me, and then I head back from Manhattan. Maybe this will even be for the best. Truly, I consider the possibility, and it is feasible. Why then can't I bring myself to do it?

The answer stares right at me. I know it my heart deep down in a part that I really don't want to take a closer look at. It's those eyes, those dark eyes that now scour into the depths of my soul. I have let myself fall in love with them. I've made the error of getting too familiar with that look on his face. I've made the error of seeing solace in these eyes; even though now, all they offer me is pain, I still look to them for joy, and I hope in talking about this issue, I'll be able to seek joy from them again. I can't believe it.

What the hell are you doing, Juliette? I wonder quietly to myself.

If I go down this path, I'll be without protection to my heart at the end of the seven days when I will have no choice but to detach from him. I should never have gotten attached to him in the first place. But there is no helping or changing this now. This is how I feel. This is how it is now.

"I need to know everything, Hudson."

"I don't want to talk about it."

"I won't force you."

"All it'll lead to is more argument and fight."

"Then, let's have the fight then. I can tell you're hiding something from me, Hudson. You know I can tell. If you look at me and think that I don't deserve to know what it is, then you can go back to bed."

Yes, it is better that way. I want to know if he feels even the tiniest bit of what I feel. Does looking into my eyes make him falter, too? Does his heart skip beats at the thought of causing me so much pain? If it does, he'll know I deserve some explanation. If not, I'll go back to bed and sleep like a baby. The answer to the question then will determine how I react. Do I return to myself and start to feel detached from now on?

I don't know what I want. Whatever it is that I'm developing for him in my heart cannot last, and common sense tells me that it's better to nip it in the bud now that it isn't so established, yet, what I want the most is to let it spread, to really feel what it's like to love a man like him.

No, not love. This can't be love. I can't be foolish enough to fall in love with a man like Hudson.

"Tell me, what is it? I deserve to know."

"Why are you doing this?" he asks. He looks troubled and obviously at an impasse.

"I don't know," I confess.

Hudson closes his eyes, struggling with his heart and brain. He nods and then walks to the couch. I take it as a hint to follow him. I sit just a couple of inches from him, and then he relaxes, prepared to speak. I'm truly afraid I realize, of what I'll hear from him.

"I don't know what Phillipa said to you, but she's a liar who I'm sure is out there to hurt you. She wants you to feel bad, to feel miserable like she does."

She's succeeded already, and the anguish I feel has little to do with her. I am angry at myself. How did I let myself go so easily? How did I let myself get so distracted and not notice my heart opening itself up for Hudson? How did I let myself get so wound up in him? Maybe if we didn't make love last night, things wouldn't be this terrible, I want to believe, but this goes beyond the wonderful time we shared. Hudson paid attention to me in a way that no one else had ever done before. It might not have been his intention, and I might have been blind to it, but it obviously had an effect on me. A devastating one I will soon, I am sure, be forced to admit.

"It's not about Phillipa anymore," Hudson says. "It's about the two of us."

What about the two of us? I want to ask. What do you mean by the two of us? There can be no two of us. There is just the contract, and you are holding up your end of the deal in the contract—nothing more, nothing less.

"Whatever she said, we can't let it come between the two of us," continues Hudson.

He keeps saying the two of us. What does it mean? What does it imply?

God, so many thoughts are running through my head it hurts.

I have nothing to say in response, so all I do is watch. He speaks again soon enough.

"Yes, I sought her out, but I think you know why. I never fancied her. I have never fancied her. I told you; she isn't my type."

"You've told me that before too," I point out to him.

"Yes, I did. But I told you to get rid of whatever assumption you were drumming up in your head about me when I mentioned the deal to you. With Phillipa, it was the truth. She never was my type, and I never felt anything for her."

Is it different for me? Do you feel something for me? I want to ask. Oh, how much I wish I could have the answer to that question.

"Alison had the idea, and I thought then that it was a good idea. Now, I see it was just a big blunder. I've never had to deal with a problem like Frank, and I let my caution of the man get the better of me. We needed to find a way to get closer to Frank, something to endear myself to him to bring a quick end to our Frank issue. We found out about the girl, Phillipa. She was special to him, and he adored her, but upon closer inspection, we saw that she was lonely. Phillipa, being a daddy's girl for too long, has never known any other manly attention that wasn't her father's. It would be easy for me to get closer to her and make her realize what she was missing. It was a terrible thing to do, but her father prompted me. It was all a calculated move. Everything I did with her was presumptive and thought-out. Everything was mechanical, and in search of a quick way to bring an end to the negative impact her father was having on my company. The dinners, the kiss, the ring, everything."

"The ring?" I ask. "This ring?"

"Yes. I got it so I could propose to her, but I couldn't go through with it. I couldn't string her along just to cut her away as soon as I figured Frank isn't a problem anymore."

"What about the tattoos?" I ask.

"It was another stupid act from me. Why do you think I tried my best to get it erased? Phillipa got obsessed with me. At the beginning, I thought I had it under control, but I was mistaken. She started to ask crazy things of me and wanted me to prove that I loved her. She wanted me to show her that I was intentional about her and that I really cared about her. I shouldn't have done it. I should have backed out then because I was starting to see this was bound to end terribly. The poor thing just wanted someone to love her, and I was using her. I felt sick with myself, but I couldn't stop. I had to go on. So, I got the tattoo. It's not something I'm proud of. It's something I will forever detest myself for. I should have summoned the courage to put an end to the madness, but I was worried that if I backed out, I would lose my company. I didn't want that."

I don't know what to say to everything he said. You made an elaborate lie and built on that lie. How can I trust that he isn't lying to me, even now?

"It's why I can't bring myself to lie to her any longer. I tell her the whole truth about how I feel about her even if I know it'll hurt her. It's better for her to find a way to deal with it all instead of forestalling a pain that'll bring in the future."

Still, I'm clueless about what to say.

"Won't you say something?" he demands after a while. "You hounded me to speak, and now I have spoken, and you suddenly have nothing to say? Do you hate me now too?"

Hate? I can't see myself hating him. And maybe that is the reason I'm caught with my voice in my throat, trying to find the right thing to say.

"I don't know whether to believe you or not," I say finally, and he looks at me, shocked.

"What? You think I'm lying?" he is yelling now.

"I don't think you're lying. It's just I don't know what I'm supposed to do with this. You, you did all of that and…" I can't go on. "I don't know," I say and get up. I consider walking out of the room, but I really want to talk about it. I want it all out tonight. So, I walk to the fireplace instead, and it fills me with memories of the two of us intertwined so passionately together. I can still feel his lips on my skin, the burn of his touch. Every single moment is burned onto my brain, and I just don't know how to figure it out.

Hudson pulls me closer to himself and I stand mere inches from him, burning with desire even now, looking into his eyes. I still truly can't believe how attached I feel to him. How he's made me want him so much that I'm afraid to breathe and even more terrified to let go. How the fuck did this happen?

His eyes. I can't help but lament because I'm sure that they are to blame. Looking into them makes me feel weak, even now. It feels me still with this crazed urge to make bad decisions. But this isn't the time for that. I must focus now. There is much bigger fish to fry.

"Look at me," Hudson says, and I truly suspect that he wants me to see beyond all of this. I wonder if he knows exactly what he's asking and knowing him I'm sure that he does. "Do you think I have any intention to hurt you?"

Those eyes are cold but sweet to me. They speak of the comfort he wants to show me, of the love and bliss. But I don't just want his eyes to tell me. I am terrified of assuming. I want to hear him speak it.

"You told her those things also, didn't you?" I ask him and pull away from him. I head for the loveseat, but I don't sit.

Hudson scoffs and hisses in anger. He walks over to a corner of the room, maintaining a considerable distance from me.

"I told you already: with Phillipa, it was different. There was an ulterior motive. It was never about her. None of what I did was about her. It was her father."

"With me, there is the contract." I point out.

"Yes, there's the contract, but it is different."

"How?"

"I'm here now, aren't I? I'm letting myself go through this tortuous moment. Do you think I don't have the option to refer you to the contract and be done with it? You, tell me! You think I'm enjoying any part of this?"

If what Phillipa says is right, maybe you are, I think to myself.

"You said it. You're a meticulous man. You take pleasure in being thorough. Maybe this is you just being thorough. This is you not leaving anything to chance."

"Juliette, what is wrong with you?" he asks, evidently exhausted. "Why can't you let yourself be happy? Just for a moment, why can't you let the pessimism perish?"

I don't know. Maybe it's because I don't want to be hurt so terribly. So, I'm believing the worst until there is absolutely no reason to believe it anymore. But is Hudson the kind of man to give me that reassurance? I don't think so. So, maybe it's the reason I can't let myself be happy.

Oh, what have I gotten myself into?

Hudson walks over to me and turns me around so I can face him. His eyes are dark, intense, filled with a mixture of frustration and desire that sends a shiver down my spine.

"What is this, Juliette?" he says, looking tortured and exhausted. "What are we doing here? What are you doing here? Why are you letting yourself hurt for no reason?"

"It's not for no reason. It's because of you."

"And here I am, assuring you I have no intention of causing you any form of pain. None. And before anyone hurts you, I'll squeeze the life out of them; I promise you that."

I remember Jasmine said something along those lines.

He touches my cheek, and a wave of relief rushes through me. I throw all caution to the wind and lean into him. Just a single touch, and all the worries that had me in a bind disappear. This is the effect he has on me. This is why I must ensure he isn't playing me like he played Phillipa. But how am I to do this? It embarrasses me that I even care to.

When our lips touch, I can't help but cry. My eyes water, and the tears flow down my cheeks, but he catches them with his finger.

"Damn, Juliette. What am I going to do with you?" he asks, then kisses me back with a ravenous hunger that ignites something primal within me. My heart races, my breath catches, and in an instant, the fire beneath my skin flares up, wild and out of control. This... this right here is why he is dangerous for me.

He needs me now, and I need him as well. There is no time or desire for foreplay here. The back-and-forth argument has inadvertently filled both of us with a thirst that can't be repressed anymore. My hands move all over his body as the kiss deepens, slow at first, then desperate, as if we're both drowning and the only air we can find is in each other's mouths.

Hudson picks me up, his strength effortless, and settles me on top of the hearth of the fireplace. A gasp tears out of me as he roughly pulls my thong aside, the fabric scraping against my sensitive skin. I'm already wet, my juices dripping onto the cold stone beneath me, but I don't care. All I want is him inside me, filling me, taking me with the raw, unfiltered need that we've both been denying for too long.

I reach for his pants, fumbling to free his hardened cock, and he helps me, both of us frantic, no words needed. The moment his length is free, I move closer, wrapping my legs around his waist, drawing him in, desperate to feel him inside me.

He pushes into me with a force that steals my breath, stretching me wide, filling me completely, and I throw my head back, a guttural moan escaping my lips as the pleasure surges through me. I dig my nails into his back, urging him on, needing him to fuck me harder, deeper, until there's nothing left but this overwhelming sensation of him pounding into me, driving me closer to the edge with every thrust.

Hudson's grip on my hips is bruising, but I love it, love the way he takes control, the way he owns me in this moment. There's nothing gentle about the way we move together, nothing soft or tender—just pure, unadulterated hunger. I bite down on his clavicle, trying to muffle the scream building in my throat, but it's no use. I'm as loud as ever, my voice echoing off the walls as he fucks me relentlessly, each thrust more powerful than the last.

The world turns on its head; Hudson and I are back in the position we swore not to be in this morning, and it's barely been twenty-four hours. But we can't help it. The more we try to deny this, the deeper the hunger runs, pulling us back to each other with an intensity that neither of us can resist.

My body is on fire, every nerve ending alive with the sensation of him inside me, his cock slamming into me with a rhythm that drives me wild. I can feel the pressure building, the tension coiling tight in my core, ready to snap, and I know he's close too—his breathing ragged, his grip on me tightening as he drives into me with everything he has.

And then it happens—a cataclysmic wave of pleasure crashes over me, my orgasm hitting me with such force that I cry out, my entire body trembling as I come hard around him. Hudson follows right behind me, his cock pulsing as he spills into me, his release triggering another wave of ecstasy that leaves me breathless and shaking.

We collapse against each other, our bodies slick with sweat, our hearts pounding in unison as we come down from the high. My mind is spinning, my body still trembling from the intensity of it all, and as I look into his eyes, I know that whatever happens next, we can't keep lying to each other. We need this, need each other, in a way that goes beyond words, beyond reason.

What the next couple of days hold for us is anyone's guess, but for now, I'm content to stay here, wrapped in his arms, my body still humming with the aftershocks of our passion. Hudson and I may be walking a dangerous line, but in this moment, nothing else matters.

CHAPTER 26

HUDSON

I wake up right after the sun rises and stir in bed slowly, letting Juliette lay on the bed before standing up. She sleeps so peacefully, like a baby. Her body is angled ever so delicately, with the duvet partially covering her naked body. She is a testament to the wonderful work of God; her beauty, her grace, and her stunning body all keep me in a trance for a while. The curtain is drawn, but there are beams of light that escape through the sides and fill the house with partial light. I watch her by the light, enjoying the sight. After drinking in her exquisiteness to my satisfaction, I turn away, get dressed, and head downstairs to have a cup of coffee. I find Alison in the kitchen, nursing her cup of coffee.

"Hello," I say to her as I join her. The in-house chef, Alejandro, whom Juliette said she spent yesterday with, asks how I like my coffee after I take my seat beside Alison by the counter.

"It's a full house these days," Alejandro says as he pours

me my black coffee. "I like it. I never get to share my coffee with people."

Alison throws him a look and he gets the hint: we'd rather be left alone to have a brief discussion. He nods, picks up his own mug and walks away. When we're alone in the room, Alison speaks up. She leans into me and she whispers.

"I spoke with her last night," she says.

And by her, I knew she meant Elizabeth. So, while I was fighting Juliette, Alison was hard at work.

"She's agreed to meet."

"That's good work," I tell her and sip my coffee.

"I didn't do much work. She said you convinced her already. All I did was discuss the location of the meeting. She doesn't want to meet in your office. There might be people watching."

"I understand that. Where did you choose?" I ask Alison.

"I'll send you the address. You're meeting with her in about thirty minutes."

"What!" I exclaim, standing up. "Why didn't you lead with that, and why didn't you contact me."

"I did. I sent you a text yesterday and called you." She gave me a knowing look but said nothing further. I can tell by the look in her eyes that she has so much more to say, but for fear of offending me, she holds her peace and focuses on drinking her coffee.

"Good work," I tell her as I head back into the room to get dressed. Juliette is still fast asleep, and I don't dare wake her. There isn't time to ponder over what last night meant for the two of us. Whatever it means, I know Alison won't approve of it. Good thing I'm not asking for her approval. After I finish dressing, I walk over to Juliette to kiss her on the forehead. She stirs and blinks her eyes awake.

"I have to go," I tell her.

"Alright," she says without a complaint. Before I leave, though, I kiss her briefly on the lips and then head out of the house. I open my phone to see the message Alison said she sent to me. It contains all the information about her meeting with Elizabeth. They met to talk late last night while I was making love to Juliette. Or perhaps fucking is the better term. A part of me though wants to stick to the former. The location she chose for the meeting is a restaurant on the outskirts of town. When I arrive, I follow her instructions and speak only to the waiter available this early.

"I'd like to speak to Venny," I say.

The waiter nods. "Follow me."

We walk through the restaurant's aisle and head to what seems like the back door, which opens to a secluded seating area. As we walk through, I half expect to find not just Elizabeth waiting for me but also Frank with a big silly grin on his face, mocking me for thinking I could turn his daughter against him. But there is no Frank, just Elizabeth sitting at a corner table and having a breakfast of bacon and eggs.

I sit opposite her. She focuses on her meal for a while before acknowledging me. The waiter stands with her, too.

"He's waiting for you," Elizabeth says finally. "He wants to know what you'd like for breakfast."

"Just coffee, please," I tell the waiter, who nods and turns away immediately.

"You don't feel like eating?" Elizabeth asks me.

"No, it's still quite early."

"Don't mind me. I eat a lot when I'm nervous."

"What's the anxiety for?" I ask her. "Never done anything like this before?"

"You mean to go against my father? A lot of times. I just have never done it with someone currently in a tug-of-war with my father—with someone he despises."

"Your father hates me? I guess that's my cue to say goodbye then? I can't live in the same house as a man who hates me."

"Don't be silly. That will only rub him the wrong way. You've poked him enough, and you've shown him you're no longer scared of him. Don't overplay your hand," says Elizabeth.

"I got under his skin last night, didn't I?" I ask and watch her stuff her mouth full of toast.

"Don't get cocky, It's not a good look on you. Last night, after I returned to the apartment and talked to my father, two things he said jumped at me. One, he said he regrets getting his foot into this deal at all. Two, he is so certain he mustn't let you win now. You'll just become him, and the first thing you'll do should you accumulate the bargaining power is kick him out. So, he'll be a fool to let you go. You'll act like you've always been acting, like you two are in good graces, and don't secretly wish death on each other."

"So, I achieved nothing in essence."

"Whatever you intended the outburst to achieve turns out to be a big mess. But I'll tell you: you opened my eyes to a new way of seeing things. It feels like I've been blind for ages but with this new insight, now, I see things differently."

"Will you help me defeat your father?" I ask her. I see no reason to mince words here. We both know her meeting with me at all is a grave sin, so why play another game with her? I was tired of games. I needed a win, and if Elizabeth will be the vessel through which I get that win, then so be it.

"Of course not," she says with a hiss.

"So, is this a waste of time for me?"

"You could leave," Elizabeth says and continues to eat. I don't leave. I watch her instead. The waiter returns with a mug of coffee for me, and I nod at him. This is the chance to enjoy another cup of coffee. The one I started back home; I couldn't enjoy because I needed to be here.

"What is this place?" I ask her. "Do they need a new supplier for their sea products?"

"Don't you worry about them. They're doing just fine. Your assistant mentioned something I find hard to believe," says Elizabeth, rolling a piece of sausage to eat.

"Alison isn't one for exaggeration. Whatever she tells you, take it at face value."

"Not this. I need confirmation. She says you have a floating source of cash. A huge floating source of cash."

"That is true."

"It's impossible. No one in their right mind will fund you," she says, still munching

"That was why we didn't go for someone in their right mind. We're not presenting you with a case based on hope. We're presenting you with one that you can evaluate and make informed decisions. I'm not looking for you to hope. I'm asking you to act."

"Well, I'll need to know who the investor is. To be sure they have the deep pockets to back you."

"You know that's not possible."

"You want me to build my castles in the skies. I need a foundation to build on here, Hudson. I'm taking a big risk being here with you. I need an act of faith from you."

"We've provided you with that. You know how it is, and we'll be able to stand against your father. Anything beyond that will be a fool's act."

"Sometimes you have to act a fool to catch a prey."

"I'm hunting a predator. One who shows no manner of mercy. There is no room for errors."

"We can't make a deal if I don't know who your investor is," she insists.

I watch her for a while, just learning about her and judging her by the way she eats. While binge eating, she takes her time, letting a considerable time pass between her bites. She has no intention of forcing herself to throw up. It looks like a calculated move from her, not just an uncontrolled gobbling down of food.

"My mother stress eats like you," I tell her.

Elizabeth looks up and chuckles like I had just told a joke. "What now? You'll find a way to convince me to work for you because your mother has an eating disorder that might be similar to mine?"

"Eating disorder? Who said anything about eating disorders? I'm just telling you about my mother," I say and continue, ignoring her haughtiness. "Her stress eating started when my father was alive."

"He must have been a terrible human then."

Is she trying to make me angry? She knows my father wasn't a terrible human being. I cross my legs and say nothing. She knows what to do if she wants this conversation to go on.

"I'm sorry, that was a low blow," Elizabeth apologizes.

"You're better than that," I say, continuing my story. "Whenever my father failed to come home for the night or if he had one of those nights when he had the jitters so much and complained about how things just weren't working out, my mother would sit in a corner and eat herself to a stupor. It wasn't a good sight, so I have seen terrible things also. I've seen what a lack of control, lack of input can do to a person."

"I didn't think you were so desperate you'd go low to garner sympathy," Elizabeth says with a hiss. "Yes, you had a rough childhood. Newsflash: it doesn't make you special. We all had demons as children."

"But your demons haven't left you," I tell her. "You still go to bed with them. They whisper sweet words into your ears, and you listen. You listen, and you're helpless when it comes to them. It's why you have so much food before you now."

Finally, I get her to look away from the food. She's watching me with such hate.

Way to go, Hudson, make an enemy of her.

I am not her father, yet I have my way of pulling rancor out of people. Unlike her father, I make it useful. I can transform it quickly to respect.

"I told you I know people like you. My mom kept eating, not because she was sad, scared, or worried for my father. All of those things were present, of course, and sometimes I'd hear her cry at night because that's when she could allow herself to cry—whenever I wasn't there. But none of those things made her eat. When it came to my father, she was absolutely useless. There was nothing she could do to help my father. That part of his life was out of her control, and the harder she tried to fight for control, the further it drifted away from her. So, she did the one thing that made sense to her. She ate, and she found comfort in it. This was something she could make happen. However, beyond that, she was useless, and the more she had to confront her uselessness, the more she hated it and the more she ate. It was a vicious cycle, and she never lived past it until after my father died, and she wasn't confronted with it anymore."

"So, you think I'm like your mother?" she scoffs.

"No, I don't think. I know. I've watched you for a long time, and I know hate seethes in you. Your father has turned his attention to people who have shown themselves useless while you, who work tirelessly to keep the company running, is treated like a maggot. That is the only reason you'd consider this meeting. You want to be more than just mere

Elizabeth. You want to fight for your position, no matter what it takes, even if it means partnering with the enemy.

"You don't know me," she hisses.

"No, I don't. But I know you don't want me to walk away with your golden chance."

I stand up to dare her and start to walk towards the door. I'm close to the door, my hand on the knob, and I fear that she has called my bluff, and now, I'll leave with achieving nothing. I can already see Alison on me, looking for a way to make it Juliette's fault. My hand brushes the door just as she calls me back.

I turn around to regard her.

"You should sit," Elizabeth says. "We have a lot to talk about."

Walking back to the table, I feel victorious. This won't be a total waste of time after all. I sit down and face Elizabeth who sets her meal aside, ready for business.

"I've gone through your public records. They're quite impressive, I have to confess. You spent a lot of time building a clientele base that stayed with you even in this hard time. How did you go about that?"

This is the part of my business that has always shocked people. They can't seem to understand how my clientele base hasn't dwindled with all the uncertainties surrounding the future of my company.

"Delivery," I say to Elizabeth, taking a good drink from my mug. "My customers know that even if the heavens were to fall, they'd get their delivery. We take that seriously, and we do not affect the quality of our products. It's basic. I went five years without making a profit for this very reason."

For five years, my books remained in the negative region. Five years of funding with my money.

"I see why you can't let my father have it. You've sacrificed too much."

"If your father made a market value offer, maybe, we wouldn't be having this discussion. There is only one reason your father can't buy me out yet. He doesn't have the funds."

"That's a bit presumptuous," she retorts.

"Oh, please. Let's not fool ourselves here. There've been words. Your father is in trouble. No one knows what kind it is, but this ongoing battle doesn't help his case. That's why you're here. You want this gone."

"It's only part of why I'm here," she says. "You're right. All of this should be mine. I have worked to earn it, but my father won't let me have it. I'll help you win this war if you'll help me win mine."

"I can't give you your father's company. I wouldn't even dare to."

"But you can make him see reason."

"How do you suggest I do that?"

Elizabeth shifts in her chair and takes a new position, which tells me this conversation just got serious. Her face takes on a serious disposition, her voice mellow and soft.

"This must never leave this room in any manner. I'll work actively to sabotage every effort you make, and you must know that you are my enemy until the day all of this comes to fruition. If it doesn't, you continue to be my enemy, and this meeting never happened."

"I understand that."

"No, you don't. What my father said about the SEC last night was no bluff. You've made him desperate, and he'll be pulling levers he has never pulled before, and I must be truthful with you; not all will be legal. He will fight dirty, and from now on, and from this moment, it is he who can get his hands filled with mud while showing the rest of the world that he is clean and who will come out on top. This isn't a matter of strategy. There isn't one. This is a matter of gut and grueling power. Do you understand what I'm saying to you?"

"Yes, I do," I tell her.

I'm no fool. I expected this; in fact, I had been waiting for it and wondered when Frank would start to play dirty. The games and back-and-forth on the court were tiring and getting nowhere. Frank had tried his other popular method, cutting me off from funds, but that isn't going as well as he planned because I have found my way around it. Now, things will get down and dirty, and yes, I am ready for it.

"Good. So, listen. Ten years ago, my father made an arms deal with a Middle Eastern prince."

"Your father is a gun runner," I cut in, not entirely surprised, but it still shocks me. There are stories about Frank dabbling into the criminal underworld, but I have always disregarded those stories.

"Yes, amongst many other things, but this isn't about the guns. At least not directly. It is about the money. When he made the deal, he had most of his cash tied up in other businesses that he couldn't liquidate, or he'd be breaking a thousand federal laws. He could have had his lackey in the SEC look the other way, but if there was anything my father was good at, it was never being moderate. His friends can't help him because they'll be exposed if they do. So, the deal came at the right time. Unfortunately for him, the United States isn't supposed to run guns to the Middle East, and he had to make use of a third party. All went smoothly, and the partial payment for the weapons was made. He transferred the weapons over, and the rest of the money was sent. But his third party is a Russian company, which, unfortunately, he can't receive his money from. This is why he wants your company. You are a cash-based company that moves goods in large quantities over the sea. The sea is large, a lot can go unnoticed there. If he gets your company, he can move his money in by cash and use the company to wash it all. Buying it also means he gets direct access to your fleet of ships and boats, and he can make his arms deals without fear of exposure or the possibility of what happened with the prince reoccurring."

"He'll get paid in cash and move his money through the seas. He runs the risk of losing a large chunk of his money to pirates."

"He's made large donations to the sea marshals constantly for the last eight months. He'll be well protected. Besides, you have your way of dealing with pirates."

"I move seafood. He'll be moving cash."

"True, but you should know my father won't have any problem handling the pirates."

"All he wants my company for is to commit crimes."

"Partially. He wants you to stay onboard because he needs you to grow the company and use it as a cover for the gun running."

This is interesting. Quite interesting.

"How much of your father's money is stuck in Russia?" I ask her.

"Just a little less than your company is actually valued at."

"That's why he won't pay the market value. That's bad market for him."

"Yes. And the longer the cash stays in Russia, the harder it is to get it out."

"So, Phillipa, none of this was ever about her?" I ask her.

Elizabeth chuckles. "No, the world doesn't revolve around my sister for my father, apparently. For him, cash is king. Cash will always be king."

"And what about you? How does any of this benefit you? How does your father's loss benefit you?"

"Worry less about that," Elizabeth says and returns to her meal.

I watch Elizabeth for a while and it becomes clear to me. She will usurp her father. She's been making her move, gathering people under her wing.

"Are you sure you want to do that?"

"He is my father. What is he going to do? Destroy me?"

I shrug. "He won't take the backstabbing lightly."

"I don't expect him to. You hold up your end of your deal, I am counting on you."

I sit back and smile. "I'll run your father into the ground."

CHAPTER 27

JULIETTE

J lay in bed with Hudson, my finger tracing the line of hair on his chest. We just made love, and I'm still out of breath from the way he took me. My body is buzzing, every inch of me still alive from the intensity of what we just shared. My thighs still quiver, and I can feel the lingering sensation of his cock, the way he filled me completely, taking me again and again until I was nothing but soft gasps and moans beneath him. My tongue runs over my lips, savoring the remnants of him, reliving every second of what had just passed.

This is the first time he's stayed in bed with me after we've been together. Most of the time, we fall asleep wrapped around each other, spent from the intensity, but when I wake up, he's gone, the bed cold where his warmth used to be. It's become a routine—him giving me everything I need, his body dominating mine, and then vanishing like a ghost, leaving me with the memory of his touch, the way he made me feel.

We seem to have fallen into that rhythm—satisfying the needs of our flesh with a kind of desperate urgency, our bodies colliding with an intensity that leaves me breathless, craving more of him, more of the way he makes me feel. And then, in the morning, I find activities to fill my time, waiting for him to return, and then we fuck again.

But this morning was different. Before he left, he kissed me. It wasn't just a casual goodbye kiss —it was deep, lingering, full of something unspoken. His lips pressed against mine with an intensity that made my toes curl, his hand cupping my face as if he didn't want to let go. The way he held me close, his mouth moving over mine, was so raw and passionate that it left me dizzy, my heart pounding long after he pulled away. The memory of that kiss will forever be etched in my mind, something I'll treat like a rare piece of art, cherished and unforgettable.

Even now, lying here with him, I can still feel it—the way he took me, his body pressed against mine, his movements slow and deep at first, savoring every moment, every gasp and moan that escaped my lips. The way he made me feel cherished and desired, his hands holding me close, his lips finding mine in kisses that left me breathless. And then, when the intensity built, when I couldn't take it anymore, he gave me everything, his pace quickening, his body moving against mine with a need that matched my own, his cock driving me wild, bringing me to the brink over and over until I couldn't hold back, my release crashing over me like a wave.

And even after he came, his body tensing as he filled me, he didn't pull away. He stayed, his arms wrapping around me, holding me close as our breathing slowed, his presence comforting, grounding me in the aftermath of something so intense, so overwhelming.

After having such a lovely morning, nothing could derail me from having the best day. Not even Phillipa, who kept pacing around the house, expecting me to speak up and ask if she was alright, or Alison, who I saw on my way to work, who gave me the death glare but surprisingly didn't come up to me. I couldn't let them sow weeds into my perfect morning, which stretched to cover the rest of the day.

After I had my shower, Alejandro showed me how to make some more recipes. After that, we baked, keeping the house constantly infused with such a beautiful smell.

"What did you do today?" I ask Hudson, feeling comfortable with him in bed. It's dark outside and we should go down for our dinner, but I don't want to move away from the welcoming heat emanating from his body. We can get food later. This right here is better than food. It's a good thing there is no family dinner tonight. Frank wouldn't dare to call for another after the last one ended in such a travesty.

"I made good deals," he says and turns to me. His fingers pull away a stray hair so he can see my eyes better. He smiles and then reaches to kiss me. "You look beautiful," he adds.

"What's that for?" I ask, feeling shy and self-conscious.

"I just wanted to look at you," he says.

"Did you meet with Elizabeth?" I asked him.

"Yes. I think she'll help me."

"Her father doesn't see her," I say, sympathizing with the poor girl. Frank is a self-absorbed and self-obsessed asshole. And naturally, Elizabeth will expect no sign of acknowledgment from him, but his relationship, or at least what substitutes for it with Phillipa, has made something obvious. Frank can pay attention to his children if he wants to; he has just chosen to ignore Elizabeth and, by extension, her brother.

"Yes," Hudson agrees with me. "She sees that his recent decisions will only lead to ruin. She doesn't want to be caught in the mix when that happens. She also wants control. She has her own vision for the company, and unfortunately for her, if her father remains at the helm of things, that is never going to happen."

"Will you help her achieve her dream?" I ask him.

"We'll help each other."

Hudson gets up suddenly and pulls away from me. He heads to the closet and starts to get into his clothes.

"What is it?" I ask him.

"Get dressed," he says. "I want to show you something."

"It's late. We have to eat."

"Don't worry, we'll eat. We'll be back here before midnight."

"Midnight? Christ, where are we going?"

"You'll see," Hudson says with a sly grin. I have no other choice but to stand up and get dressed. A few minutes later, we're driving out of the ranch house.

"Wherever we are going, can we eat first?" I ask, feeling very hungry.

"Yes, of course. Where would you like to go?"

"Anywhere, really. I just want to eat."

So, we find a fast-food joint still open and make a quick order. I remain in the car while Hudson quickly runs in and out to get the food. We sit in the car and have our meal. Sitting here with Hudson, having something as ordinary as a happy meal makes me feel so cherished. I never knew I could be so happy.

"So, who's Benny?" Hudson asks, and he almost causes me to choke on my Coke.

"How do you know Benny?" I ask him.

"You were talking to your mother on the phone while I

was in the bathroom earlier. You weren't particularly discrete about the conversation, and the name Benny came up a lot of times.

"Don't you worry about Benny," I tell him.

"Come on, I'm sure I deserve some gossip. I got you food."

That gets me laughing out loud: "Food for gossip, huh? That's a crazy exchange."

"Business is business."

"Alright, I'll tell you. Benny is my ex-boyfriend."

"Oh," he says.

"What's Oh?"

He shrugs again.

"What? You didn't think I'd have an ex-boyfriend."

"Nope, not that. I just wasn't expecting the answer to be an ex-boyfriend. I was thinking maybe a brother or cousin."

Is that jealousy I see in his eyes?

"Are you jealous?"

"Of Benny? I don't even know the guy," he snickers.

"My mom thinks he's the best man and best choice for me."

After I say that, he starts to laugh.

"What's so funny?"

"You just asked me if I'm jealous of the guy your mother is trying to fix you up with? That's the most non-threatening man ever."

"That's not fair to Benny," I say. "He's a good man."

"Why isn't he here then?" he asks me and leans into me, his tongue pushing my lips about and kissing me. "Instead, I'm the one here."

"Don't be mean. Benny is a good guy, but he's like your Phillipa; everything feels bland with him. I was with him for six months in college, and we never made love once in those six months."

"Not even once?"

"Nope."

"Is there something wrong with him?"

"I don't think so. He wanted to take things slow. Savor the moment."

"Oooof. Poor guy."

"That wasn't even a turnoff. I liked it. I appreciated it because it would have been more embarrassing if we ever tried anything, and I just never got in the mood."

"I know, right? Does your mom know that?"

"Ma doesn't care about all that. Benny is a doctor, and that's good enough for her."

"What does she think of me?"

"You?" Now, it's my turn to laugh. "You're the devil's spawn."

"Come on, you have to change her mind about that."

"Change her mind? She came to that conclusion after my review."

Hudson looks at me with shock. "No way. Demarketing me already, are we? This is all Benny's work, I'm sure of it. He's got his tentacles all around you."

"If he's got anything around me, it definitely isn't tentacles."

That throws the two of us into a fit of laughter.

We talk about random things to pass the time as we eat, and finally, we pull out of the parking lot.

"Where are we going?" I ask.

"You'll see," Hudson says as he drives on. The drive lasts about fifteen more minutes, and we arrive at the location— Tideline Sea Company.

"This is your company," I say as Hudson pulls up to a gate. A man who looks sleepy, like he was roused only recently and is doing all he can not to appear sleepy, opens the gate.

"Mr. Sinclair," says the man. "This is a surprise."

"How are you doing, James?" Hudson says as he drives past the man and continues into a complex. Streetlights light our way as we drive deeper into the complex. The further we go, the louder the sound of lapping waters.

"I can hear the ocean," I tell him, elated. I feel special. He's showing me a big part of his life.

"It's because it's night. It's all quiet now. If you came here in the middle of the day at the height of the activities, you'd barely be able to tell there is sea close by unless you see it."

He parks beside a van and steps out. I follow him out. We're in front of a building labeled General Office.

"At this time of the day, you won't be able to see how things function, but that's not why we're here," Hudson says, taking my hand. We start towards the front door, which opens before we get there. An older man strolls out of the building, dressed in shorts and a tank top. He looks like he's been swimming and has a flashlight, even though the street lamps and the moon were luminous enough. He has a big smile on his face as he stands before us.

"James called me to tell me you just pulled in. I told him he was dreaming," says the man as he hugs Hudson. They pat each other on their backs. He turns his attention to me and bows gently. "Ma'am," he says.

His geniality is so infectious that I find myself curtseying.

"Darry, how's the seas?" Hudson says.

"Treating us well. We can't complain, it's the sea. We'll take whatever it throws. Will you introduce me to the dainty lady with you?" Darry asks.

Now, I'm blushing silly.

"Darry, this is Juliette. She's my fiancée," Hudson says with such ease that I almost believed every word from his mouth.

"I see the news is true," Darry says, focusing on me again. It's nice to meet you finally, Ma'am. I thought you were a beauty in the pictures, but now I see that the pictures have done you no justice at all. You're a blessing to look upon.

"You flatter me," I tell Darry, secretly enjoying every moment of this.

"Flattery is one of Darry's best cards in the deck."

"Now, he flatters me," Darry says. "To what do we owe this August visit?"

"I want to show Juliette around," Hudson says.

"Oh, that is a business best done in the light of the day."

"And we'll do that tomorrow morning. Tonight, I have something special to show Juliette."

I look up at Hudson and judging by his words; I see that he has no intention of us leaving tonight. He lied about us returning home for the night.

"Of course," Darry said. "I best get out of your way then. If you need my help, don't hesitate to call me."

"We won't be needing your help, Darry. Go have a good night. Tomorrow, I'll speak to everyone."

"If you say so, Hud," Darry says. "Nice to meet you, Ma'am."

Darry walks past us and enters the van parked beside our car. He drives off, waving goodbye to us. Once he's out of earshot, I attack Hudson.

CHAPTER 28

JULIETTE

"You told me we would return home for the night! What did you mean we'll be here tomorrow morning?"

"I promise you, you'll be glad I made you stay till tomorrow."

"I don't have any change of clothes. Do you expect me to sleep in this?"

"You fret too much," Hudson says dismissively. "Come with me."

I keep quiet and follow him.

We go through the door that Darry exited earlier and emerge on the other side in a hallway, which I can see serves as a reception area during the day. The hall itself has been thrown into semi-darkness, and only light streaming in through the glass facade outside afforded us the ability to see. I follow Hudson as he has commanded, and we walk through a hallway that holds doors on either side. The doors are appropriately labeled. Recovery Bay, Receiving Bay, Range Area A, Range Area B. The names are diverse, but the function of each room is predictable based on the name.

"I take it you don't come here too often," I say as we walk on.

"I have three more sites like this in the country. I can't be everywhere at the same time. But Darry does an excellent job. He's a great manager. I trust him."

"Looks like you've known him a long time."

"He used to work for my father. When I got the plan to rejuvenate it all, I needed someone who was more familiar with the business. He came to mind. I approached him with my plans, and he jumped on board immediately. The seas have always been his home, and he couldn't do without them. He was just glad to have something important back."

I wonder how exhilarating it must be to have a plan, to put in the work to see that plan come to fruition, and then for that to actually happen. I can't wait to have a similar experience with my bakery. We got to an elevator and got on it.

I'm very curious about where we're going, but I know Hudson will tell me nothing, so I look forward to seeing it. The elevator stops at the topmost floor, and we get off, welcomed into another hallway. We follow this one until we come to a door labeled Lighthouse.

"It's a beautiful sight from up here at night. Come," Hudson says and leads us through the door. The first room we enter is a display unit with buttons and a constantly blinking light.

"We're not expecting any ship to come in tonight, so no one is manning it," he says as we walk past the conglomeration of keys and lights in the control center. He opens the door to the adjoining room. The tiny bed on the floor is the first thing I notice when we enter the room. It's set to the side of the room like some abandoned child's toy. It's in good condition, and there is a pillow to pair with it. This can't be where he expects us to spend the night. The thin bed will barely be able to hold me. "The men like to sleep in here if they work at night. They like to enjoy the view also," Hudson explains when he catches my eyes skimming to the bed on the floor.

Looking away from the floor, I look up, and I can see the sea through the glass. Because it's dark out there, what I see is a black mass that bobs and moves in waves. I can hear the roaring sound of the sea better this close to it. However, looking closer, by the dock, I can see two ships and several smaller boats docked.

"Why do you have more boats than ships?" I ask.

"The smaller boats are for the shallower waters. We get some of our products from the shallower end, and there is really no need to use the ships to fish there. The ships are for the bigger area."

"How many products do you offer?" I ask him, moving closer to the glass to peer closer at the ships. There are two of them, and the painting on their hulls reflects the tiny beams of light that fall on them so I can read out their names.

Lady Bug and Phantasia.

"For now, we're at thirty. We're looking to expand to fifty before the end of the year. Of those fifty, we'll be cultivating ten."

"Like a fish farm?"

"Yes, like a fish farm. The sea, while bountiful and with an endless supply, can't provide all we need. Seasonal migrations and mating affect production, and by farming in controlled areas, we can cut down on that and also boost the scale of production. It is easy to scale up what one can see. I don't know what happens within a school of fish; I can't track their birth and death rates to perfection. With this, it should be better."

"What about quality?" I ask him.

"Quality will be maintained. There are advancements in genetics and selective breeding that we will implement. We'll look to improve in productivity, palatability and sustainability."

Hearing him talk about something he's interested in feels so refreshing. This isn't business war like he's been entrenched in with Frank. This is the gruel of the heart of business itself, the technical know-how, and he has absolutely blown me away.

"This is why Frank can't take over and then discard me. He knows nothing about this business, and should he find the best men to take care of it, they don't know the fish and don't know the people like I do. This goes beyond offering them a cheaper option. Restaurants want to ensure availability, and in a business like this, where seasonal fluctuations are assured and sudden migration can impact production, it takes someone with great insight and foresight to make informed decisions that will ensure the production rate is maintained throughout the year."

"It must be a tough job making that work."

"Yes, it is. Tomorrow, I'll show you more about our production bays and packaging areas."

"I'd love to see that. Do you deal in exotic fishing?"

"Yes. We have a steady clientele that asks for special deliveries like that. Darry handles the majority of them. We don't see most of them in the seas here. Darry spends most of his time in foreign waters. He's back here because of seasonal migration. By the end of the month, he'll be prepared to go out again."

"He's a captain, isn't he?" I ask.

"Yes."

"Which ship?"

"Lady Bug. He named it after his little girl. Well, she's not so little anymore these days," says Hudson. The Lady Bug has been with us since my father was alive. She's a terrific fighter. One of the ships my father got when all of this started."

"She looks beautiful."

"When you see her in the morning, you'll know she's a wonder," he says, turning around to face me. The light in his eyes is so juvenile and sweet it fills me with joy. He looks like a young boy looking up at a kite. He absolutely loves this, I can tell. "There's something I want to show you."

Hudson walks into the other room. "Close your eyes," he calls from the other room. I do as he commands. I have my eyes shut but can feel the strain on them as a bright light comes on. I keep them shut even when I feel Hudson's hand on my waist, and he turns me around to set me in a particular position. With his hand still on my waist, he whispers into my ear, his warm breath tingling me. "Open them now."

When I open my eyes, I'm welcomed by the most beautiful sight ever. The beacon is on, and it's directed toward a part of the ocean that is so dark and blue, with the waves lapping over each other.

"Can you see it?" he asks me.

I don't know what I should be looking at, but all the same, the steady movement of the water in the area where the light shines mesmerizes me, and I can't take my eyes away from it. Suddenly, I notice a different kind of movement within the water. Squinting to get a better look at it, something jumps out of the water, and I squeal, moving away from the glass even though we are about half a mile away from the water and tucked safely behind the sturdy glass.

Hudson chuckles slightly at my fear. When it's obvious I'm not in any apparent danger, I move closer to the glass to get a better look. Another one jumps out of the water, flies in the air for a moment, and then dips back into the water.

"The light called to them," Hudson explains as he hands me binoculars.

"What are they?"

"Salmon," he says. "It's part of our effort at controlled farming."

"That's the sea," I say.

"Yes, we've created an enclosure bracket for them. It's larger than a football field. But that's too small. We'll expand depending on how encouraging the results of this experiment are. We'll be having the first harvest from them tomorrow."

"I want to watch! I want to watch!" I squeal like a little girl.

"Yes, we will," he says.

I watch the fish through my binoculars. They're jumping in and out of the water at a more rapid speed now. It seems like they're aiming for the light because, with every jump, they reach higher.

"This is amazing," I say, unable to tear my eyes away from them. "Thanks for showing me this."

"You're welcome,"

I must have spent more than thirty minutes with the binoculars against my eyes, just watching the salmon jumping hoops through the water, the next trying to outjump the last. They all are making great efforts in the leap, reaching as high as they can, getting closer to the light, but never quite catching it. After a while, the jumping subsides. They must have realized that there is no reaching the light.

"How did you get them in there?" I ask, not quite sure if this is a stupid question, but I ask it anyway.

"We created the housing first. We designed the one capable of holding ten thousand fish and installed it in the water. That way, they can't swim off, and they are far from the deeper part of the ocean, so foreign species can't pollute them. The area courted off for them is controlled. We introduced five hundred fish, carefully selected breeds, and let them mate inside the water. An equal number of males and females. We feed them and provide a regulated homing condition for optimal biological functioning. Salmon aren't supposed to be found this close to the dock, so the conditions of the ordinary water here aren't right for them. We make it right."

God, his voice is like music to my ears. I feel like I'm watching an expository movie on salmon as I watch them, with Hudson as the narrator.

"We can monitor them better this way instead of having them live wild."

"Are they reproducing well?" I ask.

"Very impressive. Judging by the turbidity of the water, we're guessing around eight thousand salmon are present in there now."

"From five hundred?" I ask, shocked.

"Yes, which is why we're increasing the capacity in the next season. If this silly issue with Frank gets out of the way soon enough, I'm thinking a five hundred percent increase, and then we can repeat the same at the other outlets."

"What about other fish species?? Do you have other plans for them?"

"Of course. But one step at a time, right?"

"Yes, yes," I say, feeling incredibly proud of him. "This is very impressive, Hudson."

"Thank you," he says, moving closer so we can watch the salmon together now. They've quieted down except for the occasional jumpers who still hope to get to light. Standing here with him feels surreal, and the sheer amount of change that has happened in my life in this short period of time feels immense, almost unbelievable. If I wasn't living it out, I'd have called it a lie.

Do you think you can fall in love with me in seven days?

CHAPTER 29

JULIETTE

*H*e'd asked me that back in Dallas. Back then, I was so cocksure it was impossible. Why would I fall in love with this asshole who cared little for others? Now, I'm not so sure what I feel. Standing here with him makes me so happy, so blessed. At this moment, I don't want the seven days to run out.

"Did you bring her here?" I find myself asking. I don't understand why. Is it an inherent urge to sabotage my own happiness or just a coping mechanism to keep me on guard and constantly remind me that Hudson isn't the right man for me, no matter how he makes me feel now?

He moves away from me, his body language showing how angry he is.

"Are you serious right now!" he asks his voice as cold as eyes. "That is what you're thinking of in this moment?"

Hudson walks out of the room, leaving me alone. He heads back into the control room. I stand alone and feel like crying, but the tears don't come. Instead, I watch the dark seas, now unable to make out any fish jumping.

Why did I ask that? Why can't I keep my damn mouth shut! After a while, I join him in the control room. I stand by the door, watching Hudson fiddle with the control. As he does that, the intensity of the light outside changes as well as its direction. After a while, I walk over to him and kneel before him. He focuses on the light, pretending like I'm not there.

"I'm sorry," I tell him.

I get nothing back from him. Just a cold lack of acknowledgement of my presence.

"I don't know why I did that, okay. I just wanted to know."

He glanced briefly at me but then turns his attention back to the light. After a while, he sighs and turns to me.

"Why are you so intent on examining us? On questioning it. It feels good. Unbelievable even, I don't know myself that we should look more closely at it just yet.

"I know," I say. "Or maybe I don't know." This though is a lie, so I decide to say the truth.

"I'm just … I think I'm scared Hudson."

"Scared? Of me?"

"Maybe. Maybe of us. I don't know how not to take a closer look because I didn't expect it and it's diving me crazy not to know what to make of it. And you seemingly don't as well."

He turns away again, the light calling for him. He tweaks some more buttons and resets it to its initial configuration.

"Again," he says. "I think we should simply just enjoy the moment."

"You and me, we're here, aren't we? That's all we are sure of. We are. We don't know what tomorrow will hold. Hell,

I'm worried out of my mind what new move Frank might take. But when I'm here with you, I can get that worry out of my mind. I can focus on the joy you give me."

This … his take somewhat amuses me. "You talk about that like I'm nothing but a distraction."

He thinks about it for a while before he speaks. "And would that be so bad? Remember, we are both together to help each other out. You help me steer clear of Phillipa, and I pay you so you can get your bakery. This thing between us is all an addition. Why should we worry ourselves further about what it might hold? Why not just enjoy the moment, one day at a time." His voice softens. "You really can't do that?"

"I don't know," I say and stand up.

Enjoy things one day at a time. Looking at the clock blinking on the control board, I can see it's past midnight already, which means Hudson and I have just about three days more to spend here in Manhattan. If he resolves his issue with Frank within the next three days, will he no longer require a distraction? Do I then lose all importance to him?

I return to the viewing room; the sea won't stop calling to me. There are no answers in there, yet, I return to it every time.

The solution to this is simple: What do I really want?

I don't know.

It's hard, close to impossible to think long term. When I close my eyes, do I see Hudson in my life, in say, the next six months? No, I don't see him. What I see, however, is my bakery. I see myself as a business owner, proud and fulfilled. That is the only future I'm certain of.

Maybe he is right. My worries are unfounded. I'm stressing myself over something that will unfold in time.

Three days ago, I would never have guessed I would be in the lighthouse with Hudson Sinclair, happily watching salmon jump in the sea, yet here I am. I don't know what the next couple of days will hold either, so why do I stress over it?

I do know what is before me now. I do know what I want now. Hudson. I want to feel, let out the desire I feel for him. I want it to completely consume me.

In the midst of it.. in the midst of him with me I know that my questions dissipate and in its place is a certainty that feels more real than anything that I have ever known. These moments of pure magic I know now are what haunt me, and I'm desperate to feel it once again.

This seems to be it. This seems to be the answer and it's just as Hudson said. I need to get myself caught up in the moment and not worry needlessly about the future, so I walk back to the control room but don't get there as Hudson is on his way to the viewing room.

"We should head out. I prepared living quarters for us."

"I don't want to leave yet," I tell him, my voice laced with desire.

"What do you want, then?" he asks me, his eyes locking onto mine, full of dark promise.

Before I can say "you," Hudson's lips crash onto mine. I'm not surprised—he probably sees it in my eyes, feels it in the way I look at him with raw need. As his tongue invades my mouth, tasting me, I become fluid in his embrace, melting into him.

Falling deeper, I submit totally to the mindless hunger that overtakes me. He guides me with his body, his passion wrapping around me like a vice until we reach the glass. He stands with one arm over my head, pushing against the glass, while his other hand lifts my chin, forcing me to meet his gaze as his tongue slides deeper into my mouth. There's nothing gentle in the way he handles me—his touch is rough, demanding, and it ignites a fire inside me that only he can quench.

His free hand roams over my body, squeezing, groping, claiming every inch of me. I gasp, grabbing at his broad shoulders, needing to hold onto something as he bites down on my neck, tasting my skin with a hunger that mirrors my own. I'm barely able to hold back, my breaths coming in ragged gasps as I feel the desperate, raw desire between us, tangible and electric.

Eventually, he turns me around, his hands rough as they pull the zipper of my dress down. He's desperate with it, his breath hot against my neck, and his frustration with the delicate frills of my attire makes me smile. But soon enough, he gets what he wants—my dress slides down, pooling at my feet, leaving me bare except for the thin lace of my bra and thong.

I kick the dress away as he unclasps my bra, his fingers impatient, needing to feel my skin against his. When he finally gets it off, he doesn't waste a second. His hands are on my breasts, cupping the full mounds, his thumbs flicking over my hardened nipples. The sensation shoots straight between my thighs, making me moan, the sound low and needy.

And then he gets more forceful.

My chest hits the glass as he takes a sudden, forceful grip on my waist, pinning me there as his hands slide down to my hips. My breasts are squished against the cold surface, the chill of the glass assaulting my nipples, sending shivers down my spine. Hudson's hands move to my thong, and when he can't seem to be patient enough to get it off, he rips the flimsy lace away with one swift motion. The forceful snap and the slight sting make me gasp, my body trembling as wetness floods between my thighs.

He doesn't hesitate—his fingers are on me, sliding through my slick folds, finding my clit with expert precision. He presses down on it, circling it with his thumb, and I can't help the moan that escapes me, my body arching back against him. I hear him unzip his pants, the sound sending a fresh wave of heat through me. He leans into me, his cock hard and throbbing against my ass. I reach back, desperate to guide him into me, but he slaps my hand away.

"Keep those to yourself," he growls into my ear, his voice rough with need. He bites down on my earlobe, his breath hot against my skin. "You can scream, let it all out. No one is here to hear you."

And then he thrusts into me, filling me completely in one hard stroke. I'm barely able to hold back a scream, the sound tearing from my throat as his cock stretches me, fills me to the hilt. The sensation is overwhelming, a mix of pleasure and pain that has me clawing at the glass, my nails scraping against the surface. He's relentless, fucking me with a raw, primal intensity that leaves me breathless, my body pressed tight against the glass as he takes me.

My knees buckle, but Hudson is there, holding me up, his grip on my hair and hips keeping me steady as he pounds into me. His movements are rough, possessive, each thrust harder and deeper than the last, and I can feel myself unraveling, the pleasure building to an almost unbearable level. My moans turn into screams, my body trembling with the force of it all, but he doesn't let up. He keeps fucking me, his cock driving into me over and over, hitting that perfect spot inside me that has me seeing stars.

"Fuck, Hudson," I gasp, my voice barely audible, but he hears me. He grinds against me, his cock so deep inside me I can feel every inch of him, and it's too much, too good. I can feel my orgasm building, the tension coiling tighter and tighter inside me, ready to snap.

Hudson pulls at my hair, using it as leverage as he slams into me, his breath hot against my neck. I can feel him losing control, his thrusts becoming erratic, desperate, and it pushes me over the edge. I cry out his name as I come, my body convulsing around his cock, the pleasure so intense it's almost painful. My vision goes white, my mind blank, and all I can feel is him, his cock buried deep inside me, his hands on my body, claiming me completely.

He groans, a low, guttural sound that vibrates through me as he finds his release, his cock pulsing inside me as he spills into me. He keeps thrusting, riding out the last waves of his orgasm, his grip on me tightening as if he never wants to let go.

We stay like that for what feels like an eternity, our bodies pressed together, breath mingling as we come down from the high. When he finally pulls out of me, we both collapse to the ground, spent but sated. Hudson pulls me close, his lips brushing against my forehead as we lie there, tangled in each other, the world outside forgotten.

No words are needed. We both know we'll be doing this again, and soon.

CHAPTER 30

HUDSON

*W*ith the first breaking rays of the sun, I stir awake. Juliette has her head on my shoulder, and her body is fully relaxed against mine. She trusts me now. I can see in the way she's let herself be totally free with me now.

Last night was amazing. After we made love, the two of us were totally spent, and for a while, we considered just passing the night up there in the tower but doing that was risking getting found in the morning by my workers. I could call Darry and tell him to order that no one is to come into the lighthouse until I ask them to, but I didn't want to disturb him, so we dressed and found our way to my suite in the industry complex. There, we both went to sleep immediately, welcomed by the soft cushioning of the bed, and we saw we made a good decision to come up here.

Now, the day has broken, and there is a lot to do. Even though I don't want to, and I want to keep watching her sleep, I shake Juliette awake. She stirs in her sleep and turns away from me, evidently not ready to get up yet.

"It'll be a long day," I tell her as I get out of bed, walk to the window, and pull the blinds apart. Light floods into the room, causing her to groan. But finally, she gets out of bed.

"Why can't we stay in all day today?" she asks.

"I need to see my workers this morning before we head back into town, and I promised to show you how things work here. We don't have much time to spend here. I have to be back in town before noon."

There are some final touches I have to put into the plans that are already underway.

She frowns but gets out of bed. We take our showers together, and that takes longer than planned. After having our shower, we dress, and soon, we're out of the suite, heading towards the industry complex. Just as we're about to get into the car, Darry pulls up beside us in his minivan. He jumps down, and by the look on his face, I can tell something is wrong.

"What is it?"

"I think it's Frank," he says.

"Frank? Is he here?"

"No, but there are men at the main office saying they're from the SEC. They have a stack of documents that says they're allowed to put a stop to production. We have to harvest the salmon today, Hudson. If we don't, we won't be able to meet the demands we have on the ground already."

Frank, the thought of him fills me with fury. Elizabeth said he'd do something like this. I just didn't expect it to come this fast.

"If you stretch production, speed to its maximum, how long can we delay the harvesting and still meet the demands?" I ask Darry.

"Two or three days. Anything beyond that, and we're in dangerous territory," he says.

"I'll take care of it," I reassure him. "Come on, let me talk to the men and reassure them."

"That'll be great," he tells me, jumping back into his van. I drive ahead of him, returning to the industry complex. We park in the central parking area, and the eerie silence is disturbing. I get out of the car with Juliette right beside me. Having her here fills me with pride. This is my girl, and I want to tell the world but first, I must handle this Frank business.

I look at my wristwatch to find the time is already past eight and on good days, the industry should be running at full power already. I walk into the common area and can see the men from the SEC. They are gathered in a corner, looking absolutely clueless as to what they're supposed to be doing. They are doing a perfect job of disturbing production already. I'm sure Frank will be proud. Or at least proud of whoever he strong-armed into sending his people here.

"Get the men to meet me in the main area in three minutes," I tell Darry as he walks over to address the men. I head towards the main area, which is a big hall large enough to accommodate all my workers. At least all the ones working here in my Manhattan factory.

"Do you want me to stay back here?" Juliette asks me, looking around, and not sure what she is supposed to be doing.

"No," I say to her, reaching for her as I open the door to the main communication area. "I want you right by my side."

She looks very satisfied with that and follows me into the room. I stop at the front of the room. She stands by my side, and we both watch my workers enter. When they're all gathered, Darry walks over to me and whispers into my ear that they're ready for me.

I cough to get their attention, even though many are already watching me, waiting to see what I have to say to them.

"It's nice to see all of you again. I had hoped we'd meet this morning under better conditions. You all, I'm sure, know my fiancée, Juliette."

They say hi to her, and Juliette waves to them.

"I hoped to show her how we run things here. We'll have to visit that some other time. For now, I have to address the situation at hand. We will provide to the men out there whatever it is that they need. We have committed no crime, but Frank wants to bully us into surrendering. I want to assure you, like I have always done, that will never happen. Mr. Dubois won't get ownership of this company, not as long as I'm alive. Production will be temporarily put on hold for now, but we'll be back up again soon. So, if you have your loved ones around, go spend the day with them. If you don't, go enjoy what the town has to offer."

I see hands raised. They have questions.

"Will this break affect our pay for the week?"

"No, you will be paid as usual."

"What about our salmon? We were supposed to start harvesting today."

"Let the fish enjoy the water for a little longer," I say, and the crowd laughs.

"We've heard that Frank Dubois will finally pull some lever to buy you out," someone in the crowds says.

"All of Frank's levers are broken. He would have pulled them a long time ago if they weren't. Frank has no leverage over me, and as long as we remain solid as a team, each member diligently carrying out their duties, we'll be just fine.

Frank wants us to worry; he will try to sow dispute within our ranks, but we must make that difficult for him. Tomorrow, you'll resume work, and you'll be addressed by your team leaders; for now, have a good day."

My tone is simple enough: Enough questions.

They all pick up on that and walk on, leaving Darry behind.

"Will you talk to them?" Darry asks me, referring to the men outside.

"I see no reason to. I should head back into town."

I walk out of the room and start towards the main entrance, but Juliette and I get accosted immediately by one of the men from SEC.

"Mr. Sinclair, please give me a minute of your time," the man says and runs over to me.

"Just a minute," I tell him.

"I wanted to let you know we were sent here by Ruffy Lark."

I know him, not so much, but enough to know he is one of Frank's lap dogs. No wonder they were here before the factory opened for the day's work. Frank is intent on absolute sabotage.

"I see Mr. Lark does a thorough job," I say.

"Yes, he does. He also wants to speak to you," the man says, handing me his cell phone. I have the urge to ignore the call and walk away, but I take it and talk with the man on the other end.

"Mr. Sinclair. I'm lucky to find you at one of your industries this morning."

One of my industries. So, they've successfully shut down all my units this morning. Well done, Frank.

"What do you want?" I ask Lark, my voice letting him

know we're not buddies and I don't intend to waste time socializing with him.

"Frank can't make it to your industries. He's occupied with a lot of work. If you were to turn on machines, my men there would be deaf to it all and would report to me at the end of the day the results of their investigations. I hear there are some very nice resorts around town where they can spend the next ten hours or so."

He is trying to warming himself up to me. This is another one of Frank's lackies who can see that the man might not win this and doesn't want to make an enemy of me. Unfortunately for him, I want to win this fair and square.

"Your men have a duty to fulfill here, Mr. Lark. My men won't get in their way and will provide all that they ask for and that they're legally allowed to access. I think this is what keeps society functioning. Everyone doing their job perfectly well."

"Of course, of course," says Mr. Lark with a note of disappointment in his voice.

"They'll get to work immediately."

I have no intention of getting indebted to one of Frank's men. That is a terrible idea.

I end the call, hand the phone back to the man, and finally walk out of the hall.

"Are we returning to the ranch?" she asks me.

"Yes," I say. "We'll pack up and leave. Frank has said we're not welcome there anymore."

This action is a clear indication that the faux civility we both were practicing is done with. In war, there are casualties and no mercy for who comes out the loser.

We get into the car, and before we drive out, I call my other factories. Everything is at a standstill. No work can be done, and everyone is waiting for my directive.

My directive remains the same. We don't go on the offensive just yet. We watch to see what more Frank has up his sleeve.

As we finally drive out of the complex. I get a call from Alison.

"I just heard," she said. "Where are you?"

"Leaving the Manhattan complex. I was going to show Juliette around, but that isn't possible anymore."

If Alison has any objections to that, she keeps it to herself. But I can hear her displeasure in her voice. "What do we do?"

"The only thing we can do. We sit and wait," I tell her.

"We need to retaliate," she says.

"No, not now."

"What do you mean not now? We can't afford to have the industries shut down for two days. We can't let ourselves begin to have trouble with revenue. It's the only thing working for us now."

"We'll take a small hit. We'll survive this pain. Just hold on," I tell her.

"Do you have a plan?" she asks me.

"Of course. I know exactly what to do."

Elizabeth gave me all the ammunition I needed. Now, I just have to find the right time to fire.

"We still have revenue coming in from Rakeem's company, right?"

"Yes," Alison says.

"Good. That will suffice for now. Is there anything else?"

"Yes," Alison says. "You need to go to the mansion. Go with Juliette. There is someone there for her. He says his name is Benny, and her mother sent him."

CHAPTER 31

JULIETTE

*B*enny? In Manhattan? Why would he be in Manhattan? Why would my mother send him here when I told her we'd talk when I returned home? It makes no sense at all. Hudson watches me as he pulls into the parking lot. He seems to be enjoying this.

"You think he's here to win you back from me?" he asks with a big grin.

"You'll not tease Benny when we get in there," I tell him, and my countenance tells him I mean it because he quits messing around immediately. We get out of the car and walk into the ranch house. While it was just last night that we were here, it feels like ages ago. A lot has happened in that short time. Hudson and I spent time at the lighthouse, spending such a memorable time together, a time that I didn't want to end, filled with bliss, desire, and joy. I was the happiest I had been up there watching the sea. It seems I get to be the happiest I have ever been with Hudson, yet at the same time, he finds a way to make me so sad and angry. How can one man be able to pull me to the end of both spectrums of emotions? It's always a roller coaster ride with him. I've been with him for barely five days, but I've gone through a wild ride of emotions, ten years' worth.

"Why do you think he's here?" Hudson asks.

I'm just as clueless as he is. Benny has no reason to come find me in Manhattan. We haven't talked in years, even though I know he's been in communication with my mother.

When we walk in, we find just Elizabeth and Phillipa waiting for us, and Benny sits in a chair, not looking entirely proud of himself. He looks a little shy, and with Elizabeth and Phillipa on either side of him, he looks out of place.

"Hey, Benny," I say, ignoring the others and walking over to him, but Phillipa gets in my way. She stands between me and Hudson, hands at akimbo and ready to fight.

"Get out of my way," I tell her.

"Or what?" now she threatens. "I know what you are, you fucking leech."

What the hell is she talking about?

"Yes, your secret is out, and I know what you've caused Hudson to do. We found out about everything, the fake engagement. You two were only here to fool us. And it's you. It's all because of you. You got your claws into him. Now, you'll extract those claws."

She wags her finger at me so dangerously that I have to duck to avoid getting my eyes poked.

She really is crazy. Jasmine was right. I can see the craziness in her eyes, the way they dart around, wide and wild, daring me to make a move. This is her home, and this is her family. There is nothing I can do here.

"What is this?" Hudson says, stepping towards me. He

moves to get me out of Phillipa's way, but Phillipa stops him, reaching up to him and rubbing his jaws with her finger.

"You don't have to play her game anymore. Her secret is out. You don't have to protect her anymore. I know she's the reason we can't be together, and I'll rectify that now. It will all be okay, trust me. No one will come between us anymore once we take care of her. It will be me and you, forever."

"You're an even bigger fool than I thought if you think I'll let anyone use me or pull me into a game. I don't know what you've heard or who you have been speaking to, but the answer remains the same. This can't happen. Never."

Phillipa looks shocked, but she recovers quickly and smiles.

"You'll change your mind, Hudson. You'll have no choice but to marry me. You'll see. I promise you."

She looks chagrined. The sweet Phillipa I saw the first night at the party is gone and in its place is the devil. Or maybe she's always been like this, and I didn't pick up on it. She moves back, chuckling cynically, and finally, I walk over to meet Benny, who won't even meet my eyes.

"What did you tell them, Benny?" I asked.

"The truth," Elizabeth answers. "I have to say, I had my suspicions, but I could never prove them, so I let them lie."

"What are you all talking about?"

I can tell our ruse is broken, but there seems to be something else going on, something they are hinting at that beats me. First, Phillipa, and now, Elizabeth. They are talking like I orchestrated all of this, like I made Hudson agree to this fake engagement, and it wasn't his idea all along.

"The ring," Elizabeth says and stands up. "The ring was what caught my eye. It's expensive, not something Hudson will just cough up for any random person. She must be someone special, and if she is that special, how come I never heard of her? How has he kept her a secret for so long?"

"I would have found out!" Phillipa declares. "I know everything that goes on in Hudson's life. I make sure I do so I can be there for him should he need me, but I never saw any evidence that he had someone."

"He would have at least mentioned you in passing. If he loved you so much to give you that ring, he wouldn't be ashamed of you or keep you a secret for so long. Something wasn't right. Imagine our shock when Benny showed up at the door this morning."

"What did he tell you?"

"That you owe money and all of this with Hudson is a ruse."

I look at Benny, but he won't look into my eyes. He made a good effort to avert his eyes.

"Then it made sense," Elizabeth continued. "You two came to a deal, and you are posing to be lovers, so my father won't ask you to marry Phillipa."

"He loved me," Phillipa chips in. "He loved me before he went away, and I knew he would come back to propose to me. I knew it was happening, but then you came in with your devilish scheme and you destroyed it all. You used your employment with the agency to gain access to Hudson and then you played on his doubt, you told him lies and told him you'd play his fiancée if he paid you."

What the hell are they talking about? That isn't even what happened. Yes, the engagement was a ruse, but none of this was my idea—none at all.

"You're wrong," Hudson chips in. "Yes, this is a ruse. There is no engagement between Juliette and me, and it is all a lie. But you're the reason for the lie." He points at Phillipa. "It was my idea. I didn't want to come to Manhattan and still have you being delusional that there'd be anything between us. I've told you countless times that it won't work, but you can't seem to understand that. I knew if I had a fiancée you'd back away. But that still didn't seem enough for you because you're sick."

"You don't have to lie for her, Hudson. It's okay. I understand. It's the kind of man you are. You can't help it. You saw she was troubled, and you offered to help her. But it's fine now. She doesn't need your help. I'll pay off her debt. You can let go of the ruse."

"Don't you understand," Hudson says and moves closer to Phillipa so he can speak right into her face. He looks frustrated with the lady who is so adamant about believing only what is in her head. No matter how many time he has tried to convince her, she just won't accept that Hudson doesn't love her. "All of this wasn't for you. It was because of your father. I got closer to you because I knew your father was eyeing my company and you were one of the possible solutions to make him back off. I heard he was desperate to marry you off, so I thought if I offered to do that, he'd abandon his want for my company, but I have since learned that isn't the case. Your father will simply be killing two birds with one stone if I marry you. He'll now even fight for the company more and use our conjugal bond to his benefit."

"You don't love me?" Phillipa asks, tears falling down her eyes.

"No," Hudson says, very curt and direct. "I never did. You're a good girl, Phillipa, a beautiful one, and there will be men who will raze down cities for you, but unfortunately, I am not that man, and I will be doing a disservice pretending to be that man. You'll find a man for you out there, I believe it."

Phillipa stares at him for a long time and I watch the light go off in her eyes. She turns around and walks out of the house, dragging her feet along, I see the tears falling as she walks away and I'm feeling sorry for her. But at least, that is done. She has no reason to hang on to delusion anymore. She shuts the door behind us and spins all of us back into action. Elizabeth looks from me to Hudson.

"I'd never guessed it was a ruse. You two played it very well. Very well."

Elizabeth was playing along with Phillipa all along. I understand now.

"Excuse me," I say to that and leave the room with Benny as Hudson moves closer to Elizabeth, no doubt to discuss the embargo her father has placed on his company.

I know no other place within the house to lead Benny to, so I walk him to the bedroom.

"Did I do well? Did they buy it? Are you free now?" he asks when we're alone.

"What?" confused I ask him.

"The lady who came to see me told me I just had to expose the secret. I have to tell you, Juliette, I was very hurt when I saw it. You and me, I thought we had a chance."

"We had that chance, Benny. See how it turned out? We're not meant to be together. But what are you talking about? What lady came to see you?"

"Why are you asking me that? Didn't you send her?"

"No! I didn't send anyone to you!"

Now, he looks confused and walks to the nearest chair to him so he can sit. "But she told me she was from you and that the engagement was a ruse. She said I just need to come to the house and tell the truth,"

"What truth is that?"

"She said you owed money, and this is your way of paying it. She told me how to say it, how to paint it all like it's your fault. She says that way, you'll be free faster. If the family finds out it's all a charade, Hudson will have no choice but to let you go. I agreed to do it because I thought I was helping you. Oh my god, I have been so foolish."

"It's fine. It's fine. Just go on. What else did she tell you?" I ask him.

"She said you'll deny it all, but it's all part of the script. She asked me not to meet your face, so it feels like I'm intimidated by you. She told me all I was supposed to. Down to the letter."

"This person, what else did they tell you? Did they tell you their name?"

"Yes," he says. "It was why I believed them. I googled her and saw she worked for him. For Hudson."

"What's her name?" I ask even though I know the name already.

"Alison."

CHAPTER 32

HUDSON

I watch Juliette lead Benny away. When they turn down the hallway, my phone starts to ring, but I ignore it. I have to talk to Elizabeth.

"Your father made his move this morning," I tell her. "All my factories have been shut down. No production."

"Which of his puppets is he using?" she asks me.

"A man called Lark. I talked to him this morning and he told me we could come to an understanding. Production can continue."

"Did he tell you what he wanted?" Elizabeth asked, chuckling.

"No, I didn't let him tell me. I declined his offer to bail me out. To accept his offer means to be indebted to him. I don't want to start incurring debt to people I don't know just yet."

"If this takes longer than you can accommodate, you might have to use him."

"I don't think it will," I tell her and once again, my phone starts to ring. I reach for it to see who is so desperate to reach me. I expect it to be Alison, but I'm surprised to find it's Jasmine. Why would Jasmine be calling me at this time? I wonder but ignore it. I'll get back to her later.

"Can your secret source of funding keep you afloat for the short time your revenue will take an impact?"

"Yes. Your father is keeping all this quiet, so it should be easy to capture whatever cash we get from them as actual sales. Once real sales are back up, we shift them to an external source of funding. But that aside, I need your help with something. I think it's time we nip this in the bud. Finish it all, once and for all, and to do that, I need evidence. Something concrete to work with."

Elizabeth is quiet and contemplative for a while. She knows there is no going back once she does this.

"Alright, I'll get you something. Remember, keep me out of this, totally or it's gonna blow up in your face in a way that's unsalvageable."

"Come on, Elizabeth. You know better than to threaten me."

She looked up at me, and for a while, I see that fear skip past her face, but quickly, it's gone and replaced with her resilient countenance.

"It's not a threat," she corrects. "Just telling you things as they are." She stands up, ready to leave. "You'll get a package from me before the end of the day."

"That'll be great. Thank you."

Elizabeth barely makes it three feet from me when we hear the screeching of tires outside the house. It is forbidden to park right outside the house. The garage is the only designated spot for cars at the ranch house. Elizabeth turns around and starts outside the house to see who it is. She barely makes it to the door when it swings open, and an angry Frank comes through the door. He is fuming with the rage of a thousand lions.

"Hey, Father. What's wrong?" Elizabeth tries to prod but Frank barely even acknowledges her. He moves past her and comes right at me. I watch him as he attacks me, swinging his right fist at me. He is old and slow, but not too slow for his age. It's no trouble to stop him. I push him away from me. But he comes again; this time, he moves even faster, and there is evidence of martial arts training in the way he moves. He is fast and decisive with his attacks, but I parry it all the same, not letting any of his punches catch me.

He comes again, and this time, I pull him closer, dragging his arm towards me; I turn him around and tuck both his arms behind him before I push him away. He falls on the couch.

"Father, what is this!" Elizabeth exclaims.

Her father stands up, and out of nowhere, there is a gun in his hand. I don't dally in my actions. I move out of the line of fire but get closer to Frank in the same move. The plan is to kick the gun out of his hand, but he must have picked up on that because he moves back, increasing the gap between us so my kick won't get to his hand.

"You motherfucker," he shrieks, his eyes bulging with rage.

Phillipa returns to the living room, probably drawn by all the commotion. She screams when she sees the gun in her father's hand.

"Have you no sense of courtesy? Do you not know that some things are out of bounds to the likes of you!"

"What is this about, Frank?" I ask him.

"You know what it's about! How dare you touch her! She's mine! Mine alone!"

I see. No wonder she was so desperate to get in contact with me. He knows about me and Jasmine.

"I guess she really isn't," I say and watch Frank get even angrier. "Will you shoot, Frank? Do you think you'll get away with this too? This is one way to get what you want easily, isn't it? You kill me, and you have no one contesting the company with you. It's an easy ride. But then there is just too much garbage that comes with killing me. Too much you'll never be able to get away with. Even the all-powerful Frank must know that. So, if you won't shoot, why don't you tuck the gun away, and then we'll talk."

He keeps the gun raised at me.

"Father let go of the gun. The woman isn't worth this."

"She's worth more!" he yelled at Elizabeth.

"If you do this, you'll lose everything, Father. Everything."

Frank doesn't look at his daughter, not even for a moment. He is squarely focused on me.

"He's nothing," Frank says. "He's no one. I'll get away with whatever I want."

"So, do it then," I dare him and step closer to him.

"Stop it, Hudson!" Elizabeth yells at me. "You two be sensible. I do not want blood on this carpet! Killing anyone doesn't solve anything. It only complicates all of this further. Father, if you kill him, it'll take months before the investigation into his death is wrapped up and his company is available for sale. Months is too long, Father."

Inch by inch, the anger is replaced by reasonability. He sees reason in what Elizabeth is saying. But he doesn't lower the gun.

"You'll sell to me. Hudson. You'll sell to me, or I swear by your father's grave, the SEC's snoop into your affairs is only the beginning of the woes that'll befall you."

I say nothing to him but watch as he drops the gun. Elizabeth walks to him immediately and snatches the gun from him.

"Jesus Christ, Father. All over a woman!"

"You two leave," Frank says. "Hudson and I have a lot to discuss."

Elizabeth is hesitant. "Father, I don't think it's advisable to leave you two alone, not after—"

"Get out of here!" Frank yells at her, and she walks away from him, dragging Phillipa, who has been watching everything unfold with shock in her eyes. When they're gone, Frank finally smiles. He's a predator who doesn't care about consequences anymore. He is angry and wants to take his anger out.

"Would you like a drink?" he asks me after a period of prolonged silence between us. He doesn't worry or scare me anymore. I'm sure he sees that. I know I'll beat him. I have it all worked out. Before the end of the night, he'll have lost everything.

"Yes," I tell him.

This isn't the time to play coy. We'll talk now with no façade between us. I'll tell him how I really feel about him.

He walks to the in-house bar and returns with two glasses of Glenfiddich. I collect one from him as he sits. I don't. I hover over him, watching him. He takes a big gulp of his drink before he finally speaks.

"You won't win this boy. You've given me a new reason to make sure you don't. Now, I don't even care who runs things. I'll take this from you and leave you to forever regret your actions."

Empty threats.

I scoff and drink from my cup also. "You've let yourself be blinded by hubris for too long, Frank. You've amassed too much wealth, so much control in such a short time you've forgotten what it's like to watch your back."

"What's that supposed to mean?" he asks.

"You can't look in the mirror, Frank. You're mad about my messing around with Jasmine. You can't take what you dish out when that is what you've been doing to me for months."

"That's the difference between you and me, boy. I get to do whatever I like, whatever I want, while you sit and let whatever I want be done."

"How's that going for you? Not so easy, is it?"

"Things will change now. I've been soft with you because I respected what you've created here."

"You've been soft with me because this is all you can do now. You're a toothless tiger, Frank, and all you're good at now is keeping your mouth shut so people don't see you've lost all your teeth and your fighting power. All they see is a tiger, and they tremble. But I see it, Frank. I see beyond the façade, beyond the lies and the posturing. You're in trouble, Frank, and for someone like you, who doesn't know what it's like to be in trouble, it really isn't hard to dig deep and find what kind of trouble you're in."

"What is this? What are you talking about?"

Now, I sit and drop my glass on the stool beside my chair.

"Tell me, all of this has nothing to do with Phillipa, does it? You had no intention of letting things go should I marry your daughter."

"I love my daughter," he says.

"Yes, I see it. But there is something you love more. It's your nature, and you can't fight it. She was just a pawn in all of this, a means to get what you really wanted."

I see it now. If I had married Phillipa, as he hoped, he would have found a way to make me complicit in his crime.

He would have forced me to use my ships to get his funds, and once that happens, I am forever yoked to him. He'll hold that over my head and demand that I help him out whenever he needs something moved through the seas. He had plans within plans.

"My daughter loves you. She would have been happy with you. She wasn't a part of my plan initially, but when I saw the two of you hit it off, I figured there is more than one way to get what I want from you."

"Poor Phillipa. I got closer to her just to manipulate you into accepting a deal to buy out a smaller percentage of the company."

"We both play our games, Hudson. We both use people. Like you're doing with that poor girl. When all of this is done, you'll discard her like some rag and then move on. You and me, we're not good men, Hudson. We're the worst of the worst. And the thing about men like us is there can't be two of us at the top. It's dangerous. Too unstable."

I won't sit here and try to convince myself that I'm a good man. I have done things I'm not proud of, and truthfully, when I made Juliette the offer to pretend to be my fiancée, it was with the notion that once all of this was done, we'd never see each other again. I was using her just like I had used so many people to get to my current position. People have always been stepping stones for me—maybe that stark brutality one needed to become this successful was something my father couldn't accept, and that was why he never achieved his dreams.

Maybe in the beginning, Juliette and my relationship was contractual, but now, I can't say what I feel for her. All I know is that I want to wake up tomorrow and be comforted by the idea that she is mine, that she is by my side.

"Frank, this has gone on for too long, and I'll give you a

chance to step away and keep all you've worked for for so long. Things will get messy from here on."

"I love it when things get messy," Frank says and stands up. "You're not welcome here any longer."

I walk away from him and head upstairs into the room. I find Juliette standing by the window, looking out into the garden. When I open the door, she turns around and walks over to me immediately.

"I heard some noise downstairs. Is everything alright?" she asks me.

"Yes, all is fine," I tell her and walk over to Benny, who is staring at the floor, looking lost with himself. I wonder what went on in here while I was downstairs. "You," I point at him, and he looks up at me. "You have to leave. You have to leave now!"

Benny nods. Doesn't even argue as he walks towards the door. "I am sorry, Juliette," he says by the door. "I had no idea. I am very sorry."

Then he leaves.

"What was that about?" I ask her.

"There's something I have to tell you," Juliette says.

"You can tell me on the way."

"We're leaving now?"

"Yes. You're returning to Dallas."

"What? No. I don't want to go. I don't want to leave you."

I move closer to her and lift her chin up so she's looking at me. "You're going home. I don't want you around here. I don't want you caught up in this mess."

She shakes her head. "But I don't want to leave you. I don't want to."

I pull her closer and kiss her as tears fall down her cheeks. "I'll come for you when all of this is over with. I promise you."

"Hudson," she says softly. There is something else she wants to say, but she stops herself just in time. "Will you really come?"

"Yes, I will," I tell her, and I mean it. But I need to get her out of here first, away from Frank's reach. I don't know what he'll do if he finds out that Juliette isn't just someone who is here with me because a piece of paper says she must be here.

CHAPTER 33

JULIETTE

I can spot Phillipa watching us from above the ridge as we walk out of the house and get into the car. She's sitting on a horse and is so far away that I cannot make out her disposition. As we get into the car, she is joined by Elizabeth.

I won't miss those two, but I will miss Alejandro, whom I have said a brief goodbye to as Hudson seems in a rush to get out of the house. He said he has business to take care of. From what I can gather, it seems Frank found out about him and Jasmine, and now, they actually hate each other.

"You wanted to tell me something back in the house," Hudson says as we pull out of driveway. He was on a call with his pilot earlier on, asking how soon the jet can be fueled and ready to fly. Judging from listening to his end of the conversation, the pilot said thirty minutes.

I don't want to tell him about Alison. He has too much on his plate already, and I probably know why she did it.

"Spit it out," he says, sensing my hesitation.

"It was Alison who brought Benny to town. She convinced him to lie and told him you were holding me against my will."

Hudson simply nods and continues driving.

"You're not going to say anything?" I ask him.

"Don't worry about that. I'll take care of it," he says and continues driving.

"Is she in trouble?"

"Alison? She knows what comes with what she did. She'll welcome whatever recompense I have for her. Don't you worry about her."

"I told you she was out to get me," I say with a sigh, tired about everything.

"And I should have listened to you. But none of it matters now. You're going back home, and I'll deal with Frank."

"You won't do anything stupid or dangerous, right?" I ask him.

Hudson smiles bashfully at me. "Do I look like someone who would do such a thing?"

"Dangerous, yes. Stupid, no. You're spontaneous. Who the hell thinks of a fake engagement on their feet like you did?"

He shrugs. "I had a problem that needed an urgent solution, and you were there. I confess I didn't give much thought to it, and the plan was riddled with many holes."

"It would have worked. If Alison didn't fess up, it would have worked."

The jealous girl. She worked it all out so well that to Phillipa, Hudson remains the saint in all of this, and to Benny, he is the villain. Maybe she was just worried about the company and didn't want Hudson for herself.

Well, none of it matters anymore. I'm going home. I wonder what I'll do when I get home. Do I return to the

IONA ROSE

agency or look for a new client to work with? Do I look for some other job? My contract and time with Hudson Sinclair are over. It's time to return to the real world. Hudson said he'd come to me, yet something about that doesn't satisfy me. I'm compelled to believe him, but I fear that putting distance between me and him will have him quickly forgetting all about me. He is Hudson Sinclair; he can have any woman he wants.

"We didn't see this till the seventh day," I say with a sigh.

"Don't worry, you still get paid. You did a stellar job."

"I had the best costar," I say.

We both ignore the elephant in the room. We both did a good job because, at some point, it stopped being a job. That was it.

The rest of the ride to the airport goes on in silence. Hudson helps me bring my bag to the jet.

"How long before we lift off, Reece?" Hudson asks as we settle inside.

"Whenever you're ready, Mr. Hudson."

"I won't be making the flight with you, Reece. It'll be just you and Juliette."

"Alright, Mr. Hudson."

"Please make sure she arrives at her home safely."

"Yes Sir, I'll make a couple of calls to have a car for her upon arrival."

"That'll be great."

"Thank you, Reece," I chip in.

"You're welcome, Miss," Reece says and walks away, returning to his cockpit.

I'll miss these luxury perks when I get back to Dallas. Hudson has exposed me to a life of lushness and now, I have to return to my reality. At least, I'll have my seventy thousand dollars. I have no reason to return to the agency. I'll take a week to rest when I get back to Dallas and then reach out to a realtor about acquiring a space for my bakery. I have a space in mind already. It's in the business center of town that is sure to bring in a lot of traffic. I'll have to target lunch hours as the time I'll have the highest traffic. If it gets high enough, I'll need to hire an assistant to help to deal with hiring, running the bakery, and the day-to-day activities. I have a lot of work to do, but I won't focus on that now. I'll enjoy this little time I have left with Hudson.

"You look worried," Hudson says, pulling my mind back to the present. "What's on your mind?"

"I'm thinking about my bakery. There's a lot of work to do to set it up. It feels a little overwhelming."

"But that won't derail you, right?"

"No, it won't."

"That's what I thought. I know you. I know you've got it. Nothing is so big you can't deal with it."

"Well, I hope so," I say chuckling.

"Come here," Hudson says, and I find myself gravitating towards him so naturally. God, I'll miss him so much. He settles me on his lap, his arms around my waist.

"Won't you come with me?" I ask him.

"Soon. I just want to stay here a little longer."

"I don't want to leave," I say, letting myself feel vulnerable with him. "I'll miss you. You messed with my head so much, Hudson. You've messed with me so much."

"I didn't mean to," he says and pulls me into him. I let myself fall helpless as his lips found mine.

"Are you sure about that?"

"You're not my type, remember?"

I laugh and hold his face in my hand, my fingers tracing the line of his face and feeling his stubble. He looks so calm and collected, even though I can tell he's troubled.

"How do you do it? Remain calm in the face of trouble?"

"I'm not thinking about it now. I'm here now with you; nothing else matters. You think I've messed with your head, you've done even something more terrible to me. You've changed me from the heart out. You remember Jasmine, don't you?"

Why is he talking about her now, God?

"Yes, I remember her. You just got in trouble with Frank because of her, remember?"

He chuckles. "The other day, you asked me where I was and said I was lying. You were right. I was lying. I was with her. You'd stirred so much hunger in me, and I needed some relief, so I went to see her. But I just couldn't do it."

"You couldn't what?" I ask him, wondering if he is saying what I think he's saying.

"I couldn't make love to her. That's never happened to me. But you came into my life and stirred it all up. You messed me up badly and now, all I think of is you. No one else. I don't see myself with anyone else, only you."

So, that was what Jasmine meant when she said I had him in a bind.

"Hudson," I say, scarcely able to believe what he's just said.

"It's alright, I understand it now. I see it. I know what it is."

He's looking right into my eyes, and my heart flutters. What is this? What's happening?

"Juliette, I think I know what this is. I have never let myself feel these things, and I always guarded my heart against them, but you found a way to break through them. So, I'll tell you one thing, and I want you to hold on to it. When I said I'd come for you, I meant every word of it, not because I need you out of town but because I need to focus and yeah, there's a truth to that. You've been a constant source of distraction."

"Oh, Hudson," I say, still absolutely speechless.

"Shhh," he says and places his finger on my lips. "Don't say anything. As I was saying, you've changed my life and shown me something I will forever hunger for, and that is why I won't let go of you. I need you in my life because I love you."

"Hudson, I love you too. I don't have the words to express what I feel now, but God, you make me feel jittery."

"You don't have to say anything," he says, kissing me. With tears streaming down my cheeks, I kiss him. The kiss is wet and messy, but I don't care.

I wish the kiss could last forever, but soon, we must pull apart because he has to get to work. Letting him go is the hardest thing I have ever had to do, but I have to do it. He said he'd come back; all I can do now is believe that. I let him go.

"Good luck," I say.

'I don't need it. You should say that to Frank."

"God, must you always be so cocky?" I ask, laughing.

Hudson kisses me again.

"So, did you fall in love with me in under seven days?" he asks.

"Took just six," I tell him.

"I told you it was going to happen."

"We both failed at that, didn't we?"

Hudson lingers for a while, but in the end, he leaves, and I'm alone. Reece announces that he's gearing up for takeoff, but I hear nothing of his words. I cry as the plane lifts off, looking at the outline of Manhattan's skyline. All this beauty, yet only one thing will I remember of my time in Manhattan. Only one person.

CHAPTER 34

HUDSON

I can still hear the roar of the departing airplane behind me when I get my phone out and place a call to Alison.

"Meet me at the office building in an hour," I tell her.

"We'll have to put a pin on that," she retorts. "Rakeem just got in contact with me. He wants to meet us."

"Do you know why?"

"I reckon he got news of the factory shutdown."

"Okay. I'll meet up with you in thirty minutes," I tell her, ending the call. It should be easy dealing with Rakeem, and I hope that I don't leave the Fejitos with bad news for the sake of everything I hold dear. Back in the car, I can still smell Juliette. I sniff the air, letting her essence fill me up again. I embrace that in her absence. I miss her already. It's a strange feeling, almost as though a phalange I had no idea I had was taken from me, and now, the absence of that phalange fills me with some loss. I can't put my finger on it and define it properly, but I feel incomplete.

This is crazy I hiss as I drive out of the airport and head immediately to the Fejitos mansion. There's still a lot to do today; I must ensure that by tomorrow, work resumes in my factory. Failure to do that will be a thing of concern. I look at my wristwatch. It's just a couple of minutes past noon. There's still a lot of time in the day. I relax and enjoy my drive, looking out into town at the detached look on the faces of all who walked past me. It takes me a long while to figure out that I have been comparing everyone's face to Juliette and none of them catch my attention like hers. I receive a call from Jasmine about a mile from the estate.

"I'm sorry," she starts. "I slipped up. It was all my fault. I am sorry for whatever hurt my mistake might have caused you."

"It's okay, Jasmine. This is no fault of yours. I got in bed with you, knowing the risk that came with it fully well. I'm a grown man, and I take responsibility for my actions."

"Thank you. How's Juliette?"

"On her way back to Dallas."

"You two got in a fight?"

"No. Frank made a move. He got the SEC to stop production in my industries. Things are about to get messy, so I moved her out of town. Besides, our ruse got blown this morning."

"You've had a busy day," she says.

"You have no idea. Where are you?"

"Away. Never to be in Manhattan again. The city has given me all it can. I need to find something new."

"I see. Where will you go?"

"Do you want to come looking for me?"

"I don't think so. I think I'm done looking for temporary pleasure."

"You found someone to tie you down, huh? I told you the two of you were lying to yourselves. I am happy you realized that quickly."

"I'll miss you," I tell her.

"No, you won't. You'll forget all about me and soon, you'll barely even recollect what I look like. But I'll remember you. No one who meets you will ever forget you, Hudson Sinclair. Goodbye."

She ends the call before I can say anything else, and I drop my phone on the passenger's seat. That is one door closed, never to be opened again. I wonder what she'll do now, but I don't worry about her. Jasmine has always known how to survive.

I pull into the estate, and once again, I meet Alison waiting for me. We walk into the mansion and meet Rakeem in his study again.

"I don't know whether to say you're a sight for sore eyes or to lash out," Rakeem says as we take our seats. The study remains the same.

"You have nothing to worry about, Rakeem. All is going well," I tell him.

"What's your plan to have production back on track?" he asks me. "We can't have you focusing solely on the company as a source of income. If you do that, you open yourself up, and Frank will have an easier time tracking down your source."

"I know, and before the end of the day, production will be back on."

"The end of the day. That is a wild reassurance. Are you assuring me of this?"

"Yes, I am."

"It's important that you do not fail because I have made moves in your trust."

"What are you talking about?" I ask him.

"You've developed a reputation for yourself in the last couple of months, Hudson. People have been watching you, and more importantly, they've been watching Frank even more closely because of you. People see he is faltering. They are looking to exploit a weakness in him, and it all depends on how this battle with him pans out."

If these people knew what I have uncovered about Frank and how I intend to use it, they'd pull all they can and rally behind me. But I don't need them. Not now. I have all I need, and in a couple of hours, this should be over. But I pay attention to Rakeem all the same.

I pay attention to Rakeem. There is more to what he's saying but he's taking his time to get to it and that irks me. I want it done now. I want to know what I'm dealing with.

"I have curated a list for you. You have to go through the list and get in contact with them before the end of the day. Since you're reassuring me you'll get your production back on track by the end of the day."

Rakeem stands up and walks to his drawer; when he returns, it's with a dossier, which he passes to Alison, and then she passes it to me. I take a brief look at the list and almost gasp. Big names in the financial world. The conglomeration of these men is sure to bring down Frank. They've never had an incentive to, until now. If I can add these men to the plans I have for Frank, total annihilation is assured.

"Is this real?" I ask.

"Yes. Very real. Frank's time is over. They want you to usher in a new start. A new beginning. You just need to defeat Frank."

"They're using me because I'm dispensable."

"Don't look at it that way."

"But that is the way it is. I don't care. I'll do what they want but also show them that I am not dispensable."

Oh, they'll all know I'm not dispensable, but they'll not be able to tie me down.

Rakeem smiles. "I knew I could count on you. Let's drink to celebrate this," he says and walks to his liquor cabinet. "My wife and I will be leaving the States in three days, and I want to head out knowing I have a big win in the bag."

"You will. I also want to thank you for believing me. For taking a chance on me."

Rakeem smiles and passes me a glass, and then Alison another.

"You showed me I could take a chance on you. Here is to future collaboration and a resplendent future which you will usher in."

He raises his glass, and I follow suit. Soon, we shake hands, and we're on our way back to the garage.

"You said you wanted to see me," Alison says before we get into the car.

"Not here," I tell her.

I don't want to deal with her just yet. I want to ruminate over what Rakeem just told me, and I will do that as I drive to the company building with the dossier on the passenger seat. I can see what this means for me. It might not be what the men intend for me, but it is what I must get from it. I have seen how much of an embargo being under people can cause. Frank had the finance world in a chokehold because he had the leverage to pull on everyone. I don't want anyone to have leverage on me. Never. So, I must make use of this opportunity well. I must fashion my freedom from it. My absolute freedom. That has to be it.

Alison follows me into the office and takes her seat. I pour myself a cup of coffee before I finally speak to her.

"Do you want to explain why you did that?" I ask her. There is no need to be explicit. She knows exactly what I'm talking about.

"She was distracting you," she says, feeling justified.

"I warned you not to impose yourself on me."

"I did what I thought was right for the company. I needed you at your full game and with that girl here, that wasn't possible. I saw it, and I knew telling you would never achieve anything, so I took matters into my own hands."

"Do you see that you were wrong?"

If only she knows what I have planned, then she'll understand just how wrong she is.

She thinks about it for a while and nods. "But you must understand. I meant no harm."

"Maybe you didn't. But your action shows that you don't trust me, and I can't have you around if you don't. If you don't believe in my ability to make the right decisions and to segregate my emotional decisions from analytical ones."

"I trust you," Alison says, her voice breaking. "I trust no one the way I trust you, Hudson. You must know that. You have to know that."

"Maybe I used to. Maybe you do, but I do not trust you, and I can't have you around if I do not trust you."

"Hudson, no, don't do that. We can fix this. I'll never go behind you to act in such a way, never again."

"You don't get it do you? When your ways were antagonizing, I could take that. I welcome contrary ideas and thoughts. But your actions can't contradict mine. We need to present a strong front. A united front. I don't see that happening with you again. You've been an immense help, Alison. But we must go our separate ways now."

"Hudson please, don't do this. I did it for you, Hudson. I did it because you couldn't see she wasn't meant for you. You know I am committed to you. She was nothing, nothing. I am the one for you. Can't you see it? Can't you see I did it for you? I don't mind if you have Phillipa, she's not a threat to us. It's supposed to be me and you, Hudson. Not you and her."

I sigh and stand up. Why does it always lead to this?

"You have to leave, Alison. Don't make a fool of yourself any further than you have already."

Alison blinks back the tears already forming in her eyes and raises her shoulder up. She stands up then, gives me a slight bow, and heads out. That is the Alison I know. Not the teary one who broke down just now.

It's just past midday, and I'm exhausted already. As I sink back into my chair, I get a phone call. It's Elizabeth.

"Yes?" I say.

"You'll receive a package soon. Don't let this go awry, Hudson. I'm counting on you."

There are so many people counting and banking on me.

CHAPTER 35

JULIETTE

I sleep through the entirety of the flight and don't wake up until it's time for landing. It's close to evening by the time we land and I'm feeling jetlagged. Reece helps me with my bag, and instead of going home, I head to my mother's. Standard practice requires that I report to the agency to let them know I have returned so they can start processing my payment, but I'm not feeling up to it just yet, so I text Jenny to let her know I'm back. I say goodbye to the taxi and walk up to my mother's door. I knock on the door and for a moment, I think she isn't home as no reply comes. Just as I'm about to turn around and start looking for a new cab when the door opens, and my mother looks surprised to see me.

"Juliette!" My ma says and pulls me in for a hug. "You came straight to your mother."

Yes, I did. I can't afford to be at home on my own. I can't afford to let myself wallow in too much sadness missing

Hudson, even though my mother won't let me catch a break unless I tell her all about my trip. It was the price to pay.

"Hey, Ma, how are you?"

"I was just about to start making dinner. Come on," she says, helping me with one of my bags. Together, we walk into my old bedroom. "Get out of those clothes and into something more comfortable and then come help me out in the kitchen."

"Mom, I just had a long flight. Can I just rest a while?"

She looks like she'll argue.

"Mom," I plead.

"Alright, I'll make dinner all by myself."

"Thank you," I tell her and close the door after she leaves. Well, now, I'm alone, but it's better knowing she's here rather than being in the entire house on my own. I get out of my clothes to have a cool shower, something to cool me off, and as the water cascades down, calming my nerves and soothing me, I find myself thinking about Hudson. I wonder what he's up to now. He said he has a plan to get his factories back up and working before the end of the day. Are those plans in play, and will he meet the target? After having my shower, I pick up my phone and almost dial his number, just to hear his voice, but I stop myself. He would be too busy to receive calls now. Besides, I just left him a couple of hours ago. I must learn how to tolerate being away from him.

I look at my bed and lie down on it to sleep, but it eludes me. Thoughts and images of Hudson flip through my head constantly, and to beat it, I finally get up and walk into the kitchen to join my mother.

"Look, it's the big shot who doesn't want to join me in the kitchen."

"Ma! Don't be insensitive. I was tired. I am still tired. I

just can't bring myself to sleep," I say as I jump on the kitchen counter to sit. "What are you making?"

"Casserole."

"Ma, did you know Benny came to Manhattan looking for me?"

My mother looks at me from the side of her eyes and returns to slicing her tomatoes.

"You knew!"

"I told him to go. I knew that man wasn't a good man."

"And you couldn't call me to tell me he was coming or that a woman came to see him."

"You sent the woman, didn't you?"

"No, I didn't!"

My mother frowns at me. "What do you mean you didn't? What is going on here, Juliette? What happened in Manhattan?"

I tell my mom about everything that happened in Manhattan and even before I left Dallas. There was a lot of distraction, and she had so many questions, but by the time she dished the food onto our plates on the table, I finally finished my story. I don't feel so lethargic anymore, and I find that I enjoy talking about Hudson.

"I don't know what to say to that, Juliette!" my mother says.

"Nothing. You'll say nothing to anyone. Not even Benny."

"You said he said he'll come for you?"

"Yes, he told me he loves me."

"Why don't you look so sure then?"

"It's not that I'm not sure, Ma. It's just that he is Hudson, and I am Juliette."

"Stop that! Any man will be lucky to have you and will thank their stars you're paying them any attention at all. Any man. I don't care if he owns half the world."

"Thanks, Ma. You've made me feel better. I know Hudson will come; he promised. But I still have that fear that he'll get so caught up in business in Manhattan and decide that one is more important than the other and I won't fault him for that. He's sacrificed a lot for that company. I don't want to come between him and the company."

"You won't do that," my mother says. "If he wants you, he'll make time. That's what I have found out about men. Whatever it is that they really want, they will always make time for it. Always."

We continue to eat in silence for a while.

"So, you have enough money for your bakery now?" my mother asks.

"Yes," I answer in excitement. I'll take tomorrow off to rest, but before the end of the week, I'll be looking for a space. I pray I find something cheap and good."

"You will, and I am proud of you, Juliette. I'm not proud that you ran off with a man, though."

"Ma, don't say it like that."

"You didn't call me before you got on the plane, and I had to contact Jenny when I couldn't get to you."

"You must have called when we were on the plane," I tell her.

"You could have called when you landed."

Now that I think of it, I don't know why that didn't cross my mind. From the moment I stepped foot in Hudson's office, and till I returned, I had totally become engrossed in his life, in his demands, in his aura and wonder. Little wonder how it is that I fell in love with him when, for that week, he became the entirety of my life.

"I'm sorry about that, Ma."

"You need to do better in the future!"

"Yes, I promise I'll do better. Ma. We have to talk about Benny. I don't want to have to deal with him again."

"Don't you worry about Benny? I know just what to say to him."

"He's feeling very guilty about what he did at the ranch."

"Well, he should. We both should. We didn't trust you to take care of yourself, and my bias was that you needed Benny. We both thought there's no way you'd deny him a date or not consider him if he saved you."

"You can't help yourself Ma. You just have to dabble into everything."

"I just want to see you happy."

"I am happy now, Ma."

"Yes, I can see that now. Why do you think I've not stated any objection I have towards the Hudson boy?"

"So, you do have objections?" I ask, chuckling.

"Of course, I do. I'm your mother."

CHAPTER 36

HUDSON

I've been waiting for Frank for over an hour now. I look at my wristwatch, 8:54 pm. Today has been riddled with so much to do, and with Alison gone, I'm stuck with having to do everything by myself. I've gone through the dossier Rakeem gave me and contacted all but one of them. The result of my meeting with Frank will determine how my conversation with the last person on the list goes. Sitting at the corner booth, watching people move in and out, I wonder what Juliette is up to. Even in all the raucousness, she still finds a way to center herself in the middle of my heart. That is how powerful her effect on me is.

I decide to give Frank thirty more minutes before leaving. His failure to show up means just one thing: I'll make the call, and all the cards Frank has stacked high will come crashing down on him. An expository he isn't ready for. Frank chose this venue, chose a time convenient for him, and told me where to sit and wait for him. I'll oblige him with all his eccentricities and let him play around for a bit longer. I need him to feel comfortable in the cushion of comfort he seems to think he has around him. He lives in a world of illusion, is deeply engrossed in it, and there is no helping him but giving him a rude awakening by showing him the world has moved on from him.

Fifteen minutes later, he walks through the door, and one of his bodyguards is with him. He has the guard sit a couple of feet away from me as he joins me.

"I had important business to attend to," he tells me as he sits, implying that this isn't important. "And we need to wrap this up as soon as possible."

"That depends on you and your willingness to pull off the embargo you've set on my company."

"You know the investigation must run its course. There is no pulling strings unless, of course, you're willing to let go of it now. I'll be generous. I'll upgrade my offer. 1.5 billion dollars."

"We're not here to discuss a sale."

"Oh, we're not? Then this is a waste of my time, isn't it?" Frank stands.

"You'll do well to sit down and be patient," I tell him, my face telling him all he needs to know. He frowns, but he sits anyway.

"What is this?" Frank asks as I pass him a file. He opens it, and in the dim light of the restaurant, he reads through the document I passed him. His eyes go wild. "Where did you get this?" he asks.

"You're asking the wrong questions."

"This can't prove anything," he says. "There is no evidence that arms were exchanged, and money definitely didn't get exchanged, so where is the sale you're referring to?"

"I told you; you're asking the wrong question. The right

question will be: If I have this, how many more do I have? This doesn't outrightly incriminate you. You know there are things out there that will incriminate you. What if I somehow came into ownership of everything? Every single thing.

"If you had it, you'd have used it," Frank hisses.

"You see, you and me, we're not alike, Frank. This is the difference between us. I'll give you the chance to redeem yourself. Step away, protect your image and your ability to do business within the country. That has to be more important to you than any frayed ego."

Frank chuckles. "You've outplayed my expectations here, Hudson. Made a very good action, but there is no way in hell you have the things you imply you have. No way. The only person who could have given it to you is…"

Frank stops; reality catching up with him.

"She wouldn't do that," he says, doubtful. "She'd never do that! I'm her father."

"You've been a terrible father."

"But that is no reason to commit mutiny!" Frank yelled, drawing the attention of other diners to us. "Excuse me," he says and stands up. He walks into the inner room in the restaurant and when he returns, some of the waiters come with him. I watch as the waiters walk to the other people in the restaurant and whisper into their ears. There are grunts of complaints and dissent, but slowly, the restaurant starts to empty and soon, it's just me and Frank in the restaurant. Now, we have the freedom to speak without risking being heard. Frank must have thought he'd meet with me and be on his way in no time.

The poor thing.

"Now, what lies did you tell Elizabeth for her to turn on me?"

"I didn't have to lie. I just stoked am ember that is looking to burn. You started the fire."

"Because I didn't give her the attention she was hungry for?"

"Because you didn't see your daughter in the way she was worthy to be seen and because you've gone myopic."

"Myopic," Frank scoffs.

I remove the dossier Rakeem gave to me and hand it to Frank, who eyes it suspiciously.

"Come on, it won't bite," I tell him pushing it closer to him, so he picks it up. He frowns as he reads the contents of the dossier. "You've for a long time refused to see the world beyond what your lenses have provided you, and in doing that, you've created more enemies than you should have. So many enemies that those who you call your friends do it just so they don't join the long list of men blacklisted by Frank Dubois and not because they want to. How long do you think such an arrangement will last? How long before someone finally says, this is bullshit, we deserve better."

"So, what? So, a couple of people have banded together, and they think they can usurp me. My control runs deeper than that. I can bring institutions to their knees if I want to. I can cripple businesses just because I want to. There is no stopping me."

"Like, I said, you've been myopic. So much has been going on right under your nose."

I pass him another dossier. "I didn't come to Manhattan just to party and wait around for you to hand me a nice deal. I saw the way you dealt with my father. It doesn't matter what deal I make with you; it doesn't matter even if I sell to you; you just don't have the capacity to be satisfied."

"What did you do?"

"I've been meeting with your friends," I tell him. "You

thought Rakeem was the only person I came here to see. Even my own assistant thought so too. Rakeem provided me with a source of funds, funds that if all things go as I plan, I won't need it. I had a bigger plan. To cripple you entirely, but it wasn't enough that I take away that which you use to terrorize others, I wanted you to feel pain. For my father. I wanted you to know what betrayal is like."

"What did you do?" Frank asks again, his nostrils flaring in anticipation. And is that fear? Good. He should be afraid.

"You'll know soon enough," I tell him, and at that moment, his phone rings. I wish I could listen to the other end of the conversation as he receives the first wave of bad news.

"Andrew, what's going on?" Frank says as he answers the call. I watch him, his face going from impassive to crestfallen.

"Andrew there surely must be something we can do. Moving away from us will cost you a lot. You know that. This is a perennial relationship that shouldn't be abandoned for pesky hurt feelings. Yes, I know."

There is a pause as he listens to the man on the other end.

"Andrew listen—"

Another pause.

"Yes, it was good business. You know, that was just an oversight. I promise you nothing of the kind is true."

More pause,

"Andrew, I—"

Pause.

Frank removes the phone from his ear and sets it down.

"You had the chance to make the right choices, Frank."

"How did you do it?"

"You'll never find out, but without your covetousness, it couldn't have worked out so well. Your deal with the Middle Easterners and the Russians was the perfect incinerator I needed. With that news, no one would want to risk being around you when it breaks.

Another call comes in just as Frank moves to speak. I see his hands tremble as he moves to answer it. It feels exhilarating to get Frank Dubois to tremble.

"You know, someone will do this very same thing to you along the way. It's the rule of the game. There is always someone coming along to replace you."

"I have no intention of staying any longer in the game. I came in to defeat you, now I'll bow out with my crown intact."

His phone continues to ring.

"You should answer that," I say as I stand up and walk out of the restaurant.

I sit in my car for a long time and reminisce over the long plan that was hatched to give me this result,

After the party that night with Frank, where we spoke, it was obvious there was no getting to him, and I already suspected he wanted the company for something beyond just his ego. I knew I had to find out what that was, but first, I needed allies. Allies different from Rakeem. The purpose of my allies was simple. They'll help me unseat Frank. The reason he had so much control was that a large percentage of companies banked with him, and because they did, they got access to loans and funds to stay afloat. They have no reason to leave Frank. He's been good to them. He's provided them with stability to have a flourishing business. To convince them to leave, I needed something big. Something they couldn't forgive.

Frank being Frank, that wasn't hard to come by. I looked into the public records of all the companies he worked with, dug deep into the volume of cash they moved with him, and discovered that he's been siphoning funds from all companies that were registered under him, and he has a perfect cover-up for everything. The loans he provides them.

It is counterintuitive to steal from a company when you're loaning them money. However, it is a beautiful plan when you know without a doubt that the companies will pay up. If they fail to and they fold up, you can just buy them, plug the hole you drilled in initially, and then they start to make money.

This scheme is why he has many friends in the SEC. They overlook the cooked books he offers up to certify his finances. The company he provides loans to will go through the same book certified by the SEC and find no issues in it simply because it was certified by the SEC.

It was a perfect trick. One that has lasted decades and would have continued if I hadn't taken a closer look. Too many of the companies that receive loans from Frank end up folding up three to four years later and a majority of them cite the same reason, lack of funds. How can they lack funds if they are banked by Frank, who is known to be generous to his clients? Something felt off to me, so I created a fake company, made it look real enough, and applied for the loan. I didn't expect to be accepted because if the due diligence is done, they'll easily find out the company doesn't exist.

But I got approval, and a meeting was scheduled to discuss the loan policies. I requested a copy of the policy to read through before the meeting so I could be prepared to ask questions. I read through it and found the discrepancies. I didn't go to the meeting. Instead, I met with others who have banked with Frank to discuss the policies and whatever they found strange in it. Everyone points out a clause in the agreement that doesn't sit right with them but don't dispute it because they didn't want to pass up the opportunity to be banked by Frank.

The clause more or less states that in case the company folds, Frank will be allowed to purchase it for the lowest possible value. He's bought companies for less than ten thousand dollars using this scheme.

Armed with this, I made a list of Frank's biggest money-makers and met with them. Unfortunately for Frank, he had found a way to include this clause in all the recent policies he had the companies sign. In essence, Frank is banking on them and just counting on their failure so he can buy them.

That's more than enough reason for most of them to decide to stop banking with Frank. But the question remained: who would they bank with if they left Frank?

And for that, I had another perfect solution. These big spenders have companies with large equities and can form a coalition and start up their own bank. The next issue with that is that starting a bank is crippling and will drain most of their funds. Unless, of course, they don't need to start from scratch and can simply absorb a bank that has an existing infrastructure whose collapse is inevitable. If all of Frank's big spenders pull out from his bank, it loses value quickly. If his illegal gun running scheme and loan scheme make the news, the value of his bank falls even further, and the coalition of big spenders can use the loans they've taken out from Frank's bank to buy his bank. In essence, they lose nothing and cut off a parasite.

As for who will run the bank, there were suggestions that I do, but when I told Frank that I have no intention of staying in the game, I meant it. I did provide them with a recommendation, though.

I pick up my phone and make a call.

"Hey," the man on the other end says. "Should we run the news?"

"Yes," I tell Tin, the chief editor of the paper that ran that feature about Juliette and me. I promised to give him a bigger news story if he removed that story. Now, they'll be the first to run Frank's story. Both the gun running and the fraud.

"Is the evidence you've provided valid."

"Yes. I need this big, Blow it up,"

"I know just what to do," he tells me. "Thank you."

I call Darry next.

"You should get the call to start work by tomorrow before midnight," I tell him.

"You did it huh?"

"Frank is never going to bother us again."

EPILOGUE

JULIETTE

*T*he day started a little slow, but after my morning coffee, I feel rejuvenated. I have a couple of errands to run, after which I'll meet up with a realtor, and we'll go check out some of the places I can use as my bakery. I look at my phone as I finish my coffee. Still no call from Hudson. I got a text from him yesterday that he'll call me soon. That was three days after the big news about Frank came out. I've paid close attention to the financial world in the last couple of days and strangely, Hudson's name doesn't come up at all. All news outlets say the source of the news is an anonymous tip, and there are theories that it's a whistle-blower within Frank's company.

I know it's Hudson. I can tell by how detailed the news is. And the fallback and takeover of Frank's bank and all his other businesses were so well done I knew they were all Hudson's plan,

Well, all of that doesn't matter to me. He isn't here.

I rinse my cup, pick up my hat because the sun is out already and step out of my house. Walking down the stairs, I see two men walking up to me. They are both dressed in suits and have some communication devices in their ears. I want to run back into the house, but they hurry and stop me.

"Ma'am," one of them says and shows me an ID. "We're with the FBI. You need to come with us."

"What is this about?" I ask them.

"Hudson Sinclair," the other says.

"Hudson? Is Hudson okay?"

"No, he isn't. We can't talk here. Please come with us."

I start to panic, wondering what could have happened to Hudson. Is that why he hasn't called back even though his text promised to call me?

The men lead me into their car, and as they drive on, all my request to know what is wrong with Hudson falls on deaf ears.

"Please tell me. Where is he? Will I see him?"

I get no response back, just tepid looks.

Soon, the car pulls up by the corner, and one of the men dressed in a suit gets out. He opens the door for me and asks me to get out.

"What are we doing here?" I ask.

"Come with me," he says, leading me into a building. He opens the door but doesn't step in with me. "Someone will be with you shortly."

I'm confused now. This isn't the FBI office. The space is large, mostly empty and given a good touch, I could make a good bakery out of it.

HUDSON

"How did the interview go?" I ask Elizabeth on the phone as I watch the car pull up, and one of the men walks over to open the door for Juliette.

"Good. Alison took the job. The investors were happy to have me in control of things. You put in a good word for me. For me and Alison."

"That's great."

"Where are you?" she asks me.

"About to take the most important action of my life," I tell her as I cross the road.

"The most important action of your life?" She asks, her voice sparkling with interest. "What do you mean?"

"You'll find out soon enough," I reply. "Have to go now, I'll talk to you later," I say.

Ending the call, I put the phone away, needing to focus. I nod at the men, who get into their car and drive away, and I cannot believe how nervous I am. Actually, I can believe it, and my only hope is that this will go well. I'm quite certain that I will be ruined otherwise.

God, I still cannot believe what I feel for her... how much she means to me. Pausing for a moment, I inhale a deep breath to stabilize my nerves and then release it. Mustering as much confidence as I can, I pull the door open and walk in. Juliette turns around to see who just entered.

She seems startled, and for the longest time, all she can do is stare at me.

"It would look good for a bakery, wouldn't it?" I ask her, but I don't get an answer.

She still continues to stare at me and then out the window, but the men are obviously no longer there.

And then it hits her.

"Oh my God," she says more to herself than anything else. And then she looks around at the space and then back at me.

"Wait." Her eyes go wide then, and her hand slaps across her mouth.

"Oh my God."

I can't help my smile as I watch her, feeling my nerves dissipate. The important part is yet to come, but as I watch her face brighten up with sheer happiness to see me, I feel a very strong, unshakeable sense of hope that all will go well. That this will be a success and that I will be able to start the next best phase of my life.

She runs at me, and I'm surprised. But nevertheless, sharing in her enthusiasm and always ready to catch and protect her, I brace myself for her hug as she jumps on me.

I stagger slightly at the force, but I don't let her fall. Never. Instead, I hold her thighs, feeling the entire world melt away as my senses register nothing beyond her. *'Unfucking believable.'* I hold her tight, breathing in the smell I had missed so much.

"Hudson," she whispers over and over in the crook of my neck. "Hudson."

She doesn't say any more after this, and I completely understand.

Eventually, though, she pulls away from me and looks into my eyes.

"The men..." she says, "was that all you?"

I can still see the hint of worry in her eyes and hope that I would tell her that it was indeed all me so that she truly wouldn't have any cause whatsoever to worry.

"Yes," I tell her. "Were you worried?"

"They said you were in trouble!" she says and hits my arm. "What do you think? Of course, I was worried."

"Ouch!" I exclaim, welcoming the pain. "I'll take it that regardless, you are more than happy to see me."

"Shut up," she chuckles. "And yes, yes, I am."

She hugs me once again, and the most serene, wonderful silence passes between us, and then I proceed to mention the elephant in the room.

"I bought this place for you," I tell her.

I know she already suspects it, and of course, it takes her a little while to process. She pulls away from me, and while I can see the excitement in her eyes, I can also see the fear.

"I suspected as much," she said. "It would be perfect for a bakery."

"Yes, it would," I replied.

"I'm excited, I swear," she said. "So excited I didn't know how to react but also concerned. You already gave me more than I could have ever hoped for when I started this whole thing. You didn't need to do this."

"Well," I say, nervous all over again. This is the defining moment of my life, and as the next words come out of my mouth, I can't help but worry and pray that I'm saying the right things. That she won't reject me.

"Well, it is important that my wife has the best things in the world, and really, I don't see how seventy thousand dollars is enough to start a bakery."

"I have more money saved and—" Juliette starts and then stops. "Wait, did you... what did you just call me—your wife?"

There's nothing left to do now but to show her with words that I hadn't misspoken. I had meant every single word that had left my mouth.

Finally, I go to one knee and take her hand in mine. "You have the ring already," I say. "But this time, for real, no fake engagement. Will you marry me, Juliette?"

She doesn't respond as she continues to stare at me, still in somewhat of a shock. I'm very concerned now because perhaps I should have put on more of a show. Have some balloons floating in the air or something? Or perhaps I could have taken her on a trip? There were so many options, and so in this moment, when my life was hanging in the balance, I couldn't help but wonder if this was enough. I wanted to get her the bakery, to show her that I care deeply about the things she loves the most. Maybe I should have filled this empty goddamn space with a million balloons.

"I spent the last few days away from you and realized one thing. Juliette, all I want is you. Every other thing is secondary. If I have you, I'll be the happiest man I can be—"

"Yes," she says. And then her smile goes so wide that my heart skips several beats. "Yes, I'll marry you, Hudson. With all my heart, yes!"

I nearly can't believe it, but not until she's reaching for me do I stand up and kiss her. I've wanted to do that since I saw her walk across the street. I've been starved of those lips for so long. She throws her whole heart into it, and I feel it and reciprocate. She moans as our lips merge, sparking pleasures that we've learned.

"Let's do something naughty here," she leans into me and whispers into my ear. Her eyes widen, and I know exactly what she wants, especially as she starts to look for a private space.

"Really?"

"Yeah," she replies. "I can't wait. I need you. I'm so fucking excited. I'm going to lose my mind."

"I have absolutely no complaints," and so I agree.

I'm nearly unable to contain the warmth in my chest as I watch her try to find us some privacy. Whatever we do here would be fucking for sure. Raw, primal, no constraints fucking. Fast and intense, our emotions spilling all over the place, but I know it will be the perfect christening to the future before us. I would be making love to her, once again taking her as mine, and I want nothing more.

"Yes," I reply, grabbing her hand and taking her with me. "I know just the place."

Squealing, she follows after me, and my hold on her tightens. I know that I will never let go.

I lead Juliette down the hallway, my heart pounding in my chest with anticipation. The reality of what just happened still hasn't fully sunk in. She said yes. She's going to be my wife. The thought alone is enough to make my entire body buzz with excitement, but the way she's looking at me now—with that fiery hunger in her eyes, that raw need—is what pushes me over the edge.

We reach a small, secluded room at the back of the building. It's mostly empty, just a few pieces of old furniture covered with dust sheets, but it's perfect. I shut the door behind us, and in that instant, the world outside ceases to exist. It's just the two of us, and the electric tension that's been simmering between us for too long now explodes into a wildfire.

Juliette wastes no time. She pushes me back against the wall, her hands already tugging at my shirt, her breath hot and ragged as she kisses me with a fervor that leaves me dizzy. I respond in kind, my hands roaming her body, feeling the softness of her skin, the curves that drive me wild. Our kiss deepens, becoming more urgent, more desperate, as if we're both afraid this moment might slip away if we don't hold onto it with everything we have.

She breaks the kiss just long enough to pull my shirt over

my head, her eyes dark with desire as she takes in the sight of my bare chest. I can see the need in her eyes, the way she's practically trembling with anticipation. I don't waste any time either; I reach for her dress, my fingers deftly finding the zipper and pulling it down in one swift motion. The fabric falls away, revealing her to me, and for a moment, all I can do is stare. She's breathtaking, her skin glowing in the soft light, her body every bit as perfect as I remember.

I pull her close, my hands running down her back, feeling the warmth of her skin beneath my palms. I want to take my time, to savor every inch of her, but the hunger between us is too intense, too overwhelming. I press her against the wall, my mouth finding hers again, my hands already working to free her from the rest of her clothing. Her bra comes off with a quick snap, and I take a moment to admire her breasts, my hands cupping them, my thumbs brushing over her hardened nipples. She gasps at the contact, arching her back, pressing herself into me, her need matching my own.

I can't wait any longer. My hands move down to her panties, sliding them down her legs, my fingers grazing her soft, smooth skin as I do. She's completely naked now, her body pressed against mine, and I can feel the heat radiating from her, the way she's already so wet and ready for me. I can't help but groan, the sound low and guttural in my throat, as I let my fingers explore her, finding her slick and swollen, her body responding to my touch in the most delicious way.

"Hudson," she breathes, her voice trembling with desire. "Please…"

That one word is all it takes to break what little control I have left. I pull away just long enough to undo my pants, letting them drop to the floor. My cock is already hard, throbbing with need, and when I look at her, standing there, naked and waiting for me, I nearly lose it. But I force myself to hold back, just for a moment, because I want this to be perfect.

I step forward, closing the distance between us, my hands finding her waist, lifting her up so her legs wrap around me. I press her back against the wall, the cool surface, a stark contrast to the heat between us. And then, with one powerful thrust, I'm inside her, her wetness enveloping me, pulling me deeper as she cries out in pleasure.

"Fuck," I groan, the sensation overwhelming as I start to move, slow at first, savoring the way her body grips me, the way she's already trembling in my arms. But it doesn't take long for the urgency to take over. The need to fuck her, to claim her as mine, to make her feel every ounce of the love and desire I have for her.

Juliette's nails dig into my back, her breath coming in short, ragged gasps as I pick up the pace, thrusting into her harder, faster, our bodies colliding with a force that sends shockwaves through both of us. The sound of our flesh slapping together fills the room, mingling with her moans, her cries of pleasure as I drive her closer and closer to the edge.

I feel her tighten around me, her body tensing as she nears her climax, and I know I'm right there with her. My hands grip her hips, holding her steady as I fuck her with everything I have, the primal need taking over, the desire to make her come, to make her scream my name.

"Hudson," she gasps, her voice barely audible as she tilts her head back, her eyes squeezing shut, her entire body trembling with the intensity of what's about to happen. "Oh god, Hudson..."

And then it hits her. Her orgasm crashes over her like a

tidal wave, her body convulsing around me, her nails digging deeper into my skin as she screams out my name. The sound drives me over the edge, my own climax ripping through me with a force that leaves me breathless. I bury myself deep inside her, spilling into her as I hold her close, our bodies shaking together, our hearts pounding in unison.

We stay like that for a long moment, both of us panting, our bodies still locked together, the aftershocks of our pleasure still rippling through us. I can feel her heart beating against my chest, her breath warm against my neck, and in that moment, everything feels right.

Eventually, I pull back just enough to look into her eyes, my hand gently brushing a stray lock of hair from her face. She's smiling, her eyes glowing with happiness, and I can't help but smile back, my heart swelling with love for her.

"I love you," I whisper, my voice hoarse with emotion.

"I love you too," she replies, her voice just as soft, just as full of emotion.

I lean in and kiss her again, this time slower, more tenderly, savoring the taste of her lips, the feel of her body still pressed against mine. And as we stand there, wrapped in each other's arms, I know that this is just the beginning of our future together, a future filled with love, passion, and endless possibilities.

We eventually find ourselves on the floor, wrapped in the warmth of each other's embrace. I can feel her heartbeat slowing down, matching mine as we lay there, our bodies still entwined, the light from the window casting a soft glow over us. I run my fingers through her hair, my touch gentle, as we bask in the afterglow of what we just shared.

"Juliette," I murmur, my voice barely above a whisper. "You're everything to me."

She smiles, her eyes closing as she snuggles closer, her breath warm against my chest. "And you're everything to me, Hudson."

That's all Folks

COMING SOON...

THE WRONG BROTHER

CHAPTER 1

Jenny

Every time I blink, it's like flipping through a magazine, each page showing a different perfect scene. They don't look real, any of them. This entire night feels like a fantasy...a place too beautiful, with its sprawling garden around the lake, all wrapped up in starlight and soft music. The whole scene glows with all the golden lights strung from the tree branches, shimmering in the lake's reflection.

I'm tucked up in my perfect hiding spot, curled up on a sturdy branch on one of the estate's many trees. From here, I can see it all...the glimmering water, the guests in their finery drifting across the lawn like they're in a movie.

This whole night is some kind of enchanted scene, and I'm just a spectator on the edges, looking in.

But I'm not here for them. Yes, they are beautiful and glamorous, but my eyes are glued to the shining star of the movie...Brett Jackson.

His blond hair practically glows in the crowd, bright and golden. He sticks out like a beam of light among a sea of dark-haired men. He's laughing, that perfect laugh of his, and every time those marvelous teeth flash, I feel a jolt in my chest, like I can't breathe right. It's like he's lit from within. He is completely at ease. For he was born to be in this kind of crowd. And all around him, the women giggle, hanging on his every word, leaning in close to touch his arm. Their eyes sparkle with interest, and I feel a tight, hot knot of jealousy twist in my stomach. He isn't that funny...he's never been that funny.

I hate the way they look at him. The way they laugh, practically swooning, their eyes eating him up. I know he's charming, but they don't know him like I do. They don't know about the time he lifted me into his arms when I was little, scooping me up to protect me from that cranky dog everyone thought was harmless. They weren't there that day... weren't there when he smiled down at me and promised I'd be safe as long as he was there. They don't understand that he's been mine ever since. My heart's been his since the moment he rescued my stuffed animal from that dog's slobbery mouth and handed it back to me like it was nothing in the world.

Ever since then I've been biding my time.

One day… when I turn eighteen, I'll be ready, and he'll see me as more than the chauffeur's daughter who lives above the garage. I'll finally be part of this world, part of his world. But right now, all I can do is watch from the shadows, feeling like my heart will burst just seeing him laugh with someone else. It's torture, pure torture, knowing he's so close yet so far away, and all I can do is stay hidden up in this darned tree.

Just then, he glances away, moving from his little circle of admirers, and for a second, it feels like he's looking right at me. My breath catches, and I freeze, feeling my whole body go still as if by some miracle he's finally noticed me. But then I realize…he isn't looking at me. His gaze has slipped past and is scanning the crowd. My heart sinks, realizing I've just imagined it.

But someone else is looking.

A darker, heavier presence, like a shadow passing over the ground. I spot Brett's older brother, Zack, watching from across the lawn, his eyes scanning the crowd with that intense gaze of his. My heart speeds up for a different reason now. Zack isn't exactly evil, but there's something about him that feels heavy, like he knows more than he lets on, and he's always watching, always lurking on the edge of things. I shrink back into the shadows, hoping he doesn't see me up here. He makes me feel like he knows my every little secret, like he sees everything I'm trying to hide.

Before I can sink any lower, I hear my father's voice calling out from below.

"Jenny! Jenny! Why on earth haven't you been answering your phone?"

I clench my teeth, trying to blend into the branches, willing him not to notice me. But his voice comes again, sterner this time. "

Jenny! Stop trying to hide, you brat. I know you're there. I can see you. I've told you to stay out of that tree. Get down here right now!"

My stomach twists with a sinking feeling as my father's voice echoes again, stern and unyielding. I know there's no hiding now. With a reluctant sigh, I begin to climb down, inching my way carefully from one branch to the next. The bark scrapes against my palms, rough and uneven, and I cling to each branch as though it might save me from the lecture I know is coming.

The leaves brush past my cheeks, whispering against my skin like a secret. I'm only a few branches from the ground when my foot slips and my hands lose their grip on the rough bark. Before I can even gasp, I'm tumbling through the branches.

The world blurs into a swirl of leaves and twinkling lights, my heart pounding in my chest as gravity pulls me down. I feel the sting of branches scratching against my arms and legs, snagging at my clothes as I tumble faster towards the ground.

And then...thud.

I land flat on my back, the impact jolting through my spine. For a moment, everything is still, the breath knocked out of me as I stare up at the sky, stars scattered like glittering shards in the vast darkness. My heart is racing, my pulse pounding in my ears as I lie there, feeling every inch of me throbbing from the fall.

The sounds of the party fade around me, muffled by the ringing in my ears. Slowly, I become aware of my father leaning over me, blocking out the stars. I blink, disoriented. His expression is a mix of worry and irritation. The world snaps back into place, the voices and laughter of the ball swirling faintly around us.

"You're going to break your neck one of these days," he says with a frown.

CHAPTER 2

Zach

The night is perfectly orchestrated…at least, it should be.

Guests cluster around the gardens, champagne in hand, their laughter drifting lazily in the night air. My brother, Brett is as ever, surrounded by a bevy of admirers, each one with eyes full of the ridiculous fantasy that he will choose her. Most of them have come with their parents, who are also hoping Brett might finally show interest in one of their daughters. They won't approach me; they know better. My patience for small talk is nonexistent. The ball may look like a social event, but it's meant to keep the Jackson family's business running at full throttle.

I weave through the garden, catching the attention of a few key executives who have gathered in small groups, each one is here tonight for more than the champagne. I stop by one of the circles, and almost immediately, Richard Lawson, one of our lead architects, leans in.

"So, Zack, about the Manhattan project," he begins, his voice loud to compete with the sound of the live music. "We're making quite the statement with this one. Have you seen the latest foot traffic numbers? We're going to be smack in the middle of it all. Tourists, locals...they will have the Jackson name in front of them daily."

"Exactly the plan," I say, nodding. "We're not just adding another high-rise. We're creating something that draws people in. Floor-to-ceiling glass, strategic lighting that highlights every inch. This building won't blend in. It'll stand out, even in the middle of Manhattan."

Lawson's eyes light up, clearly energized by the vision. "We've run simulations on it already. It's going to be one of the most noticeable structures on the skyline...right up there with the best of them."

Andrew Barron, another executive, chimes in. "And it's not just the aesthetics. With a space like this, we're also setting the standard for high-end office rentals in the city.

298

Companies are already reaching out about securing floors. We're creating a brand in itself."

"Which is why we're carefully curating the tenants," I reply, my tone sharpening slightly. "We need long-term contracts, names that add prestige. We're Jacksons...this isn't a revolving door for anyone who can pay the rent."

Just then, the mayor strides over, extending his hand.

"Zack," he says, shaking my hand firmly. "I hear your new project is going to change the face of Manhattan."

"That's the goal," I respond, meeting his gaze. "But we could use a little cooperation with zoning."

He raises an eyebrow, clearly expecting this part of the conversation. "You know how it is...city council likes to see benefits for the community."

"Of course," I reply smoothly. "To that end we're building green spaces on the lower levels. A terrace accessible to the public, featuring local art facilities. We're not just putting up a building. We're creating an experience for the city."

He nods, pleased. "And air rights? How are you managing that?"

"We've already bought additional air rights from the surrounding lots," I say. "And as a show of goodwill, we're allocating a portion of the budget to refurbish the nearby subway entrance. It'll be safer and more modern."

Lawson jumps in, enthusiastic. "And by the way, we're aiming for a LEED Platinum certification. Eco-friendly design all the way. This building will be a model for sustainable urban development."

The mayor's interest piques. "The council will like that. It's good press for everyone involved, myself included."

I nod, knowing that's exactly the response we need from him. "We're hoping to submit final plans soon. I'd like to keep this moving on schedule, if possible."

The mayor's gaze is steady, calculating. "I'll make sure your plans get a proper review. And Zack—don't hesitate to call if you need anything expedited."

"Much appreciated," I reply, smiling broadly.

At that moment there's a sound of something crashing through the leaves and a sudden thud from somewhere beyond the garden. A few heads turn, confused, but no one knows what to make of it. No one's expecting someone to fall out of a tree at an event like this. I glance over, catching a flash of auburn hair through the shadows and shake my head.

It's her...Jenny, the chauffeur's daughter. I've caught her sneaking around like this before, hiding in places she shouldn't be.

It's only a brief disturbance, barely noticed by most. I move toward Brett, catching him just as he reaches for another glass of champagne. Without a word, I pull him aside to the champagne bar, handing him a fresh bottle.

"How nice of you Mr,.." he kids as usual.

"Maybe it's time to keep your admirers in line, or take them somewhere out of sight," I tell him, keeping my tone even. "This is still a business event, not a dating circuit."

He glances at me, unfazed. "What's the harm? Which one are you worried about...one or both?" he jokes, nodding to two women nearby, their eyes following his every move.

"The tall brunette is Harrington's daughter...major construction investor. The redhead? Millie Devereaux. Senator Devereaux's kid. So, you might want to consider carefully."

Brett raises an eyebrow, then smirks. "Harrington and Devereaux. Quite the pair." He pauses, considering. "Why not both?"

I roll my eyes, pushing the champagne bottle into his hands. "Whatever you do, make sure it's discreet. This is a serious event. Dad's going to notice sooner or later, and then you'll be hearing about it for months. He'll probably ban you from next year's ball too."

Brett frowns, though there's a playful glint in his eye as he accepts the bottle. "Fine, whatever keeps the peace," he says, rubbing my arm and giving a mock toast.

"Oh, and one more thing," I add. "Check on that girl...the chauffeur's daughter, Jenny. She just fell from a tree. Again."

"Again?" Brett's expression shifts, a flicker of concern mixed with surprise. Then he shakes his head, a faint, fond smile on his face. "She'll never stop climbing into trees and falling out of them. Sometimes I tell people I grew up with two brothers instead of just you. He turns around to look towards the trees and turns back to grin at me. "No worries there. Her father's got her. I on the other hand have two beautiful women to get to know a bit better if you know what I mean."

He wiggles his eyebrows as he makes his way over to them with a bottle. I do know what he means and once again it worries me that he's not focused at all on fostering connections or participating in the company's enhancement. My father is the one who's most displeased with this but my mother in the immaculate kindness keeps insisting that we should let him be.

He walks away and I turn to watch Jenny's father more or less chase her back towards their home above the garage.

CHAPTER 3

Jenny

"Jenny! Jenny!" My father's voice echoes down the hall.

I walk faster, pretending I can't hear him. He's close on my heels, furious with me for storming out in the middle of his latest lecture on "knowing my place." As if I don't know it well enough.

And of course, as I turn the corner, there is Brett, coming in my direction with his usual, lazy charm, a woman on each arm. They hold champagne glasses in their manicured hands, laughing like they'd already won him. I know where he's taking them. To the bloody indoor conservatory, where... No, I can't even think about it. About what he wants to do to them and with them. I'll lose my mind if I do.

"Jenny, you okay?" Brett asks. "Zack says you fell out of a tree."

My pulse races as he addresses me but the hysterical giggles from the women hanging onto his arms makes me race ahead even faster to hide from the shame consuming me.

"Be careful!" Both Brett and my father yell after me, but I ignore them both and run home.

I shove open the door to our little apartment above the garage and storm into my room, pulling the blanket over my head as if it can block out everything...the party sounds, the music, the laughter, all of it. But it seeps through, filling my room and my head like poison. Sometimes it feels like I'm trapped in some kind of prison, surrounded by all this wealth, yet always just on the outside. It's like I'm taunted with it, reminded every single day that I'll never be part of it, and that Brett… would never see me as anything other than the chauffeur's kid.

Below me, in the garage, are more luxury cars than most people see in a lifetime. Brett loves them. I don't even care about cars, but I know every damn model because he's obsessed, talking about them with the kind of focus he never shows on anything else. Once, when I was fifteen, I tried to kiss him, back when we were both in the garage, just him and me in his sleek, cherry-red Ferrari. But he was so wrapped up in some smudge on the windshield, he barely noticed. I thought he'd feel something, just a flicker of what I feel, but… nothing. He tossed a rag over his shoulder, not even looking at me, and I had to swallow back my embarrassment, pretending I was helping him with the damn spot on the glass.

Now, that memory burns in me, and my heart aches at the thought of what he's doing in the conservatory, with those two women laughing and fawning over him, probably already melting under his touch.

I've walked in on him before, wrapped around some woman like he couldn't get enough, and it was horrible. She was panting like an animal. Ugh!

A knock on the door breaks through my thoughts, and my father's voice follows, low and firm.

"Jenny. We need to talk."

I squeeze my eyes shut, hoping he'll leave, but of course,

he doesn't. I hear the door creak open and his heavy foot-steps as he comes in, pulling a chair to my bedside. The mattress dips slightly as he sits beside me, sighing in that way he does when he's about to start in on me.

"You can't keep doing this," he says, voice softer now. "I know what you're feeling, Jenny."

"No, you don't," I whisper, biting down the lump in my throat.

"Believe it or not, I know," he insists, his voice gentler but unyielding. "But I keep telling you that it's because you're young. It will pass. This infatuation will pass. You'll come to your senses soon enough to understand how this world works."

"Please stop," I plead. "I've heard you. I know I'm not good enough for the likes of the Jacksons. So please go."

He doesn't listen, and as always, he is adamant on trying his best to get me to come to my senses.

"Look at him, Jenny. Brett's not for you. You'll never be part of their world...you're not even in his orbit. These people... they're different. They don't live by the same rules. And Brett, he's the life of the party. Do you think he even knows you exist in the way you want him to?"

"Stop," I hiss, but my voice breaks. "Dad! I hear you. You don't need to remind me again that we are nothing. I get it."

He sighs, his hand resting on my blanket. "Jenny, I have

been trying to get you to understand and to listen to me for the longest time, but you haven't. So now, I think it's best I take matters into my own hands and fix this problem."

At this, my heart nearly sinks into my belly. "What do you mean?" I ask. "What are you planning to do?"

"Virginia," my father replies. "I'm sending you to your grandparents. They'll be more than happy to have you. You'll stay there for a while, work on the farm. I think it'll be good for you to get away, to have some time, some distance."

I cannot believe the words coming out of his mouth. I'm in so much shock that for the longest time, I just stare right back at him, open-mouthed.

"No," I say, my voice barely a whisper, but my whole body stiffens. "No. You can't do that. I can't leave… I can't… No!"

"You don't have a choice. Plus, you always loved the fields and working in the gardens. There'll be plenty of trees for you to climb there, but please be careful."

He sounds casual, like this is just a discussion, but there is a finality in his tone that I know makes it clear this is not up for discussion.

"It's what's best for you, sweetheart," he says. "This crush, this obsession…it has to stop. You need to see this for what it is."

The words sear through me, leaving me raw and open. I clench my fists, fighting back the scream bubbling up inside me. I can't stand the way he looks at me, like I'm some naive girl with foolish dreams, like he knows everything, and I know nothing.

"Just... go away," I whisper, my voice shaking. "If you don't leave right now, I'll scream."

For a moment, he stays where he is, a heavy silence stretching between us. Then he sighs, standing up slowly.

"Alright, Jenny," he says, his voice quieter, sadder than before.

I hate to hurt him. I hate to be rude, but right now my heart is breaking. He's sending me away, and who knows if I'll ever return. He's talked about moving back to Virginia as well, so what if... what if I never get to see Brett again?

He leaves, closing the door softly behind him, and as soon as he's gone, I feel the tears well up, hot and unstoppable. I bury my face in the blanket, sobbing as I clutch my pillow, the pain ripping through me like nothing I've ever felt before.

He's right. There's no hope. There's no way out of this. Brett will never see me. I'm nothing more than the chauffeur's daughter, and that will never change. And now that he's shipping me off, there's no longer any time to fix this. I imagine the farm, spending my days there, wallowing...and it hurts too much. I make up my mind then. It's not a sudden thought. Frustration and despair have seeped in over and over again through the years, and the thought has crossed my mind countless times. But maybe now, it's time to find peace.

Sniffling, I reach for my journal, my hands shaking as I flip it open. I press the pen to the page, but I can barely see through the blur of my tears, my hand trembling as I start to write my suicide note.

Preorder here:
THE WRONG BROTHER

ABOUT THE AUTHOR

Thank you so much for reading!
If you have enjoyed the book and would like to leave a
precious review for me, please kindly do so here:

Hard Boss

Please click on the link below to receive info about my latest
releases and giveaways.
NEVER MISS A THING

Or
come say 'hello' here:

ALSO BY IONA ROSE

Nanny Wanted

CEO's Secret Baby

New Boss, Old Enemy

Craving The CEO

Forbidden Touch

Crushing On My Doctor

Reckless Entanglement

Untangle My Heart

Tangled With The CEO

Tempted By The CEO

CEO's Assistant

Trouble With The CEO

It's Only Temporary

Charming The Enemy

Keeping Secrets

On His Terms

CEO Grump

Surprise CEO

The Fire Between Us

The Forgotten Pact

Taming The CEO Beast

Hot Professor

Flirting With The CEO

Surprise Proposal

www.ingramcontent.com/pod-product-compliance
Lightning Source LLC
Chambersburg PA
CBHW030156200626
46812CB00017B/2093